HOLDING ON

A Parable of Faith and
Strength

JO EVANS LYNN

FOUNDATION, Publishers, Greensboro, NC 27406

 FOUNDATION, Publishers, Greensboro, NC 27406

ISBN: 978-1-7369837-1-3

Dedication

To Gloria D. Evans, my sister, and my best friend, I never would have made it without God and you in my life.

Prologue

The First Monday in October 1936

"What's your name?" The teacher looked down her almost flat nose and twisted her sausage thick lips in disgust at the tiny girl who was surely not old enough to be starting first grade.

"Sister," The little girl didn't know why the teacher had such a disapproving look on her face. She lifted her chin, threw her shoulders back, and pulled herself up to her full two and a half feet in height. Grandma Hester said "looking" short was a state of mind and Sister had to admit that at just over four feet tall Grandma Hester never "looked" short next to anybody.

"I mean your real name, Girl."

"Sister Fullmore," the little girl peered up at the teacher puzzling over how someone too dense to understand such a simple statement could be a teacher. *Sister* was all she'd ever been called. If it wasn't her name then she didn't know what was.

"Does anyone know this child?" The teacher asked the class. She didn't try to keep her disgust from showing.

It was her fault that the brightest teacher in her graduating class from Tuskegee Institute had gotten stuck in a back-water school in Salley, South Carolina, but she would spend the rest of her career taking it out on the children in this hick town.

She'd followed her college beau to Salley-certain he would marry her once he had a job, but he'd taken one look at Julia Mae James, another teacher at the school, and forgotten all those words of undying love he'd been spreading out like a blanket of lust for them to crawl under during the last two years.

"She has some brothers in the upper school," a boy volunteered.

"Go get one of them," the teacher stared down at the child, "Fullmore? Alton Fullmore's child?"

"Yes, Ma'am," Sister said proudly.

"I should have guessed. He's the only one I know round here dumb enough to raise a child that doesn't even know her own name."

"My Daddy ain't dumb. Mama says he just thinks things through 'fore he says anything. She says it took him six days worth of courtin' to ask her to marry him."

Sister knew why people thought her Daddy was dumb and there were times when being referred to as the "Poor Fullmores" made her wonder at the intelligence of a man who would get drunk enough to sell his birthright- a birthright that had included half of the only Colored funeral home in Salley, South Carolina and a farm that had been so large at one time that his father had been able to give the land for Okey Spring Baptist Church and the Colored School and still have the largest farm between there and Columbia. But having doubts about her father herself and allowing anyone to talk about him to her face was a different matter entirely. Sister was getting more than a little ticked off.

"Child, are you carrying on a conversation with me like you're grown? If I say he's dumb. He's dumb," she grabbed the girl's arm, pulled her right hand open flat and slapped it twice with a ruler. "He is dumb," she drew each word out as long as a single sentence.

"Ma'am just because you're a teacher..."

"Sister, shut up," her brother Oscar arrived just in time. "Ma'am, her name is Sister. Sister Fullmore, Ma'am."

"You are just as dumb as you are ugly Oscar Fullmore. Nobody name's a child *Sister*. You two are trying to pull something over on me. You got me wasting time trying to find out one child's name when there are children here who want to learn. Put your hands flat on that desk and lean over," She was so angry that her voice was trembling as she reached for the paddle that always stood sentinel next to her desk.

Oscar didn't cry and Sister didn't either when it was her turn.

"Now, what's her name?"

"Sister," they said in unison.

"Well, I... I..." the teacher sputtered as she raised the paddle again.

"It's Mary. Her name is Mary Fullmore." Sister's oldest brother Aaron rushed into the classroom. Someone had gone to get him while the teacher was whipping Oscar and Sister.

"No, it ain't," Sister wasn't about to let him get away with giving her Baby Jesus' mother's name.

"Mary," the teacher repeated as she added the name to her roll, totally ignoring Sister. "What's her middle name?" She turned with a smile for the handsome young man. The first time she set eyes on him, she'd wanted to hate him because he was Julia Mae's child and because it was clear to anyone who knew Clark Mobley that Aaron was her old beau's son. But Aaron had so much personality, was so talented, and so eager to learn that he'd become her favorite student.

"It's, it's... Helen. Mary Helen." Aaron added although he wasn't sure he'd ever known her middle name, but since he knew that everyone had at least one middle name, he gave Sister one. "Come here Sister," he pulled her to the side, "Keep quiet. Do as you're told. These people ain't like Mama and Daddy. They won't stand for you sassing back, talking like you're grown."

"I wasn't sassing. I was just..."

"It's sassing here. That's the first lesson you got to learn in school. Keep your thoughts to yourself. You can't tell stuff to grown folks like you do children."

He understood her frustration. He'd felt it too when he'd started school six years ago at the age of eight. Since he had always been big for his age, his father had put him to work on the farm until a truant officer showed up one day and took him right out of the field. No one had ever heard of a truant officer coming to get a Colored child even though the South Carolina State Education Law said that all children had to be enrolled in school by age seven. Even their mother didn't know why the truant officer had come, she was just glad that the matter had been taken out of her hands and Aaron was happy to get to go to school.

Julia Mae James Fullmore had been what the people referred to as a "modern" school teacher before she'd married their father. She spanked them only for the very worst infractions and talked them around to doing right the rest of the time.

This worked with him and Albert Lee, the two older brothers, but with Oscar, Sister, and Claretha it had led them to believe that all adults were capable of discussing matters other than serious infractions with children. Clearly a fallacy he would have to straighten out before she ended up getting as many whippings as Oscar had that first year of school. He didn't want her spirit broken like Oscar's had been. He could not imagine Sister with her eyes down, saying, "Yes, Ma'am" to everything a teacher said or anyone else for that matter. How could he make her understand?

"Sister, you want to make a good impression the first day of school and saying too much to the teachers isn't a good idea."

"Why?" Sister's voice pulled him back into the present. "Why" She repeated. It seemed a reasonable question to Sister.

"Why?" Aaron lowered his voice even more, "Cause they grown that's why."

"Mama and Daddy are both grown and they let me tell them whatever I want. Anyway, Grandma Hester says that I can say whatever I want as long as it's the truth as I see it."

"Not here. At school they got their own set of rules."

"That don't make no sense; but I'll do it to keep peace." Sister finished after seeing the serious big brother look on Aaron's face.

Sister would soon find that it would take more than keeping her thoughts to herself to keep peace.

Chapter 1

Oscar was about sick of Sister. She'd been a thorn in his side since the first day of school three years ago. In spite of the fact that she had too much mouth, there was something about her that the teacher liked. It could have been the fact that she was a wiz in math and could help with some of the younger kids. No matter what it was, like other adults, the teacher let Sister behave as though she was as grown as he was.

Part of behaving like one of the older kids was coming out to play with them. Not only did he have to contend with having two older brothers so good looking that girls about fainted over them, now he had folks picking on him because Sister could best him in any game. She could run faster. She could hit a baseball farther and pin him when they wrestled.

Now, she was taking being a pest too far. She'd started to follow Aaron and him everywhere they went. He wasn't going to put up with it.

"Sister you can't go with us," Oscar grouched. He tried to look down his nose at her, but it was hard to do because she was only a couple of inches shorter than he was. God had finally answered one of his prayers- not to have sister grow taller than him. Their younger sister

Claretha who was three years his junior had out grown him by half a foot last year which only left Sister and the one year old Luke shorter than him.

"Why not?"

"Cause we're going to be doing man things."

"Y'all ain't no men."

"I don't know about Oscar, but Aaron sure is a man," Rose Hempshire put in as she slid her arm through Aaron's.

She was beaming with pride. All the girls wanted to be with Aaron Fullmore- at least one time and this was her first and perhaps only time. He didn't have a reputation for sticking with any woman, but every woman he'd been with would be willing to take him back on any terms. It wasn't just looks either. He was hard working, smart, and he knew how to make a woman feel special.

There was even talk that he wasn't Alton Fullmore's son, which was a mark in his favor. He had his mother's high yellow complexion and wherever he'd gotten that jet black curly hair the way it waved made it real easy to say "yes" to anything he asked.

"Shut up Rose. There ain't going to be no *man things* tonight unless going to the movies is a *man thing*," Sister spoke to Rose, but she turned to look directly at her brother. "Aaron, you promised I could go to the movies this week," Sister gave Aaron her sweetest little girl look.

Oscar's heart dropped. He knew when Sister turned those big brown eyes up at Aaron he'd give in and let her go. Thus, ruining any chance he had of getting over with Rose's cousin tonight.

"Aaron, don't let her come," Oscar pleaded.

"A promise is a promise and she did save the breast of the chicken for me last Sunday when Rev. Covington came over for dinner," Aaron pulled one of Sister's thick plaits.

Oscar couldn't argue with that. Getting any part of the chicken other than the gizzards or the feet was a major accomplishment when Rev. Covington came to dinner. The itinerant preacher who served both the Okey Spring Baptist Church and Samarian A.M.E. Zion church counted the Sunday dinners that the local Colored families took turns preparing for him as the best part of what little he got paid and he always ate and carried away enough food to last him well into the next week.

Oscar could tell that Rose was even madder than he was. They walked all the way in to Salley without Rose saying another word.

Not getting any men's things done tonight didn't mean a thing to Aaron. He wasn't all that hot for Rose, not like Oscar was for her cousin.

He almost changed his mind about letting Sister go when he remembered this, but a promise was a promise and he didn't much care whether or not Rose ever spoke to him again- there were too many women out there to let any one woman get on his last good nerve. He'd find a way to make it up to Oscar.

＊＊＊＊＊＊＊＊＊＊＊

The Fulmer's owned the only theater for Colored people in the county. It had been built of raw lumber in 1922 and by 1940 it looked like it was a 100 years old. A high center section looked like an "A" squatting on the corner of Stack Road, the main street of the Colored section of town. Lower wings on each side of the building contained the concession stands on one side and very modest indoor facilities on the other side. It was more of a barn than a real movie theater like the White folks had, but to the young Colored people of Salley, South Carolina it was a place to go courtin' on Saturday night with little or no interference from grown folks.

Oh, the grown folks knew the kinds of shenanigans that went on at the theater and in the woods between there and home on Saturday nights during the summer and early fall, but if it would keep the young men on the farms long enough for the next batch of children to get old enough to work, then what was the harm?

And if a girl just happened to get pregnant then that was even better, because the boy either would marry the girl and end up spending the rest of his life scratching out a living on the farm or the boy would run off and the girl would end up working in somebody's house and sending money home to her family for the baby.

"Why's your hair plaited?" Aaron asked Sister.

"Mama said she didn't know how long she'd be in the hospital this time and she didn't want me running around looking like a hoyden while she was gone."

Sister knew her hair was one of her best features. It hung down her back in an odd blend of black and reddest brown, wavy like the Oceesi River on a summer night. It was a thick mixture of hair that gave testimony to the truth of the stories her Grandma Hester told about White masters mixing their blood with the royal West African blood of their slaves' ancestors.

Sometimes Aaron would tease Sister about her hair. He'd say, "Sister, when I find a woman with hair like yours, I'll settle down with her awhile."

This evening though, Aaron wasn't in a teasing mood. All his thoughts were serious thoughts about his mother.

"Oh," was all he said.

Although he had tried to keep his worry hidden, Sister knew why his answer was so short. They were all worried about their mother. When she'd had their baby brother Luke a little over a year ago, they'd kept her in the hospital for three whole days during harvest time. No Colored woman laid-up in the hospital for three whole days unless she was sick unto death. Oh, there was something called a laying-in period when a woman wasn't allowed to cook because the flow of blood after the birth of a child made her unclean, but no one actually laid around. There was too much other work to do.

Grandma Hester had been madder than all get out when their mother had come up pregnant this last time. She was the local root woman. When she'd learned that the doctor had told Julia Mae that she should not have any more children, she'd given her daughter a bitter powder and told her to put it in her husband's food.

Julia Mae was too soft hearted to do it. She'd told her mother, "I can't take his manhood away from him. That's about all he's got left."

Julia Mae wouldn't even insist that Alton allow her mother to serve as mid-wife for her this time around. Hester James let everyone know that Alton was a fool to spend good money on a hospital when she had been delivering babies for over fifty years and hadn't lost a single mother.

But Alton Fullmore wanted only the best for Julia Mae. He still couldn't believe that a soot black man like him could win the hand of the only high yellow belle among the James girls. Everyone said Daisy was the real beauty among the five James girls, but Daisy was too bossy and too full of herself for Alton Fullmore. He couldn't give Julia Mae much, but he could give her a hospital and real birth certificates for each of their children.

He didn't care that three months after he married Julia Mae she'd confessed that the baby she was carrying wasn't his. Another man might have killed a woman who'd tricked him into marriage like that but he knew that she never would have given him a second look if she hadn't been knocked up. The way he figured it, it was that pretty-boy school teacher's loss and his gain.

So, every time Julia Mae started labor, Alton got her to the nearest Colored hospital. It had been easy with Aaron, Albert Lee, Oscar, Sister, and Claretha because he was an itinerant farmer and all his other children had been born in Florida or Georgia near good sized towns, but Julia Mae had wanted to come home to Salley, South Carolina. He fought it for as long as he could because he knew that anywhere within 100 miles of Salley was considered Hester James' territory and in her territory everyone did what she told them to do.

Alton Fullmore rebelled. He had grown up under a despot father who still ruled the

Fulmer's with an iron fist. No one had bossed him since he refused to go up to Columbia and learn to be a mortician and his father disowned him. Everyone thought, he felt bad about having to earn his own way, but being free of the old man was better than getting five dollars a week pay. It was worth changing his name to Fullmore and bearing the jokes to be free of the old man.

Working hard and being poor didn't bother him like it bothered Julia Mae and the children. Julia Mae was used to better. She was the belle of a family of strong women. Julia Mae was college educated and her mother was the matriarch of a family that was the closest to African-American royalty former slaves would ever achieve. The old house where Julia Mae lived as a child had the stately columns that heralded roots that sunk as deep as those of the two hundred year old trees that surrounded the house.

Aaron stood there for awhile thinking about his parents. No one spoke because everyone knew that this was his way. Aaron would stop in the middle of a conversation or a job-stand still for a time and then say something so profound that everyone would wonder why no one had ever seen things exactly that way before. Then sometimes he wouldn't say anything at all. Just start back talking like he hadn't been staring out at nothing for a few long silent moments.

When Aaron came back to himself he said, "Don't look sad like that Sister. Mama is going to be all right," Aaron smiled his reassurance.

"Promise?" Sister knew Aaron never promised anything that he couldn't deliver on and if he promised their mother would be all right she would.

Aaron didn't look at her when he said, "Tell you what, I'll go over to Springfield tomorrow and find out when she's coming home."

It wasn't until later that night as she lay awake still worrying that Sister realized that Aaron hadn't promised her that their mother would be all right.

****

"Okay, let's go," Aaron turned and started to walk in the direction of the movie. He stopped and looked back when he realized that only Sister had fallen into step beside him. Oscar and Rose stood there looking like they'd put more than they intended to in the offering plate at church.

"If y'all are going to look like that, y'all can go back home and me and Sister will go to the movie."

"Oh, Aaron, I'm not mad, just disappointed. "This should not count as my stepping out with you. Promise me next Saturday night."

"Can't do that. All my Saturday's straight through Easter of next year are gone. You want to come or not?"

"I'll go," There was still the woods after the movie. Maybe she could get Aaron to take Sister back home first.

She was even more disappointed when Aaron took her home first and rushed off saying he had to get to bed early.

****

Aaron was up before the sun was up. He thought he rolled out of bed quietly enough not to wake the other three occupants of the bed- his three younger brothers. He almost jumped out of his skin when he found a fully dressed Oscar standing at the foot of their bed.

"What you doing up this early?"

"Going with you."

"No you're not. You know Daddy can't spare both of us."

"He can't spare either of us. You know Albert Lee ain't much good for work, but if we leave now. We can maybe catch a ride back with someone and be back by noon. I got to see if Mama's all right," Since Oscar pressed his case by threatening to wake their father and thus prevent either of them from going, Aaron had been forced to take him along.

Aaron knew that Oscar would want to use up the time during the seven mile walk into Springfield talking about the movie last night. Oscar could about tell any movie that he saw back word for word. Usually, Aaron found this talent and Oscar's ability to mimic the voices of both men and women entertaining, but today Aaron's mind was set on one thing- getting to Springfield and that hospital as fast as he could. Heck, Aaron couldn't even remember what the movie last night was about. A wall of worry had clogged his ears and pressed down on his chest since that moment when he couldn't get the words out to promise Sister that their mother would be all right.

He didn't want to walk. He didn't want to talk. He wanted to run.

Chapter 2

"Aaron, you sure this is it?" Oscar's voice was full of doubt as he looked up at the building. This place didn't look anything like the hospitals where their mother had given birth to their younger siblings. The Hospital for Colored People in Lake Alfred, Florida where Sister, Claretha, and Luke had been born had a sign in front of it proclaiming it to have been "the site of a Confederate Hospital from 1862-1864. In spite of being old, the walls had been white washed and the grounds had been sparse but neat; it looked like a hospital.   But this place looked like it could have been almost anything- a stable, a country store, a Colored school house-anything but a hospital.

"We're at the end of the road that man told us to follow and ain't nothing else here where he said it would be, so I reckon this is it," Aaron tried to sound positive that he was right but it was hard when faced with a building that seemed a complete contradiction of the term "hospital".

It was a clapboard building with a front that might have been painted bright yellow forty or fifty years ago. Now, it looked faded and tired much like the buildings in those small Western towns in the movies. Aaron expected to see a bartender and a couple of dance hall girls on the other side of the doors. Why hadn't their father turned around and taken their mother back home to Grandma Hester the moment he saw this place?

"Maybe its better on the inside," They said in unison both making a half hearted attempt at laughing as they shared a "running joke."

Each time they approached the latest shack that their father had rented for them or that his current employer supplied for the farm laborers who lived on his farm, their mother would attempt to raise their spirits by saying, "Maybe it looks better on the inside."

It never did.

This time it was better. The floor was of polished slate and the walls gleamed with fresh white wash. It smelled and looked clean. There was a woman who looked even older than their Grandma Hester sweeping the already clean floor. An older man who had the proud bearing of a butler greeted them.

"The doctors don't usually allow visitors this early in the day," the old man said as his eyes swept from Aaron to Oscar, and then back to Aaron. After years of service, he recognized who was in charge. It had nothing to do with height but with the way each young man carried himself. The tall one knew who he was and liked being that person. The small one was still looking for himself because he didn't much like the part of himself that he had found.

"We just want to look in on our Mama," Aaron spoke up.

"And your mother is?"

"Julia Mae Fullmore."

"She wasn't in her bed this morning when I came in a little while ago. I thought she and her baby had gone home," In another hour, he would be caught up on what had happened yesterday and during the night while he was working at the gentleman's club.

"We just came from home. She ain't there. Where's our Mama!" Aaron grabbed the man by his collar and lifted him about six inches from the floor.

****

Sister looked up from the washboard, wiping the sweat from her brow, she could see someone walking up the road, but they were too far away for her to tell who it was. Not that she much cared who it was. Whoever it was looked like a man and she knew no man around here was going to help her with what she needed to do.

She didn't know how her mama did it. Mama could get more done in a day than Sister had gotten done in over a week. The day her mother went to the hospital she had washed clothes, cleaned the house, cooked the noon day meal for five men, made sure Sister's and her sister Claretha's hair was washed and plaited so tight that their eyes were slanted like Chinese children, and made her children's favorite checker board cake.

Sister was trying her best but she was just ten years old and smaller than most six year old children. She didn't resent the fact that as the oldest girl, she had to do all her mother's chores while she was in the hospital, but sometimes she wished that their father would make Claretha help her. There weren't but ten months between them and Sister had been doing a woman's work since she was seven years old.

She understood that Claretha was the "one"- the only one who would be able to go to school beyond the six-grade school for Colored Children in Salley. A poor sharecropping family could only afford to spare one child to finish school and become a teacher or a preacher. That one had to be deemed the best and the brightest among the children in the family and although everyone knew that Aaron was the best and brightest among the Fullmore children, somehow it had always been understood that he would not be the one. Aaron and Albert Lee had left school after sixth grade. Sister thought that Aaron had not been allowed to continue in school because he was so strong and hard working- often picking two times as much cotton as anyone else. She would be a grown woman before she learned the real reason why Claretha had been tapped as "the one" instead of Aaron.

So, Claretha got to go to school every day and stay late after school with the teacher for extra lessons while Sister missed weeks of school at a time when their mother had a baby or during planting or harvest time when she had to work in the fields or help her mother cook the big meal of the day.

"Standing here woolgathering and feeling sorry for myself ain't getting these clothes washed," Sister scolded herself as she bent down to slap another of the men's shirts against the washboard in the creek. She hated washing clothes in this creek. It was a poor excuse for a creek. It held barely enough water in it to call it a creek because it had been bone dry since June- not nary a drop of rain. The water was bracken grey and the clothes never looked as clean as her hard work should have made them look. But going to the river to wash with the other women would add another two hours to her wash-time and Sister didn't have an extra two hours to spend doing anything.

"Sister, Sister! Didn't you hear me calling you?" She looked up as the man she'd seen way down the road suddenly became her brother Oscar.

"No, I didn't hear you. I don't have time to talk. You and Aaron are in trouble anyway. Daddy said he didn't give y'all permission to go into town to see Mama."

"Sister, Mama's dead! That's why I'm back here without Aaron. I came to tell Daddy. I came..."

She didn't hear the rest of what he said. After her name, the next two words had turned off the blood to her brain leaving her both deaf and dumb.

Her lips were moving but nothing was coming out. Finally she asked, "Dead?" She said the one word like a question. She couldn't put the two words together. Mama. Dead. It didn't make sense.

"Dead. When we got there, we couldn't find her. Aaron went crazy-threatening to kill someone if they didn't find our Mama," he paused to catch his breath.

"Finally, this old black woman who was sweeping the floor said, "She bled to death. I told them she was one of Hester James' daughters and they sent word to your Grandma that her daughter was dead. Miss Hester came and got the baby girl and had her son, Boy take the body to the Fulmer Funeral Home," telling this part of what he knew seemed to drain the last of Oscar's meager strength. He sunk down to the ground like an empty bag of potatoes as he broke down sobbing.

Sister reached out to touch his shaking shoulders, but her hand fell to her side inches away. She didn't know how to comfort her brother. Crying wasn't something the Fullmore children did much of because as their mother said, "Crying doesn't do any good and most people look real ugly doing it."

"Does Daddy know?" Sister asked when she could speak.

"I don't know if Grandma Hester sent anyone over to tell him. You know she'll blame him for Mama being dead 'because she didn't want Mama to go to the hospital. Aaron sent me to tell Daddy just in case and to tell Daddy to meet him at the funeral home. You go tell Daddy. I can't. I just can't," he looked up at Sister all the time he was crying dry heart aching sobs.

This was just like Oscar. Sometimes he acted like Sister was the older of the two rather than the other way around. When they got into trouble, she took the blame and when he needed something when Aaron wasn't around, Sister was the one to ask for it. She'd always felt closest to him not only because he was nearly as short as she was, but because he needed her.

There was always something needy about Oscar and it had nothing to do with the fact that he was short and ugly with not one redeeming feature. He'd never grown much hair and had a head start on being bald in his teens like other James men. Where all the other boys in the family had eyelashes thick and long enough to make a woman weep with envy, Oscar's eyelashes were as scarce as the hair on his head. His West African dark skin' didn't have the smooth look of melted chocolate like their other brothers Albert Lee and Luke. He'd had some kind of skin problem when he was six and their Daddy wouldn't let Grandma Hester use any of what he called "her Mammy made ointments" on him. So, instead of his face healing smooth like Uncle Boy's children's faces had when they'd had the same ailment, Oscar's face had healed with a rough crater appearance. No, he'd never be handsome, but like a mother with an ugly duckling, Sister had taken him under her wing. She would have done anything at this moment to protect him from the hurt that seemed to be radiating from him right into her soul. The only way she could think to help was to go tell their father.

Dead. Mother. Dead. It didn't make sense.

Chapter 3

Alton Fullmore didn't stop his work for the noon day meal. He was too mad to eat. Early spring planting was hard enough without Aaron and Oscar going off like that. He'd saved enough seeds to plant plenty of watermelons and sweet corn to sell on the side of the road and it would take all three of them working ten to twelve hours a day to plant enough to do what he wanted to do.

He looked over at Albert Lee. The boy tried but he just wasn't cut out to be a farm laborer any more than Alton had been cut out to be a mortician. Albert Lee was too much like him. The boy had been working on that same row for over three hours. He needed Aaron and Oscar.

This was the best chance he'd had in a long time to get Julia Mae the real house he'd been promising her for years. One of the families that owned a decent house in the Colored community- running water, two bedrooms, and a front room for company-was moving to Columbia. Their oldest daughter was a school teacher and she'd found jobs for her father and brothers at a mill. Chances like this didn't happen often in a town as small as Salley and Alton meant to get it right this time.

Wouldn't the folks around here be surprised when he finally was able to put his family into a decent house? He frowned at the roof of the shack that was barely visible from this end of the field. His Julia Mae deserved better. Julia Mae was used to better. Her mother, Hester James, was the matriarch of a family that was the closest to African royalty former slaves would ever achieve and the old house she lived in when he'd married her had the stately columns that heralded its past as the main house of a Southern Plantation.

He smiled at his day dream until he looked up and saw Sister. He dropped his hoe and starting running towards her. It had to be something real bad to make Sister leave her work.

"What you doing out here, Sister? If you've come to explain why those sorry brothers of yours aren't out here helping me, I don't want to hear it," he offered the simplest excuse he could think of.

"Oscar's back, but I left him sitting on the stump crying over Mama."

"That's nothing new. Oscar always misses your Mama more than anyone else because she acts like he's the baby boy 'stead of Luke."

"That ain't it. He's crying because she's dead," Sister blurted it out like that out of anger, in part for the way he always talked about Oscar and the other part because every step of the way out here she got angrier and angrier about her mother being dead.

The doctor had told her father when Luke was born that his wife shouldn't have any more children, but her father said anything that kept a woman from getting pregnant was going against God's will. And he said that he wasn't going to allow Grandma Hester to give his wife anything to keep her from carrying his seed.

"Aaron said that you should meet him at Fulmer Funeral Home where Grandma Hester had them take Mama's body," Sister watched her father fold like an accordion and drop crying on top of a row of freshly planted watermelon seeds.

Sister didn't offer him any comfort as she turned to start doing what she could to make their house presentable. As bad as her mother being dead was, the fact that everyone would come to that shack that they called home for the wake and after the funeral for the family meal was even worst.

No one other than the traveling minister had come near their house since they'd moved back to Salley. It was like being as poor as they were contagious. Although everyone was some kind of poor, most of the Colored people had one thing that separated them from being "dirt poor"- a wooden floor, running water in the house, a house garden with more than a few herbs-something. Their house had none of that. The last time the minister had come, her mother fed him out of a picnic basket on the stump claiming that the house was too hot from her cooking. No, Sister thought, her mother didn't deserve to be laid out in a one room shack with a packed dirt floor and an outhouse so close you could hear every turd drop.

****

"She doesn't look like she should be dead," Oscar moaned against Sister's shoulder as she practically held him up as the family viewed the body for the last time before they closed the casket.

"That's because she shouldn't be. She should be home baking us a checkered cake or teaching Little Luke how to count," Sister couldn't get the anger to make room for the hurt. It wasn't fair that a woman had to keep having babies until she died from it just because her husband said so.

"Kiss your mama good-bye, Sister," Grandma Hester said as she pried Oscar away from Sister.

"Grandma I..." Sister didn't know how to say it. How could she admit to anyone that she did not want to kiss her Mama good-bye? All the other children, except Emma Margaret, the baby, had kissed their mother. Their father had kissed her. In fact, several of the men in the family had been forced to pull Alton Fullmore back from almost climbing into the casket with her.

They were waiting on Sister.

"Go on gal. There ain't never been a James woman that was scared of another James woman living or dead," her grand-mother was too close to doing the unthinkable-disgracing herself by crying in public-to consider the ten year olds' feelings. Julia Mae had been her heart. She'd washed and ironed thousands of petticoats, shirt's, fancy dresses, and anything else the White folks were willing to pay her to wash to send Julia Mae all the way into Columbia to become a teacher. And what happened? She gets knocked up by the first good-looking man that gives her the eye and then gets herself married to the only broke Fulmer in the county. "I said go ahead and kiss your Mama good-bye, Sister."

"I'm not afraid of Mama. It's not that. It's just…" Sister gave up trying to explain as she moved closer to the casket. It was easier to lean down and kiss her mother's cold, too firm cheek than to explain that what held her back was not fear, but a desire to keep in her heart the feeling of that warm embrace her mother had given her as she made her repeat one last time all the directions she had given her before leaving for the hospital. That Mama- the one she wanted to feel in her soul at the end of each day was alive and warm and smelled of rose water, but instead after the kiss, she was left with the feeling of a Mama who was dead-cold hard dead.

****

"Sister, you ain't supposed to be serving people. We're the grieving family," Aaron said as he accepted a plate loaded with fried chicken, potato salad and buttered biscuits.

"You know those folks hanging closest to the table are the ones that ain't brought a thing, but will be eating like it's their last meal whether they're family or not. Sit here waiting to be served and you might starve," Sister sat on the floor and rested her head on the side of his thigh.

"I'll have you know little Miss Thing that this is my third plate," He smiled and waved Silesia Jones away. "Thank you darling, but I think this plate here will be plenty."

"You think you're all that 'cause all these silly girls fancy themselves in love with you," Sister tried to say it like a put down, but too much pride in her big brother mixed in and spoiled the affect.

"Know I'm something. A body got to know that about them-self if they're going to make it in this here world. You're something too little girl. You're smart enough to do anything you want."

"Being smart doesn't mean anything around here. Who you know smarter than Mama was? What good did it do her in the end? Round here, a girl child is just somebody to work and have babies 'til they die," she threw the questions at him not expecting an answer.

"I'm not as smart as you and Mama, but I know there's more to a woman than working and having babies."

"Oh you just thinking about the fun you have between their legs."

"Sister, I done told you about talking about things like that. It ain't lady like." Aaron looked around to make sure no one was close enough to overhear them. He admonished her simply because his mother had taught him that he was partly responsible for helping to raise the younger kids right, but when they were alone, he let Sister talk to him about most anything grown up or not. "Sister, I'm the last one to talk down on that part of a woman. It's one of the two best things God ever made."

"What's the second one?" Sister asked even though she already knew the answer.

"Fried chicken," Aaron declared as he took another bite out of the chicken breast. "I ain't kidding Sister. Women might start out liking me because I'm good looking, but they keep liking me because I understand that there's a lot more special about women than that. I am going to make sure that any man who wants to step out with you understands how special you are."

"Special?"

"Yeah, real special, I..."

"Aaron come here," Grandma Hester's sharp command cut across the rest of what he had to say.

"Yes, M'am." Aaron stood up with a puzzled look on his face. Those three words were three more than his Grandma had ever said directly to him.

She led him out to the front porch before she said another word. "Go over to the house and get your things. Boy here is going to take you in to Columbia to get some work."

"I got work right here M'am. Daddy needs me to finish spring planting and the younger ones need..."

"He ain't your Daddy. You old enough to have figured that out by now and it ain't right asking a man to raise somebody else's child. I told your Mama that 'fore she married him. You're grown now. Time to make your own way," the old woman finished in an oak hard voice that didn't leave room for debate.

The older people on the porch had gone quiet. Aaron was too embarrassed to argue or beg the old woman to let him stay. One look at the man who had raised him was enough to let him know that there was no help coming from that direction.

Sure, Aaron knew by now that he wasn't Alton Fullmore's natural son. There'd always been enough people to hint at it and when he'd turned eight and still hadn't started school, he'd asked his mother why. She'd explained that since he was so big for his age, Alton figured he could start earning his keep. She didn't feel that she could object too hard because Alton had claimed him and treated him pretty good.

"Can I go say bye first?"

The old woman nodded in agreement.

Sister and Albert Lee were huddled together trying to figure out what Grandma Hester could possibly have to say to Aaron. Other than to order them about, she never had much to say to the men in the family.

"I'm about to go and I..." Aaron couldn't get another word around the lump in his throat.

"Go? Where're you going and why you going today?" Sister demanded.

"I'm going to Columbia to find work. Why today? Cause Grandma Hester says so."

"What did Daddy say? Daddy has the say so over us. Not Grandma Hester. What did Daddy say?" Sister looked around the room for her father but he wasn't where he had been a few minutes ago.

"Daddy didn't say nothing. Not nary a word," Aaron didn't need to say more. Unless their Daddy was willing to speak up and fight for him, Aaron's fate was sealed.

Sister followed Aaron to their house. "Aaron, I'm going with you," she cried as she threw herself into his arms.

"I wish you could little girl, but it's going to be hard enough finding work and a place to stay for myself without worrying about you too."

"I can find work just like you can. I can do anything a grown woman can do."

"I know you can, but the fact is, no one but the folks around here are gonna look at you that way. Now, they gonna see a child and later they gonna see a pretty girl. Either way, I can't protect you in a city that big and work too."

"Aaron, Sister, I just heard," Oscar came running. "I'm going with y'all."

"There ain't no y'all. There's just me that's going. I' tell you what Sister, as soon as I get me a place to stay and a job, I'll write you and send you a piece of money every month." He didn't tell them about not being their Daddy's child. He figured someone would tell them soon enough and he didn't think either of them needed anymore hurt right then.

"You promise? I don't care nothing about the money. I just want to know you're all right," Sister held on to him as tight as she could.

"I promise," Aaron said as he crossed his heart. "Y'all just look out for each other and the little ones and I'll come back to see you when I can."

"You ready?" They hadn't noticed their Uncle Boy standing in the door way. "Come on Aaron. I want to be back as far as my sister Clara's place before it gets too dark." He turned and went back to his wagon. He didn't want to hear the children crying and carrying on. It wasn't up to him. If his mother said Aaron was old enough to go in to Columbia and find his own way then there wasn't much anyone other than Alton Fullmore could do. Right now Alton was too torn up with grief and guilt to deal with Hester James. That was too bad for Aaron, but it wasn't Boy's place to nay-say his mother over a youngun that wasn't even his.

As Aaron rode away it was all he could do to keep from covering his ears to block out Oscar's and Sister's cries.

"Aaron stay with me."

"Aaron take me with you."

"Aaron don't go."

They stood there crying long after the dust in the road settled and the wagon that carried their brother away was nothing more than a speck in the fading sunlight.

"Shut up Oscar. He's gone," Sister whipped her eyes and pulled Oscar out of the road.

Sister swore then that she'd keep the promise that her mother made her swear to almost daily, "Promise me Sister that you won't get mixed up with a man because of his looks or a man who drinks or a man who can't afford to buy you a big house."

Chapter 4

"What's this mess? Sister, I know your mother taught you better than this," Alton Fullmore spit the bite of egg custard pie back onto the plate.

"I didn't have any eggs Daddy and I know how much you look forward to your egg custard pie for Sunday dessert. I did the best I could," Sister appealed to her father.

Egg custard pie. It was one of the special things their mother had done for their father. The children only got a checkered board cake a few times a year, but Julia Mae made sure that as long as she could hunt up two eggs from the four scrawny chickens they managed to keep during the hardest of times, Alton had the best egg custard pie this side of Charleston. Sister's egg custard pie was nearly as good as her mother's had been-when she could find eggs.

"Girl, you can't make egg custard pie without no eggs. You didn't have any eggs for breakfast nary a day this week. I haven't seen any signs of a fox or a wild dog around here or more than the eggs would be missing."

"Grandma Hester said I could use butter milk and lard sometimes when I didn't have no eggs. At least the crust turned out good," Sister tried to placate her father. She was having as much trouble as he did understanding how suddenly there was not an egg to be had especially from Em their most reliable hen.

"Daddy, I thought I heard voices out near the hen house last night," Claretha volunteered this information with a smirk on her face. She'd been waiting for this moment all through dinner. She'd tried to call attention to Oscar a couple of times saying how much better Sister's biscuits and mashed potatoes were than their Mama's had been. Either comment would have gotten a rise out of him any other time. Not today. He hadn't even looked up-just sat there with one hand over his face. Sister noticed that he wasn't eating but she didn't say anything. She just slipped his food from his plate onto hers because their father had this big thing about wasting food.

"Did you recognize any of the voices, Baby?" There were two children younger than Claretha, but their father still called her Baby and treated her like the baby of the family.

"Just one," She paused for effect. "Oscar's voice."

Everyone turned to look at Oscar. He'd been so quiet since Aaron had been sent away that no one except Sister noticed that he hadn't complained about the lack of eggs all week or about an egg custard pie that was nowhere near as good as their mother's had been. He was always Sister's toughest critic when it came to doing anything that their mother had done. The clothes weren't clean enough, his Sunday shirt wasn't ironed right, and nothing Sister cooked was nearly as good as anything their mother had cooked.

"Well, Boy?" Alton Fullmore didn't raise his voice but somehow the next words cut through the air like the crack of a whip. "I'm talking to you, Boy."

Still Oscar didn't say anything. He kept his head down and his hand over the lower part of his face.

"I think one of the voices could have been Pete Jackson," Claretha smiled knowing what effect that name would have on their father. He caught Oscar, Pete Jackson, and a couple of other boys gambling behind the church two Sunday's back. He'd made good and sure Oscar hadn't had a penny to gamble with since then.

"P...P...Pete Jackson? You, you had that f...fool Pete J...Jackson up here to the house near your sisters?"

Oscar still didn't say anything.

Sister was beginning to get nervous. Their father was stammering and whenever that happened for as long as she could remember; their mother had always signaled them to leave the house. He only stammered when he was drunk or real mad. One night, when Sister was about five, she could remember sleeping in Aaron's arms in the woods late into the night and last Christmas they'd had to stay in the woods until the sun came up waiting for their mother to open the door as the signal that it was all right for them to come home. Aaron wouldn't take them so far away that he couldn't hear their mother if she cried for help. Their father never hit their mother, but he would rant and rave all night long about every wrong that had ever been done to him and throw whatever he could pick up at anything that moved except Julia Mae. Alton Fullmore was a quiet, good natured man except when he got drunk or real mad. He was a mean drunk, but he was even worst when he was mad enough to stutter.

"I'm going over to Ned Jackson's place and if I find out y'all have b...been over here g...g...gambling..." He was too angry to finish as he went stamping out the door.

It took him almost two hours to get there and back, but all three of the older children were sitting where he left them at the kitchen table. Albert Lee was where he always was on Sunday, with Grandma Hester. He was the only man child in the family that she allowed to hang around her. Their Daddy said Albert Lee was so sissified that it didn't matter if he stayed over there all the time.

No one moved when they heard the slap of their father's brogan shoes on the front step and the sound of something they couldn't identify dragging behind him.

He walked around the end of the table and stood pinning Oscar between the kitchen wall and the table.

"You know what I found out Boy. Don't you," He slapped what he'd been dragging behind him on the table. It was a thick switch made up from three green vines from the muscadines vines that grew wild in the nearby woods. The vines were woven together and one end was wrapped around his right hand several times.

"You know the Jackson boys said you invited them over here to gamble. Said you claimed you had something better than money to bet. They were thinking you meant one of your sisters, but they found out all you had were some damn eggs. They said they beat you up and took the eggs. What you say?"

Oscar didn't say anything, but he did look up for the first time. The swollen lip and purple black bruises on his cheek gave vivid testimony to what the Jackson boys said.

"Boy, I'm gonna beat that gambling fire out of you. I ain't never seen a gambling man die with more than a pack of cards in his pocket." He grabbed Oscar up from the chair by the collar. "Say something Boy."

Oscar looked him in the eye and said, "I'd rather die with a pack of cards in my pocket than with South Carolina dirt between my toes."

It was the cruelest thing he could have said. The Fullmore children were forced to go barefooted except for the coldest months of the winter. There had never been enough money for an everyday pair of shoes and a Sunday best pair like most of the other children had. Only once had they owned two pairs apiece and Aaron had provided those by playing and singing at the juke joint up in Aikens. Aaron had been so proud when he'd presented Sister, Claretha, Albert Lee and Oscar two pairs of shoes apiece that Christmas morning. But instead of being happy for the children, Alton had started stuttering and cursing. As long as the shoes fit them, he'd only permitted the children to wear the shoes to church and to school after their mother displayed a rare bit of James Woman Spirit- threatening to leave him and take her children over to her parent's house.

Alton back handed Oscar with the same fist that held the switch and tore the shirt off his back with the other hand.

"I don't care what you do to me. I'm leaving here and going in to town to stay with Aaron." Oscar stared defiantly at their father.

This statement fueled his father's anger even more. Last month they'd finally gotten word that Aaron was all right. He was working in a juke joint where his singing and playing the piano was the main attraction.

"Daddy, Daddy don't whip him. Oscar tell him they're lying. Tell him they stole those eggs," Sister yelled at Oscar while she tried to grab the switch from her father's hand.

"Girl, you better leave off before you get some of this," Alton warned as he applied the switch to Oscar's back.

She backed off. She'd taken whippings for Oscar before and he'd taken a couple with her for something she had done, but this time there was something about the way Oscar was behaving that stopped her.

Sister lost count of how many times the braided switch landed on Oscar's back.

Oscar didn't cry. When the blows stopped falling he asked, "Are you through?" And then he picked up a bundle of clothes he'd hidden under his bed sometime during the night and walked out into the early evening light. He didn't look back. He didn't say bye to Sister. He just left.

"Ain't you going too? Y'all always sticking together. Ain't you going to follow him to your precious brother Aaron? We got the Widow to cook for us." Claretha raised her hand to push Sister in the back but one look at Sister's face made her drop her hand inches away.

There was anger in that face and hurt that was almost a physical force. If Claretha was capable of feeling anything for anyone other than herself she would have been moved to feel something close to pity for her twelve year old sister who'd already felt a lifetime of hurt.

"Hush Little Luke," Sister bent to pick up the three year old who was practically climbing up her skirt. His warm little body was shaking with fear. It had been a hard thing he'd just witnessed, but it had been even harder for Sister to see. She'd learned some hard things about both her father and her brother.

The whipping didn't teach her anything new. Bible believing folks around here didn't believe in sparing the rod. No, it wasn't the whipping that incased her heart in ice. It was the look on her father's face when Oscar said what he'd said about dirt between his toes. The look on her father's face told her that her father was a man who cared more about his man's pride than he cared about his children- that's why he'd been so angry when Aaron had brought them those shoes for Christmas the year before their mother died. She'd thought his anger had been about how Aaron had earned the money. Alton had that Sunday-when-it-suited-him-religion that allowed him to drink himself under the table Saturday night then dust himself off on Sunday morning and strut into church to the Deacon's pew.

And Oscar? She looked at the opening to the door that he walked out of moments before as though it was the gate to hell. She'd learned that Oscar was the kind of man who could plan something as low down dirty as stealing food from out of his family's mouths to get what he wanted. There was no doubt in her mind that he'd been planning this ever since they'd found out that Aaron was all right and working at a juke joint in Columbia. He wanted to be away from here. He wanted to be with Aaron and a whipping was a small price to pay for that kind of freedom.

"If I go, are you going to take care of this child and do the rest of my work?" Sister picked Little Luke up to get him ready for the bed that he would be sleeping in alone for the first time in his life.

Chapter 5

It never ended. The work never ended. It seemed to Sister that all she'd done for the last three years since her mother died was wash clothes, iron clothes, cook food, wash dishes, and clean the house. She seldom made it to school anymore and the last time she'd managed to get there, she was so far behind that she'd been too embarrassed to go back.

Daddy had finally gotten them a house with a wooden floor and as much as she'd wanted one, she hated the fact that the house was in the middle of a field that must have been the only place in South Carolina that wouldn't grow anything but dust. No matter how hard she scrubbed the floors or how much of Cousin Bea's special bee's wax and palm oil concoction she applied to the wooden planks, the next day the floor needed washing and waxing again.

Today was wash day and the best thing about the house was its location closer to the river than their last place had been.

"Lord, I've gone so far out in the river that I've wet my drawers," Sister chastised herself. "I'll just take them off and wash them with the rest of the clothes. No one will know I'm cooking and cleaning bare butt." She smiled at her little joke until she noticed that the drawers that she'd just pulled off were bloody. She sat down on the bank trembling and looking at the soiled drawers.

"What's wrong with me? I'm not hurting," she questioned herself as she touched her stomach. A body that was bleeding on the inside should hurt somewhere. There was nothing unusual about the few aches and pains in the muscles of her shoulders and arms. This was what every wash day felt like. Arms feeling like they had been pulled from the sockets and little points of pain radiating up the veins in the back of her hands from wringing out clothes all day was regular Wash Day Pain. No, there was nothing unusual about those pains.

Maybe this is what happens when a girl works herself to death. Her Grandma Hester had been warning her for the last two years that if she didn't get her father to make Claretha help her with the work that she was gonna, "Work herself to death."

Sister looked at the other women with their big wash pots and scrubbing boards up and down both sides of the river. Wednesday was wash day around here for no particular reason other than the fact that it took till Wednesday for the women to catch up on the rest of their work from "resting" on Sunday. All the women planned the rest their work week around wash day. Most of the women in the Bottoms where the sharecroppers and itinerant laborers lived were here somewhere, but Sister didn't see a single one she felt she could talk to.

Cousin Bea was the only woman Sister felt close to, but her husband Grady owned Fulmer Funeral Home and Cousin Bea was not only the only one other than Grandma Hester with running water in the house, she also was the proud owner of a washing machine. She didn't have to come all the way down to the river on wash day.

Since she wasn't hurting and no one seemed to realize that she was dying, Sister waited until she finishing washing the last load of shirts to go up the hill to talk to Cousin Bea. She looked up the hill to make sure Little Luke was alright. He was chasing a chick that had slipped between the wooden stakes of his play pen which was a patch of dirt about eight feet square. Claretha was sitting on the porch step reading. Although she wasn't paying Little Luke any attention and this was her only task, Sister didn't take time to fuss at her about it.

When she got up the hill, Sister followed the beautiful contralto voice to the back porch off the kitchen of Cousin Grady's house. Sister stood in the doorway and wondered what Bea was thinking about because it was clear from the frown on her face that the words to the cheery song weren't reaching her heart.

Sister was right. The white cotton lace dress that she was holding had taken Cousin Bea back to the days when she had worn a dress much like that one.

Cousin Bea was pretty by both Colored folks and White folks standards. Her skin would have been considered tan on a White person and she had "good hair" which meant that it didn't have to be straightened. But more than the complexion and the long shiny hair, her features were delicate finely drawn in shades of rose pink and a slightly darker shade of brown.

She and Sister's mother had been competing "belles" of their day. Everyone said Bea won when she married Grady Fulmer, the twin with all the money, but Bea had been in love with Alton.

It would have been funny if it had not hurt so much that everyone except Alton and Grady could see that she was just as pretty as Julia Mae. The brother's had entered into a kind of competition for Julia Mae's hand. Both thought they had lost out to that handsome school teacher until Julia Mae suddenly married Alton.

Even when six months later they found out why she'd married Alton, Grady stayed angry. For years, Bea had felt like a consolation prize and she hurt every time she went into the graveyard to put flowers on her first born little son's grave because from there she could see the bright bouquet of yellow roses that were always fresh on Julia Mae's grave. Everyone else thought Hester James put the flowers on her daughter's grave, but Bea had heard the brothers arguing about it. Grady knew that his brother would figure out that the yellow roses were his because yellow roses had been his token when he courted Julia Mae. Grady put the roses there to hurt Alton, but it hurt Bea more.

When Bea looked up from her washing to see Alton's tiny image in the form of Sister, she couldn't help but smile until she noticed the tears that had dried on the girl's cheeks. "What's wrong Baby Girl?

Sister smiled through the tears. Cousin Bea had never stopped using the pet name. Sister had been the first girl born in a family of boys in almost twenty years and although she had remained the only girl for barely 10 months, Bea had let her keep the title of Baby Girl. Sister loved her for that.

"I think I'm dying, Cousin Bea. Look," She held out the soiled drawers for Cousin Bea to see.

"Oh, Baby Girl, I keep forgetting how young you were when your Mama died. Guess she didn't have time to explain about how a woman's body works. You're not dying. You've just become a woman. That's all. Come, I'll explain things and show you what you need to do."

Sister was mad as she walked home. What was God thinking? First women had to do all the work around the house, help with the planting and harvest, and have babies till they died.

Have babies.

Sister stopped with that. Since her mother's death, she'd been a kind of mother to Little Luke. It seemed the only time she got to stop and sit awhile during the day was when she was cleaning a hurt or bruised knee or comforting him after come mishap. She couldn't see a man doing the kind of nurturing a baby needed. "Okay, God. You got me on that one," she looked up and nodded her approval.

She walked over to the little play yard that her father had constructed for Little Luke. She put him in it when she was working outside. It was made of wooden stakes placed too close together for him to squeeze out or for any of the larger farm animals or dogs to get in. Little Luke wasn't there.

"Claretha, where is Little Luke?" Sister screamed as she ran into the house.

"What are you yelling about? I had Daddy take him in to Wagoner to Aunt Clare. She's got all those girls and she said in church last Sunday that he was the cutest little thing with those dimples in his cheeks. Said she wished she had a little boy just like him. I thought you'd be glad. It's less work for us with him gone."

"Less work for us? What do you mean us? The only work you do is to go to the mail box every day. You ain't never done nothing for that child but call me. How long they been gone?

"Too long ago for you to catch up to them."

"We'll see about that." Sister took off running down the road toward Wagoner, South Carolina where their Aunt Clare lived. She couldn't lose Little Luke too.

Everyone who loved her got gone. Died. Sent away or ran away like Oscar had done a month ago when Daddy whipped him for gambling away all the chicken's eggs.

She ran until she got a painful catch in her side. She ran until her chest hurt. She ran until her body shut down and she collapsed in the middle of the road.

Her father found her there on his way back from Wagoner. When he couldn't wake her up, he took her to Hester James. The old woman's wrath when Julia Mae died had taught him a valuable lesson: Let Hester James do all she could to save one of her own.

****

When Hester James couldn't figure out what was wrong, she sent for the young Colored doctor who had moved into Aikens last summer. He determined that Sister was suffering from exhaustion and an enlarged heart.

Grandma Hester's cure for both ailments was to send Sister to live in Greensboro, North Carolina with her daughter Daisy. Alton didn't put up much of an argument and Sister just didn't care either way. Mama was gone. Grandma Hester had never let the baby Emma Margaret come to live with them so she might as well be gone. Albert Lee spent every waking moment with Grandma Hester. Aaron was gone. Oscar was gone. Now, Little Luke had been sent away too. No one who loved her stayed.

Chapter 6

"So, you're Sister?" Daisy Evans took her time looking over the young girl who had been given into her keeping. It seemed that as the only married woman with no children in her family her home had become the place to send orphaned teenage girls. Since she'd left home to live on her own at 15, everyone expected her to know what to do with wayward teens. Daisy hadn't considered herself wayward. She wanted to continue her education beyond 8th grade and when Hester James said "no" she got a visiting cousin to take her into Columbia to Benedict College. All she'd told them was that she was Hester James daughter. That was enough to get her foot in the door and by the time they found out that Hester James wasn't going to pay for her education Daisy had earned enough money doing rich Colored girls laundry and giving them White girl hair styles that she could pay her own tuition.

Daisy hoped that this one would be easier to handle than Glady the young cousin that she had been caring for the last four years had been. At least this one still had the look of a child. At 13, Glady's body had been that of a full-grown woman and it had taken Daisy all of four years to rein her in.

The eyes that looked up at her today still had a touch of innocence combined with something Daisy had only seen in her mother's Hester James eyes-ten years of knowing for each year lived.

"Yes M'am," Sister identified herself and stood there quietly hoping to pass inspection and trying to keep the adoration out of her eyes. No one dressed in the style and class of her aunt. The herringbone, brown, wool suit with its matching hat was tailor made to fit her shapely body.

"Let's get that straight right now. It's Aunt Daisy. Nothing else. When I get older than 39 you can Yes M'am and No M'am me."

"Yes, Aunt Daisy," Sister didn't want to get off on the wrong foot with this particular relative. She knew the woman standing before her was her mother's older sister by three years so Sister knew she was already three years past 39, but she couldn't claim to know much more than that about her. Aunt Daisy was one of those relatives that lived "Up North" and only came home for funerals or an occasional Big Meeting at the church during revival season.

Once, Sister and Claretha had disagreed almost to the point of blows on whether their mother or Aunt Daisy was the prettier of the two sisters. Sister knew why Claretha said their mama was prettier. Claretha was color struck. If a woman couldn't pass the brown-paper-bag-test, there was no way Claretha would say the woman was pretty. Aunt Daisy couldn't pass the test. She was honey brown rather than high yellow like their mother had been. But Sister could see beyond the skin color to the fine boned, strong features of their ancestors- the long, elegant neck, the high cheeks, and plum ripe lips. Aunt Daisy was only about 5'2 but this was tall for a James woman. To the fourteen-year-old girl just in from Salley, South Carolina this woman embodied everything she wanted to be.

"How far you get in school, Sister?"

"I was only ten when Mama died and I had to stop to take care of the house and cook for the men." Sister knew that her answer implied that she had made it past fifth grade.

"Well, we can't put a girl as big as you in fifth grade. I'll take you to the upper school of Washington Street School.

"I didn't bring any report cards or anything. A girl from home who came up here three years ago got put back two whole grades because they say the schools up here are that much better than ours."

"Maybe, but that don't have anything to do with you. You're smart. I remember that much about you and Aaron. Smart is smart anywhere."

Sister kept trying to think of a way to explain that because she'd missed so many days of school the teacher put her back in third grade twice. She studied Claretha's and Aaron's books after she stopped going to school altogether, but she knew that wouldn't mean anything to the people at the school. When they arrived at the two story building, Sister was too astonished to speak.

"Well, don't stand there with your mouth hanging open," Daisy Evans turned around and signaled for the Sister to precede her into the building.

"Colored children go to school here?" Sister couldn't believe her eyes. It was an old building but it was made solidly with a brick foundation and the stucco exterior was painted white.

"Washington School was built for Colored children back in 1915. It went from first grade to 8th grade until the High School for Negro Children opened in 1923 at Bennett College. It went all the way up to 11th grade for a time until Dudley High School opened back in 1929. They're going to build a new school just for the little children and when the school on Lincoln Street is finished. It's going to be a big time Junior High School. I only know all that 'cause of Willie. He likes all kind of history things like that.

"Sit there," Daisy Evans said as she pointed to a bench across from the office and then turned and marched up to a fair skinned man of average height. "Are you in charge here?"

"Yes, I'm Mr. Leary the principal. May I help you?" He said in a pleasant voice that was the only thing about him that gave away his race. It wasn't that his voice was uncultured or uneducated sounding. It was the deep baritone of a full grown Colored man.

"I am Mrs. Evans. I came to enroll my 13 year-old niece in your fine school. I work at A&T and I want the best education possible for her." Daisy Evans stood patiently as he summed her up. The fitted wool suit, matching hat with a

narrow brim and polished dark brown pumps
gave him the impression that she was probably
one of the few new female teachers at the
college.

"Do you have her records?" I can't enroll
a child without the proper records."

"When I asked about her records at that
little one-room country school she attended,
they looked at me like I was crazy," She didn't
stop talking when she saw the frown begin to
form on his face. "Her mother was a teacher
before she married so she mostly taught her
children at home. I'm sure that you will find
that Mary Helen will be able to keep up."

"I don't know. We have very strict rules
about records and such.

"I tell you what, if you allow her to
attend school here for ten school days and she
can't keep up, I'll take her out of public school
and send her to Palmer Institute. I really didn't
want to do that because we just found out that
she has a weak heart and I'd rather have her
with me than living on campus. This was her
first ace. She knew that the Colored people in
Greensboro were mighty proud of the public
schools for their children. Some of them
resented the uppity Colored folks who
continued to send their children to the private
school for Colored children in Sedalia. And
then she played her second ace. She gave him
the smile that she reserved for men. It was a
James woman trade mark that was so rarely
used that any man who received one counted
himself blessed.

It worked. Mr. Leary practically melted before their eyes. "That sounds fair. We do have a $2 book fee and at least a part of that must be paid before she can get her books. There's nothing I can do about the fee," he sounded almost apologetic.

"That won't be a problem. I'll pay it all now," Daisy Evans reached into her pocketbook and handed him a ten-dollar bill. "I'll donate the change for some poor children who can't afford to pay the fee."

Mr. Leary was so impressed with someone having a ten-dollar bill in the middle of the month that he took them directly to the bookroom and pulled the math, science, English, and history books for seventh graders from the shelf himself.

Sister couldn't do anything but stare from her aunt to Mr. Leary during the entire exchange in total amazement. Everything her Aunt had said had some truth in it. Her mother had taught her children more at home than they learned in school, Sister was 13 going on 14, and her Aunt Daisy did work in the kitchen at A&T. That was where any semblance to the truth ended. Although the school was small, it had more than one room and they kept excellent records.

****

"So, this is another one of your nieces," Willie Evans smiled down at the girl who personified what he liked best about the James women- they were shorter than he was. His wife at 5'2 inches was taller than her mother and siblings, but she was still a full two inches shorter than he was. This child was even shorter - only about 4'6inches tall. "I thought you said she was 13 years old?"

"I did and she is. She's taller than my mother so I guess she's as tall as she's going to get. Her height just means that it won't be much of a problem when they put her back a couple of grades 'cause she's from a South Carolina school."

"What are you talking about Daisy? Why would they put her back two grades just 'cause she's from South Carolina?"

"That's what they do up here because they say South Carolina schools are backwards up against theirs."

"Well, that ain't about to happen with me here. Are those the books you'll be using?

"Yes, Sir," Sister spoke for the first time. She was learning fast. If she kept her mouth closed and listened to Aunt Daisy's explanation for everything, things happened that she'd never imagined. She'd gotten placed in 7th grade without ever finishing the fourth grade. She'd gotten five brand new dresses without any money changing hands. Daisy had put the three ready-made dresses on her account and commissioned the seamstress to make two more dresses. And now she was about to get an at home teacher all to herself.

"Did they tell you where they are in these books?" Willie asked as he thumbed through the books that Sister handed to him.

"Yes Sir. The teacher gave me this. She gave him a sheet of note paper with book titles and page numbers on it.

"Come sit at the table with me. When I get through with you, they'll be putting all those other children back three grades."

Daisy Belle James Evans smiled to herself as she turned to go to the bedroom to change out of her best suit before starting dinner. Although Willie never mentioned it, she knew he hurt deep down inside because he'd "wasted" the college education that his family of over forty siblings from one father, his natural mother and two stepmothers had put in nickels and dimes to pay for him to have the chance to receive. Willie used every opportunity to show off how much he knew. Yes, find a man's sore spot and you could get him to do anything you wanted him to do. And right now, she wanted him to teach Sister enough each night to keep her in school for the next ten days.

****

Sister had to keep herself from developing a crush on Willie Evans. It was hard because he was fast taking the place in her heart that had been vacant for three years. She'd decided that as a group of people men just weren't worth loving unless you wanted to get lied to and hurt. They never kept promises. Aaron hadn't sent her a dime or written her a single letter. The piece of money didn't matter, but the lack of that monthly letter had hurt so deep that Sister still had scabs on her heart.

Her Uncle Willie was a different kind of man. He not only kept promises, he made a body feel better about herself just by being around him. When Sister confessed that she fooled Aunt Daisy into thinking she was in 7th grade Willie had laughed so hard he fell on the floor.

When he finished laughing, he said, "You think you smart enough to trick Daisy Belle? If you are, you know too much for me to be teaching you anything."

"What I did ain't funny Uncle Willie. She deserves better for taking me in." Sister was hurt and confused that he would laugh about something that had made her feel so ashamed that her stomach hurt.

"I ain't laughing 'because it's funny. I'm laughing 'cause it means that you don't know anything about Daisy Belle. Let me show you something," he said as he walked over to Daisy's dresser. He pulled a package wrapped in brown paper from the drawer and spent the next ten minutes trying to remember exactly where and how it had been wrapped so he could put it back without his wife knowing that he had been in her things. "Look at this?" He handed Sister a folder.

It contained copies of her grades and the number of days she'd missed each school year and twice it had the words, NOT PROMOTED in all capital letters. Sister was so ashamed. She'd missed the rest of the year when her mother had died on March 22nd and she hadn't been able to start school the next year until after harvest. And then Luke had caught the whooping cough and she'd missed almost a month nursing him.

"Don't cry, Sister, I didn't show you this to make you cry. I just wanted you to know that

Daisy Belle made sure she knew all about you before she agreed to let you come stay with us. She didn't want to get caught up with another "wild child" like Glady. We know you got held back because you missed too many days not because you're dumb."

"Why she ask me what grade I was in then?"

"She just wanted to see what you would say. She was right proud that you managed not to tell her the truth without out-and-out lying to her. She said she thought that meant you had some potential."

"Potential for what?"

"Now, that I don't know. Help me get this wrapped back up and put away before Daisy Belle gets home."

Yes, her Uncle Willie was a man who kept promises. He promised to make sure she kept up in school and he did. Willie taught her enough to not only keep her in school for the ten days, but to put her near the top of the class for the next three years. When Sister got home each day her uncle had her lessons ready for the evening. Willie was usually home all day because he had something wrong with his stomach that made it hard for him to digest almost all meat and most vegetables unless Daisy mashed them up real fine. So, he had time on his hands that he was more than happy to spend staying ahead of Sister's teachers.

Chapter 7

Joe straightened his tie and petted his head to make sure that the Royal Crown Pomade® was doing its job. He bent over and used his handkerchief to restore the military shine to his shoes. Without noticing what he was doing, he pulled his lean, muscular body up to its -full six-foot one inch height, put his shoulders back, and pushed his chest out before he knocked on the door.

This was it, his entry into Colored Society in Greensboro, North Carolina - his first visit to Miss Daisy Evans' House - the place to be. On the Colored side of town, a body could buy liquor and drink it by their lonesome self or they could go to Miss Daisy's and have some laughs with their drinks.

He planned on having a real good time. It had been but six weeks since the war was over. He'd spent the last four years as a cook at a base in Southern Georgia waiting for things to get bad enough with the Japes for the White boys to decide they needed his all Colored Unit. They hadn't gotten to go, but he'd talked to some Colored boys who'd gone to France and Germany. They'd done more than fight flies. Done some real fighting. They had medals. He had one too. What did it matter to him that it was for a grease fire in the kitchen?

"Forget it Joe, them 'years are gone. Ain't nothing you can do about them," he told himself for the five hundredth last time as he put his hat on then took it off again when the shortest little somebody he'd seen in a long time opened the door and stared up at him.

"Good evening sir, you here to see Aunt Daisy or Uncle Willie?" she asked him. The way she looked at him made him more than a little bit mad because it hadn't been much more than a glance, but somehow he knew that she felt that it had been enough to sum him up as a man and that she hadn't thought very much of what she saw.

"Good evening Miss. He smiled the smile that had had drawers dropping all over York County in South Carolina since he was twelve.

The smile had no effect on Sister. The only ugly man in her family was her brother Oscar and he was the one she loved best. He couldn't get by on his looks like the rest of the men in the family. He'd always had to work hard for everything he got. Sister could appreciate that. Up until three years ago when they'd found out that she had an enlarged heart, she'd worked like a grown woman since before her mother died when she was ten years old.

No, a smiling, handsome man meant nothing to Sister. All she wanted to know was how much money a man still had in his pockets come Monday morning.

Almost as though he could read her mind he said, "Don't be hard on me like that. Just because I'm here don't mean I'm like the other men who come here. How long you been here?"

"Three years," she didn't know why she was still talking to him much less answering his questions.

"Have you ever seen me before in all that time?"

"No."

"See. I'm not a regular."

"Oh," Sister didn't apologize for thinking he was a drunk. They had other liquor houses in Greensboro.

"So, let's start over. Good evening. My name is Joseph Ervin Evans, Jr. recently Private First Class Evans in the United States Army. My friends call me Joe." He had taken off his hat and held it military fashion in his right hand. He realized by now that it was going to take a bit more than the usual amount of charm to impress this young woman. Even though she sounded like a grown woman, she was so tiny he was beginning to wonder if she really was full grown.

"Well, Mr. Evans," she stressed the *Mr.* part of his name to emphasize the fact that she had no intension of starting anything or of being his friend, "Come on in. Who you said you're here to see?"

"Miss Daisy," Joe said. His brother had told him to be sure to ask for Miss Daisy. Although her husband Willie Evans was a distant cousin on their father's side, asking for

Willie branded a man as an outsider who didn't even know anybody who knew somebody. Everyone knew that Miss Daisy was in charge and that her husband Willie was the entertainment.

"I'll get her," she said and walked off and left him standing there.

He stayed where she left him. The room was too dark to do anything else until his eyes got adjusted. That first thing he saw when he could see better, was a woman so fine he thought that he still must be half blind. She was almost as short as the girl who'd opened the door and it was clear from their eyes and mouths that they were related somehow but there the similarity ended. This was a woman- a full grown woman with skin a couple of shades darker than honey, eyebrows finely arched over eyes that were almond shaped and slightly slanted, high cheek bones, hair so thick and fine that it no doubt came down to her waist when she wasn't wearing it up in matching twists on each side of a single part, and lips as full and sweet looking as ripe plums. He'd heard the term timeless beauty from some of those college boys in his unit, but he'd never witnessed it. The women in his family were beauties until age forty then their warm seamless yellow skin turned brown and wrinkled like empty potato sacks. There wasn't any way of telling how old Miss Daisy was and he was sure that fifty years from now she would look just as good.

She didn't say anything while he stood there staring like a fool. Men had looked at her like that all her life and she accepted it as her due as any woman who knows that she is beautiful does.

"Ma'am, I. That is... my brother, Robert Lee Evans, told me about your place. I sure would appreciate coming in to visit for awhile." He hadn't felt this young and untried since he was a boy of twelve thirteen years ago.

"What's this Ma'am stuff? Do I look like your mama?"

"No, Ma'am. You sure don't."

"Well, come on in. Drinks are twenty-five cents and the company is free. I don't run no whore house so you can look for that somewhere else."

He started to say, "Yes, Ma'am," again but she'd already turned to speak to another gentleman.

Joe looked around. He wasn't sure what he'd been expecting in the big city, but at first this liquor house wasn't that much different from those he'd visited in York, South Carolina.

There was the usual horse hair sofa on one wall with a circle of chairs around the room. Then a closer look offered the differences that made Daisy's place special. Next to each of the chairs was a small smoking table with a metal ashtray nailed to the top and a small drawer in the front of each table that held cigarettes. There was enough room next to the ashtray for a drink and a saucer that held either a couple of pickled boiled eggs or a handful of boiled peanuts. Joe checked the floor for shells-not nary a one. Then he watched as one man put his shells in a bucket and then politely passed the bucket around to the man next to him. Joe was impressed. He'd never been anyplace that served food or where a fight hadn't broken out at the rate of at least one an hour. Here, there was much the same kind of talking and sharing stories that soldiers carried on in the bunkhouses on the base at night. The quiet hum said that most of the people there knew each other.

The food and polite manner of the men was strange but the strangest things Joe noticed was that no one was all that drunk and that the two young women there both appeared to be related to Miss Daisy. Although one was the pretty little thing that answered the door and the other one was a big boned, big busted, high yellow gal, no one treated them like they were selling anything but drinks.

He was still standing where Miss Daisy had left him when he heard a silky female voice say, "Joe, come here let me introduce you to the boys." She'd been watching him standing there taking up space and not drinking long enough. It wasn't good for business having a man standing in her place looking like someone just in from the country.

Joe smiled when he turned to follow Miss Daisy around the room fully unaware of what she really thought of him.

That was it, Joe thought. He was in. Miss Daisy knew his name. He didn't know that she knew everyone's name. It was business to her. She knew men. She knew people. She knew how to make each and every person feel special.

Joe felt really special that night except
for one little thing that should not have bothered
him at all: the girl who'd opened the door
hadn't seemed to think that he was special at all

Chapter 8

Joe had been planning his strategy for a full week. She would notice him this week for sure. He'd avoided going into the kitchen where Willie held court last week. The girl didn't think much of him coming here to drink a bit. He knew gambling would be another mark against him.

When the girl opened the door to Miss Daisy's Liquor House, he smiled and handed her a bag of hard candy.

She looked from him to the bag and then up again. "Daisy don't take nothing in trade. If you don't have any money, you need to take this and go back to where you came from," she said as she attempted to hand him back the bag.

"I got money. That's for you. Sweets for the sweetest little thing in here," Joe said as he pushed the bag back toward her. He expected her to melt into his arms.

She peaked into the bag. She loved hard candy-every flavor, every color, but she couldn't let him see that. She knew she shouldn't take anything from this man. "I don't much care for hard candy." She set it on a table when he still wouldn't take it back. "Daisy or Willie?"

"Willie, he's a relative of mine," If his patented smile and candy didn't do the trick, maybe it was time to play his ace. Maybe being kin to Willie would soften her heart.

"Willie got more kin than anybody I know. His daddy married three women and had 'bout ten children off each of them." Come on in. Willie is at the kitchen table playing cards with some friends."

Joe stepped into the front room when she moved back from the door. He was puzzled. Women just didn't react to him this way. He knew he was the kind of good looking that women liked- lean, dark, but not too dark, white even teeth, and sexy sleepy eyes that didn't miss much. It usually didn't take him long to size up a woman, but he figured that the women he was used to dealing with were much older than this one. No, he clearly hadn't figured her out yet, but what he saw right now intrigued him.

He watched her as she turned to lead him to the back of the three-room shotgun house. Though he kept his eyes on her, he couldn't help but take a Colored man's notice of his surroundings. A black boy learned early on to know three things when he entered a place: who was there, what woman was "with" which man, and where all the exits were. This kind of noticing was so second nature to the twenty-five-year-old that it hardly took his eyes from the young woman.

She was sure dressed like a woman and every curve shouted WOMAN. The mid-calf length of her hem showed him enough of her shapely legs and ankles to make his mouth go dry. And, Lord, Lord, he'd been dreaming of thick long hair like that for the last six months while they'd been confined to base because of all of the big events that had been taking place during the last six months of World War II.

"Willie, there's somebody here to see you," Sister went to the kitchen counter and got one of the bowls of boiled peanuts and poured the pickled boiled eggs out of the brine that she and Daisy spent a good part of the day preparing into a small pail and went back to the front room. Daisy Evans served the best eats of any liquor house in the county. The men thought Daisy did it because she was classy, but it was just business to Daisy. She wanted them to stay there drinking not leaving to go to Marie's Grill to get something to eat.

"Joe Ervin, man is that you? Willie said as he laid his hand face down on the table, not that it made any difference. It was a losing hand. Willie always got a losing hand. The only thing he'd ever won was Daisy James. No, that was another little lie he told himself. She'd picked him. Just walked up to him and said, "I'm ready for a new man. You'll do."

"Yeah, it's me. Come all this way up North to see my little cousin," Joe smiled down at the man who wasn't much taller than the girl who'd answered the door. Nothing ever changed about Willie. He looked like one of the cherubs painted on the wall behind the pulpit at Joe's church back home. No one would guess that he was forty-five years old. He was better educated than most of the men in Joe's family because his small size and poor health had rendered him useless as a farm laborer. His family had sent him all the way to Columbia to attend Benedict College. Willie had tried his hand at being a preacher like his family expected, but it hadn't worked out.

"Robert Lee, Willie turned to Joe's brother, sitting across the table, "You ain't said anything about Joe being up here."

"What's there to say? Joe's here," Since this was way over Robert Lee's maximum of one- or two-words Willie let it ride.

"Willie, tell me about that girl with the long hair serving drinks?" Joe asked.

"Don't even think about her. She's Daisy's niece. Come up here three years ago to stay with us. Daisy is real protective of that girl. She's been trying to get the country out of that girl but Sister won't ever be sophisticated like my Daisy." Willie didn't tell Joe that he was protective of Sister too. He knew too much about "Cousin Joe" and his way with women to trust him around his niece. Willie made up his mind to keep a sharp eye on Joe.

Joe didn't talk to Sister anymore that time or the next three times he went to Daisy's place. He learned quite a bit about her though by asking questions on the sly. He knew that her home was in Salley, South Carolina, that her mother had died when she was ten years old, and that she was fifteen- sixteen- he corrected himself, nine years older seemed a lot less than ten somehow. He knew what he was going to say. He had thought about it all week. He was just waiting for the right time.

Chapter 9

The *right time* didn't get there because he hadn't been nearly as slick about those questions as he thought he'd been. As soon as he walked in two Friday evenings later, Sister lit into him like white-on-rice.

"What you asking questions about me for?" Anything you want to know about me you best be asking me. You think these people know me? All they know is that I'm Daisy's niece. You want to know more than that you better be asking me about me," she said all this without taking so much as a breath.

If he was supposed to answer- he couldn't because he was too busy looking at her lips. They weren't full like Daisy's but they looked like they needed to be kissed. He laughed when he thought this and that made her even angrier.

"Are you laughing at me? You don't know me boy. I will beat you like you belong to me," she planted her doll sized fists on her hips and gave him what was supposed to be a very mean look.

He laughed even harder. He couldn't help it, the image of her with her ninety pound self beating him up was just too much. And the fact that she really believed that she could was even funnier. "I'm sorry, I didn't mean to laugh. You're such a sweet young thing. I just wanted to know all about you," was all Joe could manage to get out."

"I don't care how much you ask other folks; you still won't know nothing important about me. You don't know nothing about me. Don't know I'm sweet. Don't know I'm young. All Fullmore's are short," She didn't smile back. She didn't have time for the drunks who came to her Aunt's place. Liquor drinking men didn't have any money after the weekend and Sister was determined that the one thing she'd never be referred to as being again was "poor."

"Oh, but I still want to know all about you," He smiled the smile that had had drawers dropping all over York County in South Carolina since he was twelve.

The smile still had no effect on Sister. The only ugly man in her family was her brother Oscar and he was the one she loved best. He couldn't get by on his looks like the rest of the men in the family. He'd always had to work hard for everything he got. Sister could appreciate that. Up until two years ago when they'd found out that she had an enlarged heart, she'd worked like a grown woman since before her mother died when she was ten years old.

No, a smiling handsome man meant nothing to Sister. All she wanted to see was how much money a man still had in his pockets come Monday morning.

Almost as though he could read her mine he said, "Don't be hard like that. Just because I'm here don't mean I'm like the other men who come here. How long you been here?"

She looked hurt and that dried up all his laughter. She had four- brothers so she was used to being picked on and laughed at. That wasn't what hurt her now. She hurt now when she remembered when the being picked on and laughed at stopped. March 22, 1941. The day her mother died and her oldest brother was taken away from her and the other brother that she'd been closest to left home. She and Claretha, a sister eleven months younger than she, had been left to care for their father and their youngest brother. She stopped fighting boys and being a child then.

"Go on and beat me up if you want to." he said as he flashed the smile which had been making hearts flip over-since he was a boy. It worked again.

She looked at him for the first time as something more than one of Aunt Daisy's customers. She didn't have any use for men who drank. Drinking had been the reason her father sold his interest in the family business for thirty dollars and it was his drinking that caused the whole family to live with the shame of being the poor Fullmore's -the ones who didn't have a pot to piss in or a door to throw it out. No, she didn't have any use for Daisy's customers because she was going to have something in this life.

Still he was good looking, too damn good looking and that was a fact. Why did he have to show up here with his dark, smooth skin and brown eyes so dark that they looked black? She had her plans and they didn't include him or anybody like him.

"Mary Helen, why you have to notice how handsome he is," she lectured herself. You know looks don't mean spit. You want a man that's going to buy you a nice big house and dress you up fine. Tell him to get out of your face.

"What you asking about me for?" she said instead of what she knew she should have said.

"I wanted to know who that pretty little thing was that gave me such a warm welcome the first time I came in here. That's all, my name is Joseph Ervin Evans, Jr. everyone round here calls you Sister, but what's your real name.

"How you know Sister ain't my real name? He'd hit another sore spot. She'd gotten a whipping, no two whippings, on her first day of school because the teacher-thought that she was being smart mouthed when she told her that her name was Sister. The teacher whipped her and sent her to get one of her older brothers and when her brother, Oscar, declared that her name was Sister she whipped them both.

"It's Mary Helen. Not that knowing it is going to do you any good because I don't believe I like you at all."

"That's because you don't know me yet. Before I get through with you, like won't even be close to what you'll be feeling, girl."

She shook her head and walked away certain that he was in for a wide awaking. She knew he had too many marks against him, he picked on folk, he drank, and he thought, no he knew that he was handsome.

"I don't need that. Aunt Daisy brought me up here to better myself, not to get myself a man like that." She told herself that a dozen times that evening and hundreds of times more during the next three months, but it didn't do her any good.

Mary Helen even tried to give him to her cousin Glady, who'd been living with Aunt Daisy since she was two years old. Her mother hadn't died, but she might as well have been dead because she'd married a man who said he wasn't going to raise any seed that he hadn't planted. Glady wanted Joe and she couldn't understand why he would want a half sized girl when he could have a real woman.

Helen agreed with Glady. She knew that she would never have more than a fist full of tits, but Glady was a year-younger than she and she already had enough on her chest to put Carnation out of business.

****

When they went to the movies that Saturday Mary Helen maneuvered until Glady was sitting next to Joe and she was as far away from them as she could get with Uncle Willie, Aunt Daisy, Joe's brother- Robert Lee, and his wife Inez between them.

Mary Helen told herself that the only reason it bothered her when Glady kept saying, "Oh Joe, you is so strong. You gone hold my hand when I get scared," was the fact that the movie was a Western. And it wouldn't have phased her one bit that Glady kept throwing herself on top of him like they was in a bedroom somewhere and if Glady had not kept blocking that man's vision who was sitting behind her and Joe. It didn't occur to Mary Helen that she didn't know the man so it shouldn't have bothered her whether he could see or not.

"That girl just don't have no manners at all." Mary Helen fumed as she made up her mind to tell Glady about herself the instant they got back home.

"You want to change seats with me?" Aunt Daisy called down the row the third time that Mary Helen leaned so far forward that she bumped her head on the seat in front of her .

"No, M'am. I'm just rubbing my leg; I think I hit it on something coming in." She would have rolled her eyes when she said this if she'd been certain that Aunt Daisy wouldn't be able to see her.

"Your head ought to be hurting worst by now," Robert Lee just had to add like somebody wanted to hear his two cents worth.

Mary Helen sat back and didn't bother to comment on that, but it took so much of her will power and good nature not to lean forward again that as soon as the movie was over, she left all of them standing in her dust,

"What you do that for?" Joe asked catching up to her quickly since each one of his steps made three of hers.

"Do what?" she said giving what she hoped was an innocent look.

"Why you put me with that big, ugly cousin of yours? That's what."

He'd noticed that Glady was ugly. That was a revelation about him. Most men didn't see pass those big tits of hers. Maybe there was some hope for him after all she decided, but she wasn't ready to let him know that she was considering rethinking the situation.

"She ain't ugly, just different looking. I've heard lots of men say that next to Aunt Daisy, Glady got the best shape in Greensboro."

"I hadn't noticed," Joe said looking right into her eyes as she turned and stopped on the top step putting herself on his level since he was still on the walkway. I hadn't noticed because I'd already picked you."

"Picked me! Like I'm a flower or something. You don't pick me. I'd pick you, if I wanted you; which I don't. The women in our family pick our own men, so we know we're getting what we want," Mary Helen said in her tallest huffed up voice."

"They do," he said in a husky whisper as he put one hand under her hair messaging the back of her neck.

"They do," she almost shouted back trying to ignore the waves of warmth that were radiating from her neck to places that had never felt so alive before.

"Then pick me," he said in a voice so thick with something she was hearing for the first time that she thought he could hear her knees knocking.

"What you say? She squeaked out, hating the way she sounded because it made her feel smaller than her four feet six inches.

"I said, pick me because no matter who does the picking, you are going to be mine little lady."

"Be strong Mary Helen. Think about all those stories your grandma done told you about the women in the family that got picked instead of doing the picking. God help me," she prayed and preached herself a good sermon while she stood there trying to look anywhere but into those smoke house colored eyes of his that could leave a girl feeling sugar cured all the way through.

"Joe, I don't want you and God knows, I don't need you." she almost pleaded.

"You gonna do both of those things before I'm through with you girl," he said as he lifted her head with his finger under her chin and traced the curve of her bottom lip with his thumb before he turned and left her standing there wondering why men never fought fair.

The battle was on.

The more she denied him the kinder and more charming he was to her. The small gifts that he gave her probably wouldn't have made a dent in the armor of a more sophisticated woman but the bags of rock candy and wild flowers completely disarmed the girl who had been robbed of her childhood. She got no help from her Aunt Daisy in her fight to resist him, because he'd done the gentlemanly thing of asking Daisy's permission to court her.

****

"I don't know, Aunt Daisy. Joe says he likes my hair down my back,"
Sister turned her head from side to side trying to get a better view of her hair in the mirror.

"All the more reasons to wear it up sometime; makes em wonder what it looks like down."

"Joe already knows what it looks like down so where's the mystery."

"He knows what it looks like down when you looking like a child, but he don't know what it looks like when you're dressed like this. My Daddy told me about a place where a woman's hair is said to be so special only her husband is allowed to see it. This here hairdo says, "I'm special.""

"May be," Sister, looked at the hairstyle that was done up by pinning her hair into a knot at the base of her neck. Her aunt had parted her hair on the left side of her forehead starting a thick roll that continued behind her left ear, and then pulled all her hair on both sides of the part back into a knot at the base of her neck. "What did you say this is called?"

"A Chignon. It's French. All the White women are putting their hair up like this for special occasions. You just need one more little touch." She reached around and took a string of pearls from a small red lacquer box and clasped them around Sister's neck.

"Thank..." Sister started.

"No, don't say thank you 'cause I ain't giving them to you or anyone else. When I die I want to be buried with them round my neck or I'm coming back here and hurting somebody. I'm letting you wear them 'cause I guess your first time stepping out with your man is special enough for these.

"Joe ain't my man. My man gonna be one that don't drink and is rich enough to buy me a big house like the ones they building down the street from that fancy Colored hospital.

"You've been listening to my Mama?"

"No, well not just to Grandma Hester. Mama told me the same thing lots of times,"

"Humph, I'll guess Joe'll have to do while you're waiting for your man 'cause he's here. No, you sit down. I'll get it. Don't ever make a man think you can't wait to see him or that you ain't worth waiting for." Daisy smiled at her niece as she turned to answer the door.

Sister had to make herself wait the whole twenty minutes that her Aunt Daisy told Joe it would be before she was ready. She spent most of it walking back and forth in front of the dresser mirror looking at the way the polished cotton dress with red roses printed on a white background moved when she walked. It wasn't new. It was one of her Aunt's best dresses from last summer, but Joe hadn't been here last season when Aunt Daisy wore it. The dress wasn't as full in the skirt as Sister was used to. Her Aunt made her practice walking in it for almost an hour. Although Sister couldn't understand how in the world women got anywhere taking such small steps, she was determined to do precisely what Aunt Daisy said was right. She'd seen the way men looked at Daisy when she walked across the room in this very dress and that look Uncle Willie wore when he saw them watching that said, "I'm proud she's my woman."

Yes, Daisy James Evans knew what she was about when it came to men. Daisy said this dress was perfect. She said it did just what it was supposed to do 'because a woman's dress was meant to tease not to tell all her business. Daisy said it wasn't any man's business until he married the- right-to-open-the-package that James women didn't have a whole lot in the way of hips. The gathers at her waist made her hips look fuller and the bodice had tucks that made her 20 inch waist look even smaller. Sister frowned at her small bosom. There wasn't much even a dress as finely fitted as this one could do about that. Either the women in the family got enough tities to be milk cows or barely enough to declare themselves women. Aunt Daisy had done the best she could putting a little batting from an old quilt under each of Sister's breasts. Sister hadn't needed the girdle that Aunt Daisy insisted that she wear. Sister suspected that it was meant more for a chastity belt than anything else.

"Aunt Daisy don't have to worry about that, Sister told herself, "I ain't about to let no sweet talking man talk me out of my honey pot. Used goods ain't no good for catching the right man. I'm doing exactly what Mama told me to do- "Sister, don't get messed up with no man just 'cause he's handsome unless those looks come with enough money to put you in a big house, but get the ring and the house first."

"Sister, are you ready yet? Aunt Daisy called for her twenty-one minutes later.

****

"There ought to be a law against a man looking and smelling this damn good," Sister swore to herself as Joe reached around her to open the door. Everything about him was lethal to a young girl's heart. He had on a brown suit that looked like it had been tailor-made for him. Its color was so dark a shade of brown that it enhanced his good-enough-to-eat smooth, chocolate brown skin. His broad shoulders didn't look padded and the creases in his pants were as sharp as they could be. The collar and cuffs of his shirt were starched stiff enough to cut meat. Sandalwood, cinnamon and some other spices that came from places whose names were too foreign for Sister to pronounce combined to make Sister feel weak in the knees.

Sister found that she had to keep strengthening her resolve before the evening began. On second thought, maybe that girdle was just the thing she needed to help her get through this evening.

"Where are we going Joe?"

"I thought I would take you to El Rocko Club, but William says that they got this guy singing at The Club Mombassa that sounds like Nat Cole."

"Don't nobody sound like Nat Cole," Sister closed her eyes humming The King Trio's hit song *I love you for Sentimental Reasons.*

"Let's go see. William's my friend, but he's been wrong too many times to take anything he says for fact.

****

Sister's eyes were about big enough to pop out of her head. People said Daisy's House was high class for a liquor house, but it was nothing like this place.

Joe held her hand behind his back as they walked up a flight of narrow steps. The door at the top of the steps opened up into a room bigger than the whole movie theater back home in Salley. There was a bandstand and tables with oil cloth table cloths around the room and there was a large space for people to dance in front of the bandstand. And the people! Lord they were dressed up some kind of fine. Sister was so glad that her Aunt Daisy had insisted on her dressing up to the nines 'cause in Sister's estimation some of these people were dressed all the way up to the tens!

Joe led her to a table right next to the stage. "Ah, we're just in time. They're about to introduce the guy I was telling you about. Now, you close your eyes cause I know how you women are, if the guy is ugly, you won't say he sounds like Nat Cole no matter how good he sounds."

"I can be fair, Joe," Sister insisted.

"No, close them. He put his hand over her eyes until she closed them. Now, promise you'll keep them closed until he finishes."

"I promise, but I already know what I'm going to have to say," Sister shook her head in doubt, but kept her eyes closed just to please Joe.

"Folks you're in for a real threat tonight, Smokey Junior is going to sing one of today's biggest hits, *I Love You for Sentimental Reasons*. Let's welcome him with a round of applauds."

There was a spattering of polite applauds. It was clear that the rest of the audience was as doubtful as Sister was about the talents of this Smokey Junior person

And then he began to sing…

I love you for sentimental
reasons
I hope you do believe me
I'll give you my heart
I love you, and you alone were
meant for me
Please, give your loving heart to
me
And say we'll never part…[1]

His voice was a rich cross between baritone and tenor. Smooth and light like divinity frosting. No, he didn't sound like Nat Cole, but it didn't matter. His voice reached a place in Sister's heart that had been closed off on the evening Oscar walked away and didn't even bother to look back, had been lance with a red-hot branding iron since that day her father took Little Luke away, and bleed anew each time Claretha came back from the mailbox shaking her head. It was a voice meant to peel away the rawness of a new love and replace it with something sweet and enduring and without opening her eyes Sister knew that it was Joe's voice.

They were married on June 17, 1946, three months after they met. Joe worked hard but he still drank.

Chapter 10

"What's this I hear from Inez, 'bout you and Joe arguing? The bloom done gone off the rose this soon," Aunt Daisy asked it like the answer didn't matter, but Sister knew her aunt well enough to know that Daisy Evans didn't waste her time on idle chit-chat. If she asked a question, she had a very good reason for asking it.

"Ain't no bloom off nothing. Inez needs to mine her own business. I just found out I wasn't going to have a baby and I got mad and blamed Joe." Sister hadn't meant to cry when her woman's time came again this month and she certainly hadn't meant to say those mean things to Joe. She reckoned he was doing all he could, but since her only experience with a man had been with him she couldn't be all that sure. But it had been two whole months since they got married and Joe wanted to go his "man's thing" with her nearly every night.

"You told me you'd tell him," Sister didn't have to be reminded about what she was supposed to have told Joe. Aunt Daisy had fussed at her about it on her wedding day.

"I'll tell him if something don't happen soon. I've always done everything else like women suppose to before we knew about it. I don't see why all of a sudden I'm some pitiful little thing that can't do the one thing I want most."

"It don't matter what you want most. Ain't many people that get all they want. It's for your own protection. If we'd known sooner, you wouldn't have to worry about telling him now. Mama fixed me when I was still a young girl so I couldn't have no children because I had that real bad fever that left my heart weak. If Joe loves you enough it won't matter. Willie said long as he had me nothing and no one else mattered."

"Suppose Joe don't love me enough? Nobody ever loved me enough to stay with me through the hard times before. I can't take that chance until I have to. You won't tell him will you?"

"Didn't I promise you that I'd leave it up to you?" Her aunt looked angry that Sister would ask that particular question.

"Yes M'am, Sister tried to sound as contrite as she could. She realized her mistake. No one suggested that a James woman would break a promise. Promises were honor deep among the women in her family.

"Humph, it's up to you, but the longer you take the harder it's gonna be," Daisy let the matter drop. She didn't use her time talking when she could see it wouldn't do any good.

They worked in compatible silence peeling boiled eggs and adding them to the pickling brine. Though the two women didn't always like each other, they understood each other. They were both too strong-willed to ever be too close. Sister had slipped up the street to help her Aunt. She'd run out of things to clean and put up at home. Joe was the neatest man she'd ever met. He hung his clothes up or folded them neatly in his footlocker and they didn't have enough space in the yard for more than a tomato vine and some herbs for the table. She didn't know what she was going to do to take care of her children when she finally got some if she didn't get a place big enough to plant the myrrh, yarrow, and calendula seeds for the herbs, that her Grandma Hester had always insisted be kept on hand for taking care of babies. No, there wasn't enough to do at home for someone like Sister who was used to working from sunup to sundown. Joe wouldn't let her work outside the house.

Every time she offered to go to work in one of the big houses on the other side of town, Joe said something like, "Can't nobody ever say we Evans men don't take care of our family. You're my family now and I'll provide all you need."

So far, he given her all she needed except the one thing she both needed and wanted- a child.

"Aunt Daisy look, there's another man going in that house in the middle of the day. Wonder what's going on up there," Sister had counted five men over the last two hours she'd been sitting on the porch.

Daisy just looked at her. Anyone except Sister would have figured out by now that they were selling more than liquor up there. Daisy couldn't remember a time when she'd been that naïve. Colored men didn't get but two days off a year through the week a year- July 4th and Christmas Day. It wasn't unusual to see single young Colored men hanging around a liquor house or sporting house all day long on those two days but seeing men, especially some of the older married Colored businessmen in the community, going in and out of a house during a week day any other time could only mean one thing. It was a whorehouse.

"Sister, you finish these. I got to go downtown for awhile," Daisy said as she took off her apron and went into the house to get her hat and gloves.

****

Joe didn't know what he was going to do with his woman-child wife. One minute she was talking and acting like her Aunt Daisy reincarnated like she was more than the 39 years her Aunt had been claiming for the last ten years and the next minute she was bawling like a baby over something grown women knew enough not to talk about.

Who'd ever heard of a woman blaming a man because he didn't get her pregnant? Talking about maybe he wasn't doing it right! What she know about doing it right? He knew hadn't nobody but him been there.

"Man you got bigger problems than that. It took your mama eleven years to get pregnant with the first of her four children and twelve more to get to you," Joe lectured himself during the fifteen minutes Mr. Dicks gave the workers at his laundry to eat their lunch. "You got to get

Sister out of that house with Robert Lee and Inez before she makes you hurt somebody."

They'd moved in with his brother Robert Lee and his wife Inez until they could get a place of their own. One problem was that Sister expected him sit around the house every evening with her and to come straight home every evening. It wouldn't have been so bad if his brother's wife Inez would stop putting ideas in Sister's head.

All the married guys in the army had said, "Get your wife while she's young enough to "make" into the kind of wife you want." Sister was young enough-sixteen, but with Inez talking in her ear Sister wasn't "making" into any kind of wife he wanted.

Joe shook his head in disgust when he thought about that one night he'd come in and slipped into the bed next to his wife and reached to run his fingers through her beautiful long hair and felt a man's head instead. He nearly knocked himself out when he hit his head on the bed post jumping out of that bed.

It turned out that it wasn't a man in his bed but Sister. Inez had cut her hair like that Rosie the Riveter woman that had muscles like a man. Joe understood what that was all about. During the war they'd needed some of the women to do the work of men to keep the country moving, but the men were back home and the women should go back to being women. A man didn't want to be laying his head next to a woman with less hair than he had!

Although Sister insisted that it was her idea, Inez put her two cents in the next morning saying, "Maybe it takes a woman that looks and acts more like man to keep you and Robert Lee from spending all your time with a houseful of men every night."

Joe didn't like the comparison. His reasons for spending some time in the evenings away from home had nothing to do with how he felt about his wife. He actually liked his wife and didn't mind spending time with her but he knew for a fact that Robert Lee couldn't stand Inez.

Robert Lee said he woke up one morning next to Inez and she had a marriage certificate saying she was his wife. Joe didn't doubt that his brother had gotten messed up drunk enough to marry someone without knowing it. Robert Lee never could hold his liquor. He'd always been a stupid drunk. Back home, people would get him drunk just to see what kind of stupid things they could make him do.

Although the woman who claimed he'd married her didn't in anyway resemble the kind of women Robert Lee usually stepped out with- she was bony everywhere- with a chest as flat as an ironing board- while Robert Lee usually liked his women just the opposite, since Robert Lee was an honorable man at heart he stayed married to Inez but he went to Daisy's Liquor House or Shorty's Juke Joint every night whenever he was in town spending as little time at home as possible.

Robert Lee wasn't in town all that much because he was a porter for the Southern Railroad.

No one who'd ever met Inez blamed him for staying as far away as he could. She was a screecher and the worse kind of nag and it didn't matter whether Robert Lee said anything back or not. She'd keep screeching and nagging in her sleep unless he hauled off and slapped her.

And that was the other problem. Joe'd jumped in between them when he'd first come up to Greensboro and Inez had tried to scratch his eyes out. She screamed and yelled at him saying crazy stuff like, "Even if you win the fight over me, I'm staying with Robert Lee. I ain't leaving him for no farm boy just come to town."

Joe tried to explain that he didn't want her, that he'd jumped in because their Mama had raised Robert Lee and him better than to mistreat a woman. Then she started screaming that Joe thought he was too good for her and turned to ask Robert Lee if he was going to defend his wife's honor. But while she'd been fussing at Joe, Robert Lee had slipped out of the house. That had made Inez so mad that she'd tried to scratch and kick Joe. It had been all Joe could do to defend himself without hurting her. After that, as soon as Inez started screeching, Joe'd leave the house and let their arguments run their course that either ended up with Robert Lee walking out or with them in bed.

But Sister couldn't seem to understand how to stay out of other folk's business. She didn't seem to mine how loud or how much Inez screeched, but as soon as Robert Lee got mad enough to hit Inez, that's when Sister would jump in.

Last night was the worst. Joe'd walked in and found his little wife on Robert Lee's back beating him upside the head. Sister jumping on him like that had made Robert Lee so mad that he was bumping her against the wall to get her off. There was no help for it; Joe had to fight his own brother. They'd grown up together in the same house three years apart and never had one fight until last night. He had to think of a way to get Sister out of that house.

"Joe, I heard there's another liquor house right up the street from Miss Daisy's place. Folks say it's going to give her some real competition," Joe's friend William interrupted his thoughts.

"I don't think she's too worried," Joe was still mad that those people had moved into the first house on Cruz Street that had been empty in years before he got enough money together to rent it. The family that had lived there had moved back to Georgia when the man's father had died and his mother needed him to help on the farm.

"Maybe she needs to be. Glady, said the man asked her if she'd like to work for him. Said he'd let her keep half her money. She said she laughed at him and told him she couldn't spend no part of her money dead. 'Cause she knows Daisy would kill her if she went right up the street from her doing something like that.

"I suspect Daisy Evans can take care of any competition," Joe said thinking of how nice and classy Daisy's place was compared to other liquor houses he'd been to.

****

"Sir, could I please speak to Chief Skeens?" Daisy Evans knew the proper tone and eye level to take on when talking to White folks, especially to White folks she wanted to do something for her.

"About what Miss Daisy?" The young officer had nearly lost his job when he had referred to her as that Nigger woman the last time she'd come to pay a call on the chief. So he was careful to show her as much respect as it was in him to show a Colored woman.

"About a serious legal situation," Daisy Evans declared.

"Sir, Miss Daisy is out here to see you?" Daisy heard him speaking to the Chief.

"Tell her to come right in," Chief Skeens knew what she was there to talk about. He was surprised that it had taken her all of three days to get here.

Joe and Sister were able to move into the three-room shotgun house up the street from her Aunt Daisy Friday of the next week.

****

"I know you heard me, Inez screeched at Robert Lee. It was getting harder to get any feeling out of him-any feeling even white hot anger was better than nothing. It used to be that by now he would have either slapped her and grabbed her up and carried her to bed.

He pretended to ignore her as he sliced the bread like he'd always done back home-two thick slices for their older sister Martha who liked to spread her jam on real heavy, four medium thick slices for his mother and his other sister Louise, and four thin slices for Joe and himself. It didn't matter that Inez didn't like her bread sliced by hand- he could never get it the right thickness for her- the one thing he could do better than anyone else and he couldn't do it right for Inez. "Yeah, I heard you. It's the same loaf of bread I always bring home-fresh baked this morning. I even got Matt to put some honey in this little jar for me.

"Don't be making like you did something special for me. Honey gives me the hives. If you cared anything about me you'd know that after seven years. 'Stead everything is about you. I like sliced bread, but you always come up in here with a loaf that's got to be cut. I don't care nothing about that being something special you used to do for Ma Mary. Anybody can cut bread- that don't make you special to nobody but your dumb country Mama," That was it she thought he'd buck up now ready to fight her- one word about his precious mother would push him over.

Robert Lee looked down at the knife in his hand. It wasn't a killing knife-the striated edge was made for cutting bread, but she was such a small woman, if he put his full weight behind it and placed it in her heart-if he could find it- this knife would do the trick. He put the knife down. "If you want sliced bread, I'll go get a loaf."

"You'll go get some? You could've brought it when you came in. It don't make sense. Every time you come home we got to argue about the same thing."

"You're right," He watched the surprise spread over her face as he turned away from the counter to open the back door. "It don't make sense to keep coming home to argue about a loaf of bread."

"What you mean by that? Robert Lee, don't you walk out of here. You ain't been home in three weeks. I know you could have been home before now." By now she was screaming at his back because he was well down the dirt path that would bend back to Cruz Street after he turned the corner round the next house.

****

Robert Lee almost walked right into Joe. "Man, where you going this time of evening?" Joe could guess. Sister had sent him to check on Inez when she'd heard the first round of yelling. Joe wasn't worried about Inez nearly as much as he was worried about Robert Lee. Both his sisters were teenagers when Robert Lee was born and one had been married when Joe was born two years later being the only two boys in a house full of sisters and female cousins made the brothers real close. Robert Lee wasn't the type to talk about his feelings, but his face was so open that when he fancied himself in love, or his feelings were hurt everyone around him knew it. He'd never been able to keep anything from Joe, but lately he'd been closing Joe out. The last time he'd been home, Joe'd had to go to three liquor houses to find him.

"To the store to get some sliced bread," He stepped around Joe and kept walking. He knew Joe was smart enough to get his meaning.

"Ain't no store around here open this time of night. Come on up to the house and I'll give you enough for tonight," Joe was smart enough, but he didn't want to understand.

"Joe, I said I'm going to the store to buy some bread." Robert Lee said every word very slowly making sure Joe understood his meaning. He turned around, but his eyes didn't meet his brother's eyes. "Joe, I know there ain't no place open around here. Inez knows it too,"

Joe looked at his bother in disbelief. "Man don't do this. I know Inez is hard to live with, but things change- people change. Maybe if you tell her what you're thinking about doing..."

"Joe, I'm going to the store." There was something in his voice that said all the arguing was over.

Joe knew he'd never see his brother again.

Chapter 11

"Joe, two more weeks pay saved up and we got enough to move again. Ain't you happy about that?"   Mary Helen rolled over and pressed her head into the curve under his arm. She knew she'd been nagging lately.   Hadn't she given herself a firm blessing out about it while she waited for him to get in last night?

"I'm happy if you happy. Don't see much reason to move. This house is big enough for us and the baby when she gets here," he said without opening his eyes.

"I done told you Joe. I want to bring my son home to a house with a living room, two bedrooms, and a bathroom inside the house instead of on the back porch. Having to go outside in the cold like that is enough to make a body hold their pee till it backs up."   Mary Helen sighed then because she could tell by his breathing that he'd gone back to sleep. "Well, I'm happy enough for both of us," she said to herself and she believed it.   Grandma could be wrong just like anybody else. Women who got picked instead of doing the picking could end up with good men too.

"Joe let's go to that new movie at the Palace tonight," she said trying to coax him out of his usual early morning bad mood.

"Done seen it," he said without opening his eyes.

"Seen it.   When?" She felt his body tense and she knew that the next thing he said would be a lie,

"Honey, I mean - I don't want to see it. I heard it ain't good," he said trying to cover himself. Hell, why did women always start talking when a man was half asleep, cussed under his breath. Catching him off guard like that.   He knew she could tell he was lying. He'd never been good a t lying. Probably because he'd never had to do much of it until here lately. He'd been the youngest in his family and his mother-and two older sisters thought that he could do no wrong. So, when he did something that he wasn't supposed to be doing, He'd own up to it and his brother Robert Lee would get a whipping for letting him do it.

He braced himself for the storm to begin. She didn't say anything. What was the use in saying what they both already knew? That the movie was a Western and that he'd cross a line of Ku Klux Klan to get to a Western movie no matter how bad people said it was?   They were all bad as far as she was concerned.   The White folks called them "B" movies she guessed because they "be" the same old sorry story every time.

What need was there for her to say that she knew he was cheating on her?   Less than a year married and he was seeing another woman -- probably seeing some other women.

She got up and kept her back to him as she put on her robe so he couldn't see the tears that she couldn't keep from welling up in her eyes.

He got up and pulled her rigid back against his chest. "I'm sorry, I won't go without you again" he promised.

She didn't smile or offer forgiveness because of what he didn't promise.

And though he knew what she wanted to hear, he didn't say it. He couldn't because he knew himself well enough by now to know that it just wasn't in him to be faithful. He hadn't thought of it as a character flaw until that first night he came in smelling of *Evening In Paris Eau de Toilet* and cigarettes neither of which Mary Helen used. She looked at him with more pain in her eyes than he ever wanted to see again, He'd promised her that night that it would never happen again and he'd meant it too. But the thing was, Sister didn't particularly like sex. She saw it as a way to get herself a baby and be a mama.

The first two months after they got married she cried like a baby when her time of the month came and told him right out the next time he reached for her, "I don't see no reason to be doing that if you shooting blanks."

Now, how was a man to feel when his woman said something like that? It didn't make sense to Joe that every woman he'd ever been with thought he was some kind of lover except his wife. Still, he didn't mean to hurt her.

"I'll start breakfast," was all she said.

Sister would always be convinced that Joe getting her upset like that was what made the baby come t hat night --two whole weeks early. By the time she'd finished her six weeks laying-in, a school teacher and his wife were living in her dream house and nearly all the money that they'd saved was gone. Mary Helen didn't cry over it long. She broke the pickling jar that they'd been saving in and got a gallon jug from her Aunt Daisy and started saving for an even bigger house .

It took her two weeks to name the baby. During that time they called her everything from Blondie to Julia Mae, after her mother. Every name that Joe suggested, she rejected out of hand on the grounds that the name could belong to one of his women. She named her Gloria because it was the name of an angel and Dean because she thought it sounded good with Gloria.

****

Mad as she'd been and still was at Joe, she had to admit he was a good father. His oldest sister, Louise, had been a grown married woman when he was still a boy, so he was used to taking care of babies. He'd come straight home after-work, feed the baby her bottle of milk, change her diaper, and rock her to sleep. He had good hands. Gentle hands for a man his size. She never watched them together for too long because when she did she would find herself trying to forgive him and he didn't deserve to be forgiven.

Sometimes he looked up and caught her looking at them. He'd smile. She didn't smile back. She was almost immune to that smile of his now. Her heart didn't flop over anymore, just kind of eased over on its side.

"We sure do make a pretty baby, don't we girl?" He said trying to tease her out of the anger that had been building up instead of getting better since she found out that someone else had rented "her" house.

She still didn't say a word. She'd found his one weakness and she was pushing it in to the hilt. Silence. He'd grown up with two sisters, a brother, and three orphaned cousins in a five room house. Silence had been something he'd had as a spelling word, but never experienced firsthand until he was in the military. When it was lights-out-time in the barracks he'd been tired enough to sleep, but the quiet kept him awake.

"Oh, I forgot. This was in the mail for you." He stood up and shifted the baby enough so that he could reach the letter into his hip pocket.

Mary Helen gave him a suspicious look and she didn't move or reach out her hand for the letter. She never got mail. Her brothers and sister hadn't written to her the whole time she'd been up here, and she wasn't all that sure that her daddy could write.

"Take it. You'll see I'm not lying," he came to her and pushed it into her hand.

It was addressed to her all right and that wasn't the only strange thing about it. In the corner it said: Grady Fulmer, Aikens Road, Salley, South Carolina. Why would her father's brother be writing to her? Although she was close to his wife, Cousin Bea, she hadn't spoken more than a couple of words to him in her entire life. Sister felt Grady had cheated her father out of his share of the funeral home and changed his last name from Fullmore to Fulmer so that no one would mistake him for his sorry twin brother.

"You won't know what it says until you open it," Joe said like she didn't have sense enough to know that herself. Still, she hesitated so long that Joe took the letter back, handed her the baby, and opened it for her.

He began to read it aloud. "It says... He stopped abruptly, "Oh baby, *I'm* sorry." He couldn't bring himself to continue to read the brief missive to her. He chose instead to take their daughter back and let her read it herself.

Sister,

Your father is dying. Come home.

G. Fulmer

"He said little enough.   If he weren't so cheap, he could have wired for me. Daddy's probably already dead," she mumbled as she walked over, broke the jug, and started counting the fare for the train ride   home.

Chapter 12

"You ain't but three months old, but that ain't too young to learn what a Colored girl needs to know, "A Colored woman baring a breast on a dusty roadside in Salley, South Carolina isn't a good idea any time of day. So, you'll have to wait awhile," Mary Helen peered down at the chocolate brown eyes of her daughter. The baby wasn't much of a crier. The first time she'd given a gentle reminder of a complaint- feed me-change me- but the second time, it was hard to believe that something less than 12 lbs. could make that much noise.

The baby looked up at her as though to say, "I didn't know that." And then just as politely as you please closed her eyes and went back to sleep. Sister knew that it was just a brief reprieve. Though the child had good sense, she was still a baby and Sister would have to feed her the next time she woke up. She just hoped that she'd made it to the house by then.

Somehow, "right down the road" was a lot farther away now than it had been when she walked the distance from the train station to home as a little girl. She'd shed the heels a mile back that she'd worn not for comfort, but to make her younger sister, Claretha green with envy. The silk stockings that had been a gift from her husband were tucked into the pocket of the fitted shirt waist dress that showed off her pocket Venus shape to perfection.

She looked down at her toes covered in the gray-white sand of a South Carolina rural road with disgust and pushed back the hair that had come loose from the fashionable chignon her Aunt Daisy claimed made the seventeen year old look more like a full grown woman. In spite of the fact that Mary Helen had been married more than a year, Aunt Daisy still saw that pitiful thirteen year old motherless child that she rescued from a life of servitude after her mother died when Mary Helen was ten.

All her hopes of making a good impression had manifested itself in foolish pride. She could have wired her Grandma Hester and Uncle Boy would have been at the station waiting for her whether he wanted to or not. But that would have meant having to leave her baby with Grandma Hester while she stayed down here taking care of her Daddy. Grandma Hester would insist that taking care of a grown man and a baby was too much for Sister.

It didn't occur to Sister that she could simply refuse to surrender her baby to the old woman. No one refused or contradicted Grandma Hester. Her dictates were as infallible as the Pope's. So, Sister left Greensboro, North Carolina assuring her husband that she and their first born child would be met at the station. She didn't feel bad about telling such a little lie because the house was right down the road from the train station, but on this white hot July afternoon "right down the road" stretched out like the happily-ever-after ending of a fairy tale.

"You can sleep through anything," she whispered to the baby that she'd changed from one arm to the other more times than she could count. Mary Helen smiled just looking at this child of hers. Yes, hers. Her pretty little chocolate baby with eyes, when they were open seemed way too large for her face. This child was the real reason she had married Joe over the objections of her own good sense. More than anything in life, she wanted children of her own.

She pushed herself to go the rest of the way, "down the road." It wasn't so much that she was tired- being tired was a constant state with her- it was not knowing whether or not it would be too late by the time she got there that was wearing her down inside.

****

Her father wasn't dead when they got there. He lingered a week, and then another and another until Sister began to hope that the doctor was wrong.

Claretha was no help taking care of him. Claretha couldn't cook, couldn't wash clothes, and couldn't clean up. She could do nothing that was of value to Sister. That's what their daddy had allowed her to do while Sister had done all of the work. It didn't matter that Claretha was almost eight inches taller than Sister or that she was built as solid as an outhouse.

She was the chosen one and she was his baby girl. She had been the baby girl longer than any of her sisters because the four girls between her and the one their mama had died giving birth to, had all either been still born or died before they were a week old. Claretha was spoiled and selfish especially where their Daddy was concerned.

"Sister, you haven't finished yet. I want to come in and visit with Daddy," Claretha pouted from the doorway. She was a tall girl. Took after their mother in height and complexion -high yellow but she had their father's small forehead and thick eyebrows over bark brown eyes instead of grey like their mothers".

Sister didn't look up until she was sure she could say something that didn't contain a cuss word. "No, I ain't finished yet!" (She stressed the *ain't* because Claretha had been lecturing her about using the word since the teacher taught her that only the uneducated used such language). She continued looking daggers into her sister, "I could turn him and change the linen faster if I had some help."

"Sister, you know stuff like that makes me sick to my stomach. Just call me when you finish." She pranced back to the front room leaving her sister straining to lift a grown man nearly twice her size.

"I'd like to call her a bunch of stuff," Sister thought as she gently turned her father on to the side of the bed that she'd finished. "All right Daddy, we're almost there." She continued to whisper in his ear. She didn't know whether he could hear her. Talking to her father made Sister feel better. She wanted him to know that she wasn't angry at him any more for   staying drunk and gambling away what little money he earned or for   keeping her mother pregnant until she died from it. No, she wasn't angry anymore.   She actually hurt for him now. No man should end his life with nary a one of his dreams fulfilled.

He'd tried to stop drinking and gambling a thousand times. Sister had heard him promise her mother too many times to count that, "This time would be the last time he'd stop in the Bottom before coming home with the whole seven dollars he'd made that week. This was the last house they'd live in without a wood floor or indoor plumbing. This would be the last time he'd make her cry over being ashamed because all her sisters had married better than she had." The last time never came during her mother's lifetime. He stopped drinking, gambling, and worked harder after Mama died.

It was like he was trying to prove to everyone that Julia Mae had been right to hold on to her faith in him. He'd worked hard trying to get the kind of house that might tempt one of the two widows round there to marry him so he could get his children back home. He had about worked himself to death- working two jobs that alone would have been too much for one man. He'd pick whatever crop was in season. Traveling all the way to Florida to keep working and back home when the peaches, then cotton were ready. He slaved in the fields all day and in the flour mill most of the night. He'd worked even harder after Mama died. He kept saying that he was going to build a real house for his girls. Sister had gone up North with Aunt Daisy before her father and Claretha moved into this little house.

"Daddy, you got to get up from here and finish picking those peaches. Old man Floyd, says he don't know what he's going to do while you lying up here in the bed with a heart attack," she tried to lend him some of her strength.

"You can come in now, Claretha," she called to her sister as she finished fluffing the pillows.

"It's about time. Daddy, Daddy, It's me Claretha. I've come to read to you now," she slipped pass Sister and took her usual place on the edge of the bed.   Sister wasn't sure, but she thought she saw him move a tad and almost smile at the sound of her sister's voice.

"Claretha, I'm going over to Grandma Hester's for awhile," Sister yelled back as she left even though she knew they wouldn't miss her until the bed needed to be changed again or Gloria woke up and star-ted crying. Claretha couldn't stand babies crying around her. She'd talked Daddy into giving that last baby that had killed their Mama to Grandma Hester to raise and sending two-year-old Luke to a cousin. Aunt Clare took Luke in with open arms even though she already had six girls of her own.   That's when Sister had taken Aunt Daisy up on her offer to come to Greensboro. Enlarged heart or not, Sister had been determined to stay and hold on to what was left of her family. But after Luke had been given away, Sister realized that her Daddy didn't want or need anybody but his Claretha. Anyway, now with the Widow Florence baking for them and ironing their father's shirts there wasn't much for her to do.

The Widow Florence thought that their Daddy was going to marry her- she was working like she really believed Claretha was going to let any woman in that house other than to work, now that she had her Daddy to herself. Sister hadn't felt any need to stay.

"No, they won't miss me," she talked to herself as she walked down the sandy road. It was more a path than a road. A car would get scrapped on both sides by the blackberry bushes that grew so thick that they looked like one long plant crouched almost on the road.

"It's a white day," Sister thought. White, hot sun, white South Carolina sand bellowing up onto the tops of her feet all the way up to her ankles making them look even ashier than they'd looked when she started out. It was mid July so there was more white than green or brown, since the cotton was still in the field. Most people didn't like the heat of a day like today, but Sister thought it was just fine. It made her feel like she was home. North Carolina was all green, pink, red, and yellow now and they wouldn't be getting heat like this for another month. This was home and it felt like home.

After the first turn in the road, she could see her grandmother's house firmly planted in a field of cotton. It had been the master's house before the Civil War and it was clear that its' best days were behind it. The grey columns that supported the veranda that ran across the full length of the top floor at the front of the house were supported themselves by cinder blocks. That veranda was so rickety that Sister couldn't remember a time when it had been considered "safe" for the children to go up there. She loved the old house, even tired looking and wanting paint, it had "class". Her mother used to tell Sister that she'd felt like the Queen of Sheba growing up in that house.

"You look worn down to a nub gal. Ain't I done told you to make Claretha help with your Daddy? You can't take care of that baby of yours and your Daddy by yourself." Grandma Hester repeated the same advice that she had been giving for the last three weeks.

"It's easier to do it myself than to fuss with Claretha and then still have to do it anyway," Mary Helen sighed as she sat down and reached for a couple of handfuls of unshelled beans, put them in her lap, and started to snap the small ones, shell the large ones and add them to   the wash tub at her grandmother's feet.

"I know that's the truth," her grandma said while taking a long tug on   her pipe. They worked for a long time in the comforting kind of silence that busy hands and shared troubles makes.

"Why you pick that long legged, big eyed boy anyway?" Grandma Hester finally asked the question that Sister knew had been on her mind since they arrived three weeks ago.

"I   didn't pick him.   He picked me." Sister said, hoping Grandma would let it drop, but knowing that she wouldn't.

"Gal,   how many times I done told you about what happens to women   in   our family when they don't pick they man?"

Sister didn't answer because she knew that Grandma hadn't meant it as a question. You had to know things like that about her grandma if you were going to get along with her at all.

Grandma Hester was the only person Sister was afraid of. This was   true even though Grandma Hester was the only adult Sister didn't have to   look up at since she was half a hand taller and it was true even though Grandma wasn't the "girl" of   eighty-eight who had chased Sister down with a switch to make her   mine when she was a child. She looked at   the old woman out of the corner of her eye and Decided that she hadn't changed much during the years since then. All of her dresses were either white or some shade of purple and she still wore heavy, black but ton-top shoes year-round. Even under the shade of the porch, she wore an oversized sun bonnet with a brim that dwarfed her face because although her snow white hair was long enough in back to be worn in a ball, Grandma was nearly bald on top. Elegant. It seemed a contrary word to for a woman who wore high top booths and smoked a pipe, but that was what her grandma was - elegant. She could talk elegantly too, when she wanted to, because she'd been raised by a brother who had a college education. She took pride in being able to speak two languages - Nigger Talk and English.

"Well, I'm going to tell you one more time," she always began the story this way. She emptied her corn cob pipe over the rail of the porch and pulled out her pack of George Washington tobacco, and packed it in with a stick whittled in the shape of a naked woman. Although the details on the stick were explicit to the point of being risqué, Sister didn't notice because Grandma Hester had been using that stick for twice the sixteen years of Sisters life. When it was lit, she took a long pull and began the story...

> *They were all the same to him.*
> *Ugly. Their blunt features and*
> *kinky hair made it easy for*
> *people like him to think of them*

as animals that could be bought and sold.

They were the same - ugly, his mind repeated as he absent-mindedly searched the next group which was being herded onto the platform. His eyes moved past arid then returned to one among who did not belong. The hair on this one was long, thick, wavy and a dark, rich brown. Her facial features, while clearly Negroid, were sharp and stunning. Her nose was small and well formed, and her lips were full, but not the thick ones people like him expected of her kind. It was the eyes which, without his knowing it, enslaved him for life. Those large deep pools of amber were looking directly into his. They were intelligent and defiant.

All the others that stood with her were indistinguishable from all the ones that had preceded them on the block. For the most part, they kept their heads down. When one of them dared to look up, their eyes were those of frightened, captured animals. Her? Her eyes were alive with something he could not -fathom. As she stood glaring back at him, he allowed himself to inspect the rest of her body. He wondered how breast which were that full could be so firm and how a waist could be so small above such deliciously rounded hips. She was the most exquisite woman he'd ever seen. In that moment, he decided he must possess her.

He'd come prepared to purchase chattel to restock the plantation which had recently fallen into his hands through default. The son of its former owner had wasted his inherited wealth in less than a year. Once most of his money was gone, he sold the able-bodied slaves off one by one until even whips could not force the remaining slaves to produce a cash crop. Before another year had passed, he was forced to sell and he'd taken the first opportunity to attach himself to the new owner like a leech and to immediately introduce him t o hi s l ovely, but dowerless sister.

Marcus knew they had counted on his being so honored by being accepted into one of Charleston's finest fami l ies he'd ignore his wife's penniless state and allow his new brother-in-law to live with them. Under these circumstances, they would not have lost their home; they would have gained another fortune to spend.

He knew this and he had still been willing to allow them to think that they had suckered him in because more than anything else, he wanted to be accepted as a true gentleman. A couple of generations of earned wealth had not given him the air of elegance that even his wife's scoundrel of a brother seemed to ooze. He was wise enough to know that marrying into the "right" fami l y woul d get him what he wanted, and to his mind, it had been a fair exchange. To be one of them, this had been all that he ever wanted until now. Now, he wanted her.

"Oh, you have your eye on that one," the voice of his brother-in-law, Randall James, tore him away from his reverie. "You might as well forget her. Ophelia has passed the word that she'll buy her."

Marcus knew about Ophelia Arrant. She ran the most renowned stable of octoroons in Springfield. Usually when she passed the word, the gentlemen would decline to bid and then go to her "house" to sample the favors of the girl. Not bidding was the gentlemanly thing to do, but when the bidding began, Marcus realized Ophelia was going to get her for a price of a field slave. It wasn't right, so he bid, just one- to push the price up to an amount that was worthy of such a fine piece. "Just once," he told himself, but he bid again and again. He could feel the anger pulsating through the crowd and hear them whispering things like, "What could one expect from one such as he."

He knew that Randall was steeping in humiliation and would have no doubt kil led him, if he had not long ago worn out his welcome in all the finer homes in town. Marcus was aware of their anger, but he couldn't help himself. He continued to bid until she was his and he even stayed to bid on several more slaves, even though the other gentlemen had left Randall and him standing uncomfortably alone.

Marcus refused to have his prize transported to his plantation with the other slaves and Randall flat out refused to allow her to ride inside the carriage with them, so he sent one of their older slaves to fetch the landau from his town house. Before he started for home, he stopped by the house of a seamstress and went in alone to purchase some clothing for her. The only dresses she had already made-up were three his wife had ordered before she married him. The seamstress didn't have to remind him that he was expected to pay all of his wife's debts- old and new, so he bought three ready-made dresses although they weren't the right kind of clothes for a slave.

The two were the object of curious and angry glares as he tooled the landau through the town. He was blind to this, but Yeezhia was not. She survived each minute by sheer force of will. She wondered now whether this nightmare would ever end. How could she have been brought to such low circumstance?

After all, she was the petted and pampered daughter of a Dinka mother who had been sold to a rich English-Egyptian. If only her father had not been on one of his lengthy voyages when the slavers came to their village, she would have been at home now.

Her father had come to the Upper Nile as an indentured servant who had been pressed into naval service while on an errand for his master. He couldn't go back to England for fear they wouldn't believe he had not run away willingly. He'd planned to jump ship in Africa and work until he had saved enough money for his passage to Australia, or America. Somehow, he never made it. He traded with the natives and slavers. Yeezhia's mother had been the payment for a slavers gaming debt. The man hadn't thought she was strong enough to make the Middle Passage because she was small for a Dinka, a woman, thus without value. But her value to him grew each year.

Never in his life had anyone loved him as she had. He had been born the son of a poor Egyptian mother who was raped by a British soldier. His father had, perhaps, never known of his existence and his mother had transferred her -frustration and anger from the man who was beyond her reach, to his son. He had been an abused and unloved child who didn't know how to love. But with her, he felt loved and it wasn't long before he returned his young wife's love and when she died in childbirth, he gave to their daughter her name, rather than the Christian name that the missionary offered.

In recent years, Yeezhia's father had purchased part ownership in a merchant ship and had become a wealthy man, but he could never bring himself to move back to England where he had been treated so roughly as a youth, and where he knew his beloved daughter would never be accepted. He spent years trying to find his wife's family. And when he did, he allowed Yeezhia to spend a month each year with them. It was here that the warriors from another tribe had found her when they came with white men to find chattel for the slave market. The captain had immediately realized that he had something of special value in the tall, fifteen-year-old girl, so he didn't keep her below deck with the others. She was kept, instead, in a small cell where sailors who were guilty of minor infractions were usually kept.

The voyage hadn't been as bad for her as it had been for the others because she hoped that her father would return, find her gone, and come to her rescue like a shining knight. She'd believed this until her stained and torn dress had been removed before she was placed on the auction block. Even if her father came now, he would not be able to afford to buy her from this man.

Marcus didn't talk to her on the long ride to the plantation, falsely assuming she didn't speak English. She didn't speak to him, either. When they stopped in front of a very impressive, but neglected house, he got down, walked around to her side of the landau, and motioned for her to come inside.

Instead of getting down, she moved over to the driver's side, picked up the reins and whipped the hoses into a. Gallop. Marcus was too stunned to move. His mind could not fathom how a slave could dare to do such a thing. She had disobeyed him, stolen his horses, and worst of all, she'd run away. He could kill her for any of these offenses and no one would question his right to do so.

Yeezhia hadn't planned this. Her behavior had been as much a surprise to her as it had been to him. She simply rode until it dawned on her she had nowhere to go, no one to go to.

She stopped the horses, removed the bundle which contained the dresses from the landau, and walked into

*the nearby woods. She wanted to find
some water to wash herself. She soon
found a small pool which was fed
by an underground spring. She tore
a long strip from the sack-like dress
she was wearing and used it for a rag
to wash her body. She rinsed her
hair and used the rest of the sack-
dress t o dry herself. Yeezhia then
put on the prettiest of the dresses,
the white one with the long waist,
which ended in a "U" at the gathered
skirt. It had been designed to be worn
over a cinched waist and hoop skirt,
but she needed neither of these.*

*She was standing near the pool,
beautiful and defiant, when Marcus -
found her. When the hands, which
went to her throat, found thems1ves
caressing the slender column, it
occurred to him that he wanted to
kiss her, but he forced that thought
from his mind. One didn't kiss a
slave. One used them as one used a
chamber pot. So he used Yeezhia
and he couldn't understand why she
wasn't grateful he hadn't killed her
instead.*

*He owned her, he'd picked her and
paid for her, but she was never his
possession, for she never yielded to
him without force. Marcus was sure
that all he wanted was total
submission. He didn't want her love
though he knew she was capable of
giving it. He'd watched her with her
babies and seen a love in her eyes so
powerful it left him gulping for air.
She had no right to withhold that*

from him - not that he wanted it. Submission... That's what he wanted. Just once, he wanted to see her humbled. When giving her more than he -felt any slave had a right to expect did not deliver her willingly to his arms, he became spiteful.

He waited until each of her daughters looked as she had that first day he'd seen her, and then he sold them. If she'd begged and pleaded for him to save her children, he would have. But each time he separated Yeezhia from one of her daughters, there was never a tear. And each of the girls looked at him with the defiant eyes of Yeezhia.

The message that she gave each daughter-before they were taken from her, sustained them throughout all of their lives, as it has sustained every daughter of Yeezhia.

She said, "My daughter, you are no one's possession, for everything that makes you my daughter — your strength, your dignity, your beauty, your pride, your intelligence and your love — are priced beyond any purse. These things can never be taken from you. They can only be given away through your weakness or foolishness. Remember always that you are a daughter of Yeezhia. "The message was a strong one and it seemed that each time she sent one of her daughters away, some of her own strength went with her child. Though she was weakening, she never let Marcus know it. When she thought she could hold out no longer, God gave her ease.

Marcus' wife died in childbirth. Within a year, he'd married the only child of the planter who owned land adjoining his. His new wife was an old maid of twenty-six. The bloom was not only gone from her rose, but the petals had fallen off, too. She'd been unpicked because she was nearly as homely as she was spoiled. The new wife demanded that Marcus mate Yeezhia with one of the slaves. Her father owned one of Yeezhia's daughters, so she was aware of what had been going on. She was pretty sure Marcus would be unwilling to share the girl with one of his field slaves.

Marcus gave Yeezhia her pick. He informed her that she would live as her mate lived from that day forth. One of her choices was well over six feet tall, with skin the color of ebony. His teeth were strong and white. He looked about her age. Another was slightly shorter, but handsome, too. Fair-skinned and, like the first one, he was trained as a house slave. Yeezhia picked the last man. He was barely five feet tall, his skin was a rich blackened purple. He was at least a score older than she was, and his large forehead could have masked a great deal of wasted space or tremendous intelligence. None of this mattered to her.

She picked him only because he was small and, what white men called, ugly. Surely, she thought as she took his hand, he will give me daughters who will not tempt the white master. She got what she wanted. The smaller and blacker her babies were, the more she loved them. Now, every generation carries the mark of our small, "bright" savior.

"And that's why we always do the picking,"

Grandma Hester finished with a long draw on her pipe. She didn't say anything for awhile. Sister didn't either.

"He cheating on you?" Grandma Hester asked when they'd snapped the last of the beans. The way Sister's head jerked up told the old woman that she'd guessed right.

"How you know?" She was sure now that her grandmother-was omnipotent. She'd been too ashamed to tell anybody about Joe and he'd been so attentive and charming while he'd been down here when they'd come down for her Uncle C.W.'s funeral seven months ago, she was certain that her Joe had been switched when they changed trains in Charlotte.

"He's a man ain't he? Child, if you want to get some happiness out of this here life, you can't go expecting too much from a man."

Chapter 13

Her Daddy- stayed for five months. He never showed any signs of life for anybody but Claretha, just laid there until God finally called him home. Joe came for the funeral and said that he was going to take her and the baby back home to North Carolina. She was ready to go back. She was tired of being the sister whose name was called at the beginning of every sentence when somebody wanted something done.

Even at the funeral people acted like Claretha was the only one who'd lost a father. Sister rolled her eyes up to heaven begging for mercy as Claretha started another one of her screaming, "Daddy, Daddy, don't leave me Daddy -performances.

"She's the one needs comforting. You're strong enough to get through anything," Grandma Hester said as she sat down beside Sister at the family meal after the funeral.

Grandma was wearing a light purple dress, which was as close to mourning as she got for in-laws. "I remember when your mother died. I came over here to see about you and there you were standing on top of a peach crate trying to make a cake using that special checkered cake pan of your mama's. Don't know but two or three grown women that can get it right, but there you were trying to be like your mama.

Wouldn't let me or anybody else help you. It came out right good too, just a tad too much vanilla."

"I just had to have something to do that made me feel close to Mama and that's the last thing she did for us children before she went to the hospital. I wasn't being strong. I was being scared. Daddy let you keep the baby. Uncle Boy took Aaron into Columbia and left him there to find work right after the funeral. Sister looked her Grandmother in the eye. Grandma Hester looked right straight back. Both of them knew that Aaron's leaving had been by her order. Sister wanted her grandmother to say that she'd been wrong about that.

All she said was, "Aaron wasn't meant for round here. Your Mama had spunk and sass before she met that boy's daddy. It seemed like he drained all that off of her like some voodoo woman and give it to that boy. No, he wasn't meant for round here. Maybe your Mama wasn't meant for here neither. I should have let her go on and teach in Columbia. Well, at least I saw to it that Aaron got some schooling. He'll be alright.

Sister couldn't deny any of that. Aaron was too much like their mother- a beautiful, talented bird that needed to fly and there was nowhere to fly around here.

"Well, Oscar isn't anything like Aaron but he followed Aaron like he's always done. I was scared Daddy was going to put me aside like he did Aaron," Sister said.

"What happened to Aaron and Oscar was different. Aaron isn't Alton's child." It still rankled Hester James that Julia Mae had been too proud to go to a cousin in Columbia and have the child. No, she had to get married and give her child a name, like the name James wasn't good enough for any child.

"He'd been his Daddy all his life. Long as mama was living. I don't see how he could stop just like that," Sister felt she would never understand the back hand logic adults used to explain the stupid, hurtful things they did.

"Hush child. You are a James through and through. I'm here and I'd like to see somebody try to mess with you."

In spite of her continued displeasure with her grandmother, that made Sister smile because Grandma Hester still felt that she could beat the whole world.

"Grandma, how long I got to be strong, holding on for everybody?" Sister wanted to touch her grandma, she wanted to feel her arms around her, but no one touched Hester James without her expressed permission and as far as Sister knew no one had been given such permission since her husband died over twelve years ago. No you didn't just up and touch Hester James. You had to know that about her if you were going to get along with her at all.

"You keep holding on for' as long as you have to. Don't worry 'bout being strong for everybody. They got to do that for they self." She said this in Gullah, the mixed English of slaves, so Sister knew that this wasn't one of those things that came from the hard Hester James who always gave as good or bad as she got, but from the Hester James who knew people and could make them feel special like nobody else could when she felt there was something special in them.

"I don't know if I can," Sister said feeling the full weight of the long months nursing her father and the dread of wondering, no knowing what Joe had been doing all this time she'd been down here.

"Like hell you can't. Ain't you my grandchild? Ain't you got Yeezhia's blood in your veins? You'll hold on 'cause you got to." It sounded like an order, but Sister knew it wasn't. It was an expectation

Mary Helen tried to get Claretha to come live with her, but she said she wanted to be near her Daddy.   Grandma Hester said that Claretha could stay with her until she came to her senses.   Mary Helen was a little relieved even though she didn't admit it even to herself. She didn't need another "baby" to take care of.

****

The first thing she did when she got back home to Greensboro was to start looking for some day work. She figured that the best way to get that kind of work was to go to where the rich people lived and ask them if they needed help.   That was a mistake. The maids who opened the door weren't about to risk losing their positions to some eager young upstart.

"I'll try one more house," she said to herself as she stood trying to decide which of the last four houses on Cypress Street could be the one where they were just waiting for someone like her. She chose the yellow house

trimmed in white not because it was the only
house on the block that wasn't mostly white,
but because in looked like a family lived
there.   There was a tricycle in a corner of the
porch; the porch swing looked like it had
gotten regular use and although the plants in
the front yard had been pruned it was clear that
little else had been done to them. Wild
honeysuckle grew among the boxwood plants
that framed the yard just like they belonged
there. No self respecting gardener would have
allowed such a rude display of nature's will.

When the maid slammed the door in her
face, she sat right down there on the top step
until she saw a big black Cadillac pull up in the
circular drive way.

"Sir, do you k now that you got
somebody working in your house that don't
know how to treat people.   I bet she's even
mean to your children," Sister said to the man
who got out of the car carrying his coat
although it was cool enough for him to be
wearing it.

"You could be talking about my wife or
the maid, Ulla. They're both as mean as
snakes." He said as he lumped up to the porch
in the most disjointed way of walking that she'd
ever seen.   It was kind of like his head and
neck knew where he was going and the rest of
him kind of caught up in spells.   He was so tall
she was glad that she was standing on the
porch.

"How do you do? I'm Mr. Ben Wilson,"
he said while sticking the biggest, pinkest hand
God had ever created right out to her.

What was she suppose to do with it? Was he so rich he didn't care that North Carolina was in the South? Sister stared from the hand to the man's face and back again. She continued to look questioningly from his big Santa Claus red cheeks to his hand until he reached down, grabbed her right hand and pumped it up and down.

Sister was too shocked to take her hand back.

"Well? Who are you, standing here on the porch of my house judging the women folk there in?" he spoke pass the first friendly smile she'd gotten from a White person in her entire life.

"I'm Mary Helen Evans. I have to find a job that pays enough so I can buy me a house," That's it she thought. I said too much. Ain't no White man going to knowingly help no Colored person buy no house.

"Oh, you're going to buy a house? I tell you what. We need somebody for Ulla's day off every Thursday and my Mama's maid quit the other day. I'll hire you right now for both those positions if you promise me two things.

"What? She asked not even trying to keep the disappointment out of her voice. She'd known as soon as he'd started talking that this was too good to be true.

"Just promise me that no matter how mad my mother makes you, you won't quit for a year and that if you quit her it won't mean that you'll quit us too."

"That's it? That all you want? I'd
promise that I'd work for your mother for ten
years if you pay me right,"

"No, I wouldn't ask that of you even if
you were wearing wings. So, it's a deal?" He
stuck his hand out again and this time he didn't
have to grab hers.

****

Mary Helen worried about how to tell
Joe about her job all the way home. She
practiced all kinds of ways to ease it into the
conversation, but as soon as he walked in she
blurted it out.

"Joe, I got a job today and Miss Mae
Ella said she'd be glad to keep Gloria for a
dollar a day," She'd waited until nearly
midnight to tell him this and she wasn't even
mad, She'd made up her mind that every time
he came in smelling of cheap perfume and
unwashed pussy she'd just keep repeating what
her grandma had told her about men. Sister still
didn't understand why marriage vows weren't
the same as a promise or why there was
something about men that turned boys who
would cut their wrists to make a blood promise
into beings who would cheat on women they
claimed to love so likely. But if Grandma
Hester said it was the way men were Sister
guessed a woman over ninety years old was old
enough to know what she was talking about.
Sister didn't expect Joe to be faithful, but she
did expect him to help her get a house. She
didn't think that was asking too much.

"You got a job taking care of your own baby and keeping our house clean," Joe was in a bad mood. He felt bad about being unfaithful and he was mad at Sister because she wasn't even trying to keep him faithful by nagging at him. His mother had never stopped nagging his father about it. She'd cussed him out about it while he was lying in his casket during his wake because he'd shamed her by dying at one of his other women's house. But Mary Helen didn't act like she cared any more. She hadn't asked who he'd been out with so late one time since the baby was born.

"You saying this house ain't clean and Gloria isn't being taken care of like she should be?" She put her hands on her hips ready to take him on.

"I didn't say that. I said you have enough to do," Joe would have laughed at the way she stood there like a little bantam roster ready to fight if he didn't know that for her anger usually was followed by tears- not a gentle tear rolling down a pretty little cheek, but gut wrenching dry sobs that left a man's soul bare.

"I need more to do, if I'm going to be round here by myself all times of the night besides that, it takes both your jobs to keep us here.

"I'm going to do better baby," he said as he tried to drag out one of his patented smiles. They both knew he wasn't talking about doing more work or making more money when he said this. There were only so many hours in a day and Joe worked 14 of them five days a week.

"Did I ask you to do better? Long as you don't bring none of those coodie diseases home, I don't care what you do." She didn't mean that, but she could tell that he thought she did.

He did do better for a while-long enough to get her pregnant again. It was another girl and since Joe was doing better at the time, she named the baby Josephine after him and Ann because it was the only name she could think of that sounded good with Josephine.

Chapter 14

Young Mrs. Wilson wasn't quite as mean as a snake. Mary Helen could get along with Miss Kay. She found that she had a way with White folks. Mrs. Kay Wilson came from old Virginia money. She was used to having things done for her, so she was pleased that May Helen, as they started calling her, was a Colored girl that went on and did things without having to be told. She was a modern Southern woman. She'd laugh about how she been thrown out of every college for Southern ladies in Virginia and North Carolina until she'd finally graduated from that liberal college in Chapel Hill where they understood that there was more to a woman than being a "good little wife."

Old Lady Wilson, as Mary Helen called Mr. Ben's mother was a different story. She was from new money, carpet bagger money, and although she was born and raised in the South, Greensboro's Old Money let her know that she wasn't one of them. Even when she married Mr. Ben's father who owned the only Cadillac dealership in the state, their applications to the Country Club were never accepted. It still galled her how Ben's wife had sashayed into Greensboro and become a member of the Country Club in less than a month.

Old Lady Wilson had iron grey hair that made her look as hard as she was. She looked seventy-five, but she was sixty-one.   Her husband had died twenty years ago and left her with four-boys to raise and a business partner who forced her to learn about business in a hurry.

The first week, Mary Helen thought she was going to have to cuss the bitch out.   She kept laying money and jewelry around to see if Mary Helen was going to steal any of it and following behind her asking her all kinds of questions that weren't any of her business.

"M'am," Mary Helen finally said one day, "I don't mean no disrespect, but have I asked you anything about your family?"

"All you need to know about me is that I'm the one who pays you." Old Lady Wilson straightened her spine to her most prim and proper, Southern lady look.

"That's fair.   And all you need to know about me is that I do my job," Mary Helen looked her in the eye, challenging her to say more.   She wasn't impressed with that Southern Lady look.   She'd seen that same look on Grandma Hester hundreds of times.

"You got spunk, gal.   I like that in a Colored gal," Old Lady Wilson was always careful to say Colored instead of Nigger when she wasn't angry.

After that, they got along as well as anybody who hadn't been personally anointed by God could get along with the old lady. It still took Mr. Ben six months to stop asking Mary Helen, each Thursday evening, if she was coming back the next week.

When Ulla died in May, Mary Helen started working fulltime for the Wilsons.

****

"You, gone be all right Squeegie Boy," May Helen said as she sat the Wilson's eldest son down after putting a band-aid on his knee. The covering was more for show than for anything else.

"Can I go show Mama?" he asked as he turned to run off to the living room before May Helen could tell him 'no'.

It didn't work. She caught him before he'd gone two steps. "No, you know how upset your Mama gets when you go in there when her bridge club ladies is over. I know some good medicine for a hurt leg. Let's go in the kitchen and see if we can find some," she said this while she *firmly* turned him and pointed him toward the kitchen.

Squeegie hadn't thought that it would work. At four years old, he was used to not seeing his mother even when she was at home. Hers was a world of society meetings and charity organizations - Hospital Hospitality, Daughters of the Confederacy, The Empty Stocking Fund, and The Greensboro Home for Children, where Southern daughters who were suppose to be spending a spell with a maiden aunt somewhere, came to have the babies that the good ladies of the home cared for until they were adopted.

It didn't matter now that he only saw his mother for a few moments in the evening when she wafted into his room on a cloud of Channel Number 5, silk, and fine brandy on her breath to kiss him good night. He had May Helen.

"Here's the cure that I was looking for," May Helen said as she put the molasses cookies on a saucer and placed it on the table next to a glass of milk.

****

She thought about her children when she looked at the Wilson boys. Squeegie and Andy needed a bunch of mothering. Color didn't make much difference in what children needed. She hoped that Miss Mae Ella was taking good care of her children.

Mary Helen had three girls now. The last one she'd named Mary Louise after her mother-in-law and sister-in-law because the child looked like Joe's people. Besides, Mary was Jesus' mama's name and Mary Helen figured that anyone who looked like those Evans would be needing all the help they could get to get through life.

"May Helen, could you bring us some more refreshments," Young Miss Wilson called from the livingroom.

"Yes M'am," May Helen answered in the voice she reserved for when they had company, but she made a note to herself that she would tell Miss Kay as soon as her guests left not to be expecting her to stop and bring drinks after she'd started making dinner.

"They don't need them drinks this time of day no way," she said aloud to herself. She mixed the drinks, honeyed lemon juleps, the way Miss Kay had shown her, but she cut the liquor with a couple of tablespoons of vanilla extract before she added it. The drinks tasted just as strong and the ladies congratulated themselves for being able to drink so much and still be perfect Southern ladies.

"Lord, I'm tired. May Helen said, talking to herself. If I could go home and sleep for a week, I'd just be starting to get rested by next Sunday morning." She knew that she was dreaming. As soon as she got home, Joe's cousin, James Robert, was going to take them down to Joe's home in York, South Carolina so that Joe's family could see his children.

Chapter 15

The children were as good as they could be on a trip that long, but still taking care of three children in the back seat of a 1950 Chevy was more than she had patience enough to put up with at this time of day, night rather, it had been after seven by the time she got home that evening.

Joe and James weren't any help. Joe had offered to let Gloria sit on his lap, but Sister wasn't about to let one of her babies sit up there with a couple of drunks. Well, maybe they weren't exactly drunk, but she knew they had been drinking before she got home. That and the fact that she was so tired was the reason she'd suggested that they wait and leave in the morning. She'd been out voted. James had this new car and he wanted to show it off before Joe's sister's husband Jake got one.

So here they were pulling up in the yard of a house that Mary Helen hoped wasn't nearly as sorry looking in day light as it was at night, at one o'clock in the morning. *Every* light in the house was on and everyone even the children were up crowded around the door, peeping out like night owls in the forest.

"What's going on Joe? Somebody dead or something? I know you ain't brought me down here for no funeral without telling me. I didn't bring nothing with me but my green party dress." She didn't stop for answers, whipping herself into to high state of anger.

"Ain't nobody dead. Why you think somebody dead?" Joe said without turning so that he could look at her.

"I grew up in the country, Joe. Country folk ain't up this time of night for nothing," Mary Helen said still feeling that they were trying to pull something.

"James told them that he was going to bring me home today the last time he was down here. You know they're going to wait up for their Baby Boy." Joe said this as he jumped out of the car before it stopped rolling and bounded into the house leaving Mary Helen to carry the children in.

"I'll take one in for you, Sister," James Robert offered.

"No, you won't. If Joe wants me or these babies in that house, he'll come back, out here and get us like he's got some sense." She wasn't fussing at him just stating a fact.

James Robert put his head down on the steering wheel and groaned softly to himself. He'd worked a full day too and he wanted to get started on the road back up to his home in Gastonia, North Carolina which was about an hour's drive. He didn't argue with her. It wouldn't be any use trying to change Sister's mind. He wasn't much for arguing any way.

He was a short man, just a little over 5'5in, but well built and muscular for his height because he was a construction worker. It was his big eyes and equally big smile that most people noticed about him first. No. He wasn't going to argue with Sister. That was Joe's place, so he sat there thanking God that he wasn't married and praying that Joe would come back out real soon.

It took Joe two minutes to realize what he'd done wrong and another five more to get up the nerve to come back out and face Mary Helen.

"I'm sorry. I- ah - I ah thought you were coming in with James Robert." His weak explanation was greeted with a look from Sister that Grandma Hester would have been proud of.

He plucked Gloria and Josephine from the seat next to his wife and held the door for her while she struggled to get out of the car-with the baby in her arms. Joe didn't offer to help her again after she slapped his hand away.

"Well, look a here. What we got here? A-Little-Old-Girl-Maker? Joe, she is a sweet little thing. Little Mary you don't have to worry about having a boy to carry on the family name. I named my last boy Joe Ervin, after my little brother." Joe's sister Louise said all this while she looked almost hungrily at the baby in Mary Helen's arms.

Mary Helen knew right there and then that she didn't like Louise. It didn't have anything to do with her brass ankle color or her dyed red hair, or the fact that this woman had helped to create the philanderer that was her husband. She didn't like her because she wanted her baby. Mary Helen didn't know why she wanted her child. She just knew that she did. Louise already had six children of her own.

Mary Helen realized why her Mary was so special to them when she saw all of Louise's daughters at breakfast the next morning. The brass-ankle -fair skin had skipped Louise's girls as complexion does sometimes in Colored families. None of Louise's girls were as dark skinned as either of Mary Helen's older girls, but they were several shades darker than their Mama.

Mary Helen couldn't complain about the way his family treated her most of the time she was down there. His Mama started calling her Daughter and using Louise's pet name for her, Little Mary. She didn't even have to worry about doing anything for her baby. Louise offered to feed her from her own big breasts that still had plenty of milk since she was still nursing three year old Buster. She did have something to complain about when it was time for them to leave that Sunday afternoon.

"Now, Little Mary we've already talked it over with Joe and he says that it's all right for us to keep Mary Louise for awhile," her mother-in-law whispered as she tried to pry the sleeping baby from Mary Helen's arms.

"Do you think I give a damn what Joe says. This here is my child and she ain't staying nowhere less I say so." She was so mad by then that she would have put the baby down and taken on that whole house bare handed, if she hadn't been sure they'd take advantage of it and grab her child.

"Joe, talk to her," Louise ordered her brother like he was still a boy and she was the thirteen year old older big sister.

"Let's go out on the porch, and talk about this, Honey," Joe said as he reached for Mary Helen's arm.

"Honey, ain't nothing but bee's shit. Ain't no need for us to go out on the porch and talk about nothing," Mary Helen was too upset to realize that she'd said a cuss word in front of Joe's mama. Although her brothers had taught her how to cuss at the same time they'd taught her how to play baseball, she was usually very careful not to cuss around her elders.

"I said, let's go on the porch and talk about it," Joe used a tone of voice with her that she more than took exception to. She stood there like the soles of her shoes had melted into the cracks of the floor.

He picked her up, baby and all, and carried them both out of the house, slamming the door shut with his foot.

"Girl, if you ever sass me like that in front of my family again." He stopped like he'd completed the threat. He couldn't say that he would hit her because he suspected that she knew as well as he did that he would not raise a hand to her.

"Listen, you know how low Mama been feeling since she had to get a breast cut off 'cause of that cancer. She said that having that baby here would bring the joy back into her life. Why you being so stubborn? You always saying how hard it is on you working and taking care of three children. Let Mama help you out by keeping Mary Louise for a little while." He finished with his most appealing srnile.

She had to admit that what he said made sense. What would it hurt to let them keep her for a little while?

"Okay, Joe but we're coming back Thanksgiving to get my child. That's six months. If your Mama hasn't had her fill of joy by then, I'm sorry for her.

She found out two weeks after she got back home that she was going to have three children to take care of anyway. She was pregnant again.

Mary Helen worked right up to the day that Sandra was born. She didn't bother with a six week laying-in. She had work to do. She'd figured out that Joe was the kind of man who'd only go as far as a woman pushed him. And she couldn't push lying up in bed. In ten days, she was back at work.

****

Mary Helen stood at the bus stop with her fellow day workers trying to figure out why they all wore aprons over their dresses. What was there to protect? There was as sameness about the dresses. The one hue they had in common was faded: faded gingham, faded sprigged muslin, faded calico. None of them looked special enough to be remembered in their work clothes. Most of the women they worked for were "new" South. Liberal enough to only require uniforms on special occasions, but Southern enough to see nothing wrong with paying $15 a week for labor that combined cook, laundress, housekeeper, maid, and babysitter into one person.

Mary Helen gave up worrying about how they looked and started worrying about how to get Joe to rent Miss Tunie's house. Miss Tunie was an elderly maiden neighbor who had dozens of nieces and nephews, but no children of her own. They'd been fighting over the honor of taking care of the dear lady for months. Miss Tunie had confessed, in confidence, to Mary Helen that they believed she had some money hidden away. She didn't. But she didn't see any harm in letting them believe it until she was dead. The nephew who'd won the tug of war wanted an answer by the end of the month, when he and his wife were coming up from South Carolina to take Miss Tunie to live with them.

"Joe, Miss Tunie's nephew says that he's going to rent her house out for twenty-five dollars a month." Mary Helen slipped this in while Joe was helping her get the girls ready for bed. They had developed a routine in which she bathed and dressed the children for bed and Joe tucked them in and either read or told the children stories. This was another thing that made it hard for her to stay mad at him. Sister had never met a man who was so helpful and nurturing with children.

"That right. I suppose you got it all figured out how we can save money by moving in there." There wasn't a drop of enthusiasm in his voice.

"Joe, I want that house. It's a start. We got to start somewhere. We got to start now or we might not..." She couldn't finish it. She couldn't even let her mind finish the thought that at twenty she could see herself ending up in the same three room house she'd started married life in. "Say you'll think about it Joe. Just say you'll think about it."

Before he could answer there was a knock on the door.

"Sorry to be coming by this late y'all," William Bothwell said as he stood in the door way holding his hat. Mary Helen called him Weasel, had been calling him that since that first night she met him at her Aunt Daisy's house. Mr. Sampson up to wait until Officer Penn made his rounds tomorrow," he finished trying to make himself seem real important.

"Thank-you, We - William," Mary Helen made herself thank him even though she had a feeling she wasn't going to appreciate his little favor after she read the message.

When she read it, she collapsed into the nearest pair of arms. She never knew whether they were Weasel's arms or Joe's arms. They were Joe's.

"Man pick it up and tell me what it says," Joe instructed Weasel as he fanned Mary Helen with his free hand.

"I, I can't read Joe," Weasel admitted as he stood there holding the message upside down.

Joe started to hand his wife to Weasel, and then thought better of allowing the man's hands on her. He walked over-and laid her down on their bed in the corner of the front room.

He returned and took the paper from Weasel. It said:

SISTER. CLARETHA. DEAD. COME. HOME.

G. FULMER

Chapter 16

Claretha. Dead. Claretha. Dead. Mary Helen read the wire so many times while she was going down on the train that it looked like it was a hundred years old by the time she got to Columbia, South Carolina. She felt as old as the wire looked when Uncle Boy picked her up at the station.

"How?" She asked him.

"I don't know Sister. They called us to come up to that boy's house that she was supposed to be engaged to. Didn't say what was wrong. Just that it was an emergency. That Claretha needed us. When we got there she was dead in the back bedroom with a hole in her chest so big you coulda seen the bedspread through it if there hadn't been so much blood. Ain't never seen so much blood before in my life. And I done kilt more hogs than I can remember." He was shaking when he finished and Sister found herself giving more comfort than she was given. He was so torn up she didn't want to ask him more, but she had to know.

"Who killed her? Who killed my sister?" Sister said, ready to fight. She could deal with the anger better than she could deal with the pain.

"They say she kilt herself. Sister don't look at me like that. I ain't the one saying it. That's what everybody else saying," He moved as far away from Sister as he could get. He knew what kind of tempers those James women had.

"Why they saying that? Claretha might have killed somebody else, but she was too stuck on how good her body looked to mess it up like that," and when she said this, Sister was positive that no one could convince her otherwise.

"Where's Joe and your children? Uncle Boy said trying to change the subject.

"Home," Sister said. She knew what he was trying to do and she decided to let him. It wasn't any use trying to get any more information out of Uncle Boy. Even if he knew more than he was telling, which she doubted, he wouldn't tell her any more than Grandma Hester'd told him to tell her. Sister knew she couldn't talk without sounding like she was mad at him and she knew how much it upset Uncle Boy when anyone was mad at him.

He was a small purple-black man, with the shiny baldhead that was the birthmark of all James men. They were all born bald, grew hair slowly, and started losing what little they'd grown by the time they were seventeen. Uncle Boy had spent his whole life being bossed around by everybody, but mostly by his Mama, Grandma Hester. He'd learned early what it took not to get on her wrong side -not speaking unless he was spoken to and doing exactly what he was told- and he'd practiced it -for so long that most people thought he was stupid. Sister knew better, but she left him alone.

They spent the rest of the fifty-eight mile ride to Salley in silence. She was quietly reflecting on what really had happened to Claretha and he pretended that it took all of his concentration to keep his ancient '39 Ford truck on the road.

It was eight-o-clock in the evening when they got to her grandmother's house and even though there was still plenty of day light left on this evening early in September, Mary Helen knew eight-o-clock was Grandma Hester's bed time. Nothing had kept her up past that time during all the years Mary Helen had known her, so she wasn't expecting to see her coming out onto the porch when Uncle Boy rounded the bend at the top of the road.

"Boy, go on in so I can talk to Sister, and tell that yellow wife of yours to get away from the door trying to listen." Grandma wasn't asking him, she was telling him and although he was fifty-seven years old, she knew that he'd cornply.

"Sister, before you start asking any fool questions, I want you to read this here letter on top of these others in the box. Then you can ask me all the questions you want." Grandma Hester gave Sister the letter and sat in her rocking chair to start working on lighting her pipe.

Sister sat down too when she recognized the handwriting on the envelope.

Sister,

By the time you read this letter I will be dead. I couldn't bring myself to marry Colin cause in my heart I know that the only man I could ever love is dead. Sister, you never understood about me and Daddy and I don't expect you to now but I am going to be with him. I laid out what I want to wear and here is a picture from the Marseille Catalog showing how I want my hair. I don't want nobody washing me and dressing me but you Sister. Make sure they bury me between Mama and my Daddy.

Claretha

"Lord ain't that just like Claretha, to die and leave more work for me to do." Sister tried to hand the letter-back to Grandmother, but she shook her head and gestured like it was a thing too foul to touch. When Sister continued to hold it out, she took it and put it in her bosom.

"What's the rest of these?" Sister asked as she turned over the next envelop in the stack. "Oh, my God, this is Aaron's hand writing!" Sister sat down as she opened it.

Sister,

This will be my last letter for awhile. Me and Oscar are joining the Navy before they take us in the Army. Only reason why I kept writing this long is cause I promised. I just remembered that you didn't promise to write me back, but I wish you would just to let me know you're alright. Use this money to get you an Easter dress.

Love Aaron

Sister turned the letter over. Nothing fell out. All 32 of the other letters were empty too. It was like she told Aaron, she didn't care that the money was gone, she cared that Aaron had gone away to fight a war thinking she didn't care enough to write him back. The imagine of Claretha coming back from the mailbox time after time shaking her head burned into Sister's mind. It was a good thing that Claretha was dead because it saved Sister from killing her.

* * * * * * * * * * * *

The next day Grandma Hester went with Sister to the Fulmer Funeral Home and sat quietly while Sister washed and dressed Claretha in the clothes she'd laid out to be buried in. When Sister finished dressing her younger sister Claretha wore a light blue dress with a lace in-lay that made the scooped neckline look modest and pearl white buttons down the front made her look older than nineteen. It had been their mother's best dress and Grandma Hester and Sister'd wanted to bury her in it ten years ago, but Alton Fullmore had given it to nine year old Claretha instead.

Sister dressed Claretha's hair as close to the picture in the Marseiel Catalog as she could get it, at least the part of Claretha's hair that showed. She was careful to follow all of Claretha's dictates but one. She buried her so that their mother was in the middle.

****

"I wish all those people would just go on home," Sister said as she sat on the porch next to her Grandma's rocker.

"I know that's the truth. They ask you any questions? Cause if they is messing with you, I'll go in there and wear them out," Grandma Hester said as she started up from the chair. She was wearing her finest dress. It was so dark a shade of purple that you had to get right up on it to tell that it wasn't black. She only wore it when a James woman died.

"No, M'am they ain't saying nothing to me," Sister was quick to say. The last thing she needed today was for Grandma Hester to get started. "They're talking to Aunt Lila and Uncle Boy trying to find out what they know"

"Humph, like I would tell either one of them any of our business," Grandma Hester said with more than little contempt in her voice. Uncle Boy was a James, but he wasn't *a*

James Woman and as far as Hester was concerned that meant he was barely related and his wife, Lila, meant even less.

"Who that coming now?" Grandma nodded toward the cloud of dust that signaled that a car was coming a half mile before it was visible from the porch.

They waited silently because neither one of them much cared who it was. Neither one looked mildly surprised when the sheriff got out of the dusty, black car. His skinny neck stuck out of his collar like a lone string bean that had been left in the field. He was the kind of man Grandma Hester called slack: slack butt, slack chest, and probably slack of the other stuff men were supposed to have. He knew that the White folk in Aiken County didn't respect him because they knew that his Daddy got the job for him by paying for votes, but he expected the Colored people to respect him because he wore a badge and he was White.

"Evening Hester," he said not even bothering to take off his hat.

Grandma Hester didn't say anything.

"Hester I'm going to have to have that letter that girl wrote for evidence." He shouted it, figuring that the old lady who had to be at least ninety years old was probably deaf.

Grandma Hester said nothing.

"I said, I got to take that letter Claretha left in for evidence," he yelled it loud enough this time to bring most of the people who were in the house out to the porch to see what was going on.

"Evidence of what?" Sister answered him with a question, since she knew her grandmother well enough to know that she wasn't going to say anything.

"Of who killed her," he said this slowly like he was talking to a dimwitted child.

"She killed herself. Since when can you put somebody in jail for killing theyself?" Sister said this like she was speaking to an equally dimwitted child.

"That's for the law to say after we done investigated." He was beginning to sweat. It wasn't supposed to be this hard. His Daddy had sent him out here by himself 'cause he was going to be questioning an old Colored woman, but now all these niggers were crowding around and he couldn't think what to do. He'd look like a plumb fool if he took a hundred-year-old woman in for withholding evidence.

"Since when they started investigating Colored people's deaths?" Sister sassed back at him. She'd taken his measure and decided that she could handle him,

"Since I became Sheriff. I got to have that letter before I go back to town," he almost pleaded with Sister.

"I can't help you. It was given to Grandma Hester, and if she can't tell you where it is I reckon nobody can," Sister said and sat back down on the porch like he was already gone.

"Anybody here know where that letter is?" The sheriff yelled to the crowd on the porch.

There were general mutterings of "No" and "I ain't even seen it."

"She might've even burned it for all y'all know." He caught and held on to this idea like a man pulling his boot out of mud three feet deep. "That's it. She done burned it. I'm going back and tell them that she burned it."

He walked back to his car as slowly as what dignity he had left would permit and drove off leaving a trail of dust that took an half hour to clear.

"Where is it Grandma?" Sister asked later as they still sat on the porch.

"Where nobody, but a James woman will ever find it,"

Sister thought for a few minutes, and then she knew where it was. There was a place that Grandma Hester'd shown her when she turned twelve where you had to touch both corners in the right place at the same time to open a hidden drawer.

"Grandma is right, no one but a James woman will ever -find it," Sister- thought. "Here comes another car. Lord, why won't people leave us alone," Sister was so tired her knees were knocking.

"You go on inside and lay down in my room. Won't nobody mess with you in there," Her grandmother waved her into the house. Sister went because she knew no matter how crowded the house was no one would go into Grandma Hester's room uninvited.

Hester James took the telegraph from the man read it...

WILLIE DIED. FUNERAL. YORK. S.C. WEDNESDAY.

She counted the days on her fingers- five days. They must have figured that since Sister was already in South Carolina, she wouldn't have any trouble getting there for the Wake on Tuesday. Hester James folded the piece of paper and put it in her pocket. It didn't matter that it was for Sister. Hester James made the decision that Sister didn't need to see it. "That child has been through enough these last days to keep her hurting for awhile. Daisy don't need that child there." Hester James settled her mind on a plan as she slid into bed next to Sister that night.

****

Sister kept her eyes closed for a few minutes longer when she woke up the next morning. It wasn't often that she got to sleep in as late as 6:00a.m. Since she'd been down here, her grandma had let her sleep late while she cooked breakfast and started the other chores for the day. Sister was smiling until she stretched and touched something in the bed next to her.

"Grandma, what's wrong!" Sister was terrified. No one had ever awoken early enough to catch Grandma Hester in bed. Sister's first thought was that she must be dead, but when she put her hand to her neck she could feel her heart beating. She was still alive. Maybe they could save her.

Sister ran and got Uncle Boy and his wife up and got one of the relatives who had stayed over after the funeral to go get the doctor. The doctor wasn't sure what was wrong. He figured that she'd had a stroke or a seizure of some kind. There wasn't much he could do but wait to see if she got any worst.

"Don't worry Sister. I seen this before," Boy said. Mama had this same thing a couple of times before. She had it once when they tried to take me into the army during that First World War. She said just before she got sick that it wasn't no way she was going to let them take me when D.W. had gone and left the farm and I was the only man she had left. After they left me here, she got up and started back doing what she had been doing before. Folks called it a miracle but I suspect that it had something to do with getting her way."

Sister didn't think this time was like the other times. No one could think of anything Grandma Hester wanted her way about and Sister had watched over her for hours at a time and never saw a single movement or sign of life.

But it happened just like Uncle Boy said, after five days, Sister woke up to find her grandma in the kitchen cooking breakfast after starting two kettles of homemade lye soap and washing six twelve-foot lines of clothes.

One day later Sister was on the train going back to Greensboro, wondering what Joe was doing and hoping that there would still be enough money in the flour sack at the bottom of the bushel of apples to pay Miss Tunnie's nephew the month's rent in advance that he wanted.

Chapter 17

"Me and Gloria killed Uncle Willie today," Josephine confessed.

"Killed Willie? Joe gave his daughters a puzzled smile. He would never stop being amazed at the things children could get into their heads.

"Yes, sir," Josephine said and Gloria nodded sadly in agreement.

"Y'all ain't no killers. Baby..."

"We did Daddy. Let me tell you," Josephine cut him off. They wanted his forgiveness but not before he knew the whole story.

"Okay, I'll listen." Joe said tiredly. He didn't know when he'd had a week worse than this one. First, his wife gets word that her sister was dead and then today he had to get off work two hours early because of an emergency at home. The policeman, who came to his job to get him, claimed he didn't know what was wrong. The first thing in Joe's mind was that something bad had happened to one of his girls. He expected the officer to take him to the hospital. He was almost relieved when he took him home instead and when he saw Gloria standing there holding Sandra in her arms and Josephine standing next to her, he felt so good that it took him a few seconds to realize that they were crying like babies. They were babies-six and four and a half still qualified them as babies to him even though both of them reminded him of miniature Mary Helen's.

"This is what we did, Josephine continued..."

When we stay with Aunt Daisy, Uncle Willie keeps us most of the time.

"I know Baby that's 'cause he's been sickly all his life. That don't have nothing to do with y'all," Joe interrupted to reassure the girls.

"Just listen Daddy. Go on Josephine," Gloria refused to be comforted before he knew what they had done. "We know he was sick Daddy. I can't remember a time when Uncle Willie wasn't sick. We just knew that there was something wrong with his stomach and Aunt Daisy only let him eat stuff like light bread soaked in milk, Graham crackers soaked in milk, oat meal and watery grits. We thought she was being mean to Uncle Willie."

Josephine stared Gloria into silence as she continued.

"That's right Daddy. He said it was kind of a game helping him get around Aunt Daisy, and me and Gloria liked helping him. Every day, as soon as Aunt Daisy was gone long enough for us to be sure that, she had gone too far to come back, Uncle Willie would send us to the little store at the end of the road to get some "real" food for him. "Real" food was what he called anything that had to be chewed before it could be swallowed.

As soon as Gloria and I got back from the store, Uncle Willie cooked his "real" food. He'd laugh and talk until his food was done but when he sat down to eat, he never talked and we didn't talk either. He looked real happy eating that food."

Joe could imagine how Willie had looked. The few times that Daisy had allowed Willie to have regular food on a special occasion like his birthday Willie had savored each bite and chewed each mouthful as long as he could. It was almost embarrassing watching him eat because it was like watching someone enjoying having sex.

"This morning was different," Josephine drew Joe's attention back to her story. *"As soon as he started eating, Uncle Willie leaned over and grabbed his stomach. Blood started coming out of his mouth. Gloria jumped up and ran down the road to get Miss May Ella. I couldn't move Daddy. I just sat there and looked at Uncle Willie rolling on the floor."*

Miss May Ella came and saw how sick he was and she got a cab to come and take Uncle Willie to the hospital and then she walked over to the college to tell Aunt Daisy. Everyone forgot about us. Gloria ain't even seven yet and they left us here all by ourselves," Josephine paused for a word of sympathy from their father but Gloria wouldn't allow it.

"We knew it was because it was our fault that Uncle Willie had got sick. So, we just sat and waited for the policeman to come back for us." Gloria cried until her body shook with dry heaving.

Josephine gave her a mean look before continuing, *"After awhile, Aunt Daisy got home. She told us that Uncle Willie had been very sick when she got to the hospital but by the time she left him he was doing much better. She said that he was walking around telling jokes to make the other sick people laugh. She cleaned up the floor and fixed us jelly sandwiches for lunch. We thought everything was going to be all right but just when she was putting us in her bed for our nap someone started beating on the front door. Aunt Daisy picked up the poker from next to the wood stove. She stood behind the door as she opened it to see who was there. It was that policeman again.*

He said, "Mrs. Evans, the hospital requested that I come to inform you that your husband, Willie Evans, died this afternoon at 2:46 p.m. His body has been taken to Smith's Funeral Home."

Someone screamed and someone started to cry. I think it was me screaming and Gloria crying. I know Aunt Daisy didn't do any crying or screaming. She told the policeman that she couldn't go to the funeral home until he went and got you because she was taking care of us. She didn't say nothing to us. She just got out Uncle Willie's best suit and started brushing it with a whisk broom then she washed and ironed his shirt. She didn't say nothing until you got here. She must hate us for killing Uncle Willie," Josephine finished with her head bowed.

Joe looked at the girls for a while. His features softened, and he pulled them into his arms and hugged them tight. He wasn't a kissy person except with his little ones. He knew exactly what they needed right now.

"I'm only going to say this once," he started, "so I want you girls to listen. Willie was a grown man. He knew what he was supposed to eat. The doctor told him what he had to do to live. I guess living wasn't as important as eating to Willie. You girls were just minding a grownup like you're supposed to do when you went to the store for Willie. I don't ever want to hear this nonsense about you killing Willie again. He killed himself and that's a fact."

They cried with relief. It wasn't their fault. If Daddy said it wasn't then it wasn't and he never lied to them.

Chapter 18

"The fair is in town Joe," Weasel said as he tried to match his step to Joe's. Guess y'all won't be going this year since you got death in the family?"

"What them children know about death in the family. Children need to have some fun whether there's death in the family or not. They not having fun ain't going to bring nobody back." Joe jumped on Weasel a little harder than he normally would have.

He was tired. Working two jobs and taking care of three little girls and a baby alone was hard work. He couldn't really say that he was alone because Miss May Ella and the rest of the women helped all they could the early part of the day and evening since Daisy took Willie's body back to South Carolina to be buried in the family plot at the church. Miss May Ella had taken over fixing their hair since Daisy had been gone and laying out their clothes for each day. She even made sure he'd put the clothes on right and took care of them during the day while he worked. By the time he got home each evening they'd been fed and were ready for bed. But at night and first thing in the morning the children were all his. That Josephine was driving him crazy asking questions every two minutes and Gloria was getting on his nerves trying to help with things she wasn't big enough t o do.

A man couldn't plan with little children. He'd made up this plan, that should have worked, where he put the clothes that Miss

May Ella had laid out on them and put them in the bed with him. That way he'd save a whole extra hour in the morning to get them fed and over to Miss Mae Ella. Instead, his plan had cost him two hours and a cussing out by his boss man, because the girls had pissed all over themselves and him. A grown man couldn't go to work smelling like piss, so he was forced to bathe and redress everyone.

"They need some fun. Hell, I need some fun," Joe said to himself as he made a decision.

"I'm taking my babies to the fair," he announced, as he scooped each of them up and planted very wet kisses on their cheeks. "What are we going to do with that one?" he said, looking at Sandra, the baby. "I know. Gloria, take Sandra to your Aunt Daisy while I re-comb Josephine's hair. Tell her that I'll pick her up in the morning." Like Mary Helen, Joe always thought out loud, posing questions that he answered himself.

Joe sang the Platters latest hit, "Smoke Gets in Your Eyes", while he twisted Josephine's hair into something like plaits. "Your mama thinks she's the only one can make you babies pretty, but I been watching her. You look every bit as good as you do when she does it; if I do have to say so myself!"

Josephine was glad that he did say so himself, because the dresser mirror told her that she was a hot mess. The plaits were already coming loose at the ends and he'd tried to halt this by tying whopsided bows on the ends of each plait. She decided that Buckwheat didn't have anything on her. Not that it mattered to the four year old because her Daddy's eyes were shining and they always had a good time when

Daddy came home with his eyes shining and a hint of gin on his breath. She knew it was gin because she'd heard her Daddy tell Uncle James, "I drink gin 'cause it ain't no sin." There was more to the rhyme, but when he realized that she was listening, he changed the subject.

She loved her Daddy. He was the fun one. He answered all of her questions and never spanked or scolded her. Mama was mean. Mama never smiled and she fussed at Daddy all the time.

As soon as Gloria got back, they set out walking, even though there was a city bus which went straight out to the fair grounds, Joe flat out refused to ride the city bus where Colored people were required to sit in the back.

"We're walking girls. Why I'm going to pay a whole dime to ride second class when I got feet that take me first class wherever I go?"

That night his feet took all of them first class. He carried Gloria on his back with her legs wrapped around his forearms and Josephine in his arms.

Joe sang "Sixty Minute Man" all the way there, but it seemed to the girls like only seconds before he was setting them down.

"I'll carry Gloria since she's the littlest. Josephine you hold on to one of my pants' legs, and don't turn loose until we get back home." Joe instructed the girls.

"Yes, sir," they piped in together ready for the adventure to begin. It was the first time there had been money enough for them to go to the fair.

The fair was a symphony of sounds and smells. Good smells. Joe detoured as far away from all the cows and pigs as he could get and steered them away from the exotic animal exhibits.

"Don't want to see them. Don't want to smell them. Been around enough animals to last me a lifetime," he mumbled.

"We'll ride first, Girls," he said as he marched them over to   the merry-go-round where a nice lady agreed to hold one of his girl's hands while he rode with the other one if he'd do the same for her while she rode with her little boys.

They rode it and got back in line four times before he was ready to go on the next ride.

"This here is my favorite ride Babies. The Ferris wheel," Joe reverently said the name of the thing that looked to the girls like a monster with thousands of multi-colored eyes and a gigantic head with dozens of mouths that kept stopping to spit up its human meals. They didn't tell their Daddy this.

A lot of people must have felt the same way that Joe did about the monster, because it was the longest line they'd stood in so far. It took over thirty minutes for them to get to the front of the line.

"You can't get on here with those younguns?" A fat, red faced man said when it was finally their turn.

"I'll hold on to them real tight," Joe said.

"No, you won't. Cause you ain't getting on here. If one of those little pickaninnies falls out, it'll cost me a whole night's work." He didn't waste any more time talking to Joe as he motioned for the next person in line to come forward.

"Joe didn't step back not because he took exception to his daughters being called pickaninnies. Now that he looked at them under the bright lights of the fair, they did kind of remind him of the children back home who used to play in the fields while their mothers and fathers picked cotton. He stood there because he really wanted to ride that Ferris wheel.

"Joe, I'll ride with you and Weasel will be glad to hold the children. Won't you Honey," Glady sounded really pleased with herself. She knew that Joe wasn't going to be able to avoid her company this time. She'd never stopped trying to get Joe, but he'd done everything he could to stay away from her.

"Go on, nigger," the man behind Joe said.

Joe hesitated one more second before he handed Mary Louise to Weasel and pried Gloria's and Josephine's hands off his pants' legs.

"You watch them good," Joe told Weasel.

Weasel knew that Glady was using him. It'd been her idea for him to talk Joe into going to the fair. Yeah, he knew he was being used, but he also had enough sense to know that getting used was the only way a man like him got to be with a woman who looked as good as

Glady Just having people see him walking down the street with Glady was enough to keep him happy for weeks. So, he stood there being used while they rode the Ferris wheel five times.

"Joe, Do you want me to tell Weasel to take the children home and we can go down to Miss Mable's Place," Glady said clinging so tight to Joe that he felt like he'd have to soak for a week to wash the smell of her off him.

"No, I don't want you to tell Weasel nothing. I done told you gal. I ain't messing with you," Joe tried to ease a little farther over on the seat.

"Why, Joe. Ain't no telling when Sister gonna be back. A man needs a woman and you ain't gonna find no more woman than me in this town." Glady filled in what little distance he'd been able to make between them.

She wasn't about a let it drop. Joe was the only man who'd said, "No" to her abundant charms. She knew he was sleeping around, so why not with her?

"Glady, there're too many women in Greensboro for me to be messing with Mary Helen's cousin," he said this thinking that it would shut her up.

"Sister ain't nothing to me Joe. We cousins so many times removed that it ain't really being related no more."

It was their turn to get off and Joe leaned over like he was going to help her down. He didn't even stick out his hand as he said, "She's something to me Glady."

Glady didn't give up. Everywhere Joe and the children went the rest of the evening, she was there propositioning him.

"I'm going to feed my children. Then I'm going home." Joe announced when he turned again and found Glady and Weasel on his heels. Joe made sure that the children tasted every kind of food the fair had to offer.

"Look, Daddy," Josephine said as she pointed to the red rings the candy apples made around her sister's mouths.

Joe laughed too, but he was really thinking about how to get rid of Glady and Weasel. Then he remembered that he was walking.

"Weasel, I think it's about time for that last bus to leave for town." Joe said as he munched on some greasy fries topped with vinegar and salt.
"What. Glady said, Is the bus bout to leave? Come on Weasel. I ain't walking nowhere," Glady pulled Weasel away from a whole paper cone of fries.
"Now girls let's go have some real fun," Joe said as he finished off Weasel's fries. I'm going to win some prizes for my babies."

It took all that was left of his week's pay, but he didn't stop until all three girls had bright painted glass piggy banks.

They were some happy some bodies on their way home that night! Joe taught the girls a poem about "Jump back, baby, jump back" by Paul Laurence Dunbar his favorite poet. By the time they reached home he had changed it up a bit, the girls were saying, "Jump back, Daddy, jump back," as he did a jig each time, they came to the refrain giving them a ride that was almost as good as the merry-go-round. It went something like,

Seen my babies home last night,

Jump back, Daddy, jump back.

Held their hands and squeezed them tight,

Jump back, Daddy jump back.

Heard them sigh a little sigh,

Seen a light gleam from they eye,

An a smile go flitting by—

Jump back, Daddy, jump back.

Oh, they had a time until they rounded the corner of Gorrell Street and Cruz Street.

Didn't I turn those lights off, children?" Joe inquired as he came to a sudden halt under the streetlight.

"Yes sir, the girls replied in unison, even though they'd all been so excited when they left, they wouldn't have noticed if he'd left the door wide open and every light in the house on.

"Well, if I didn't leave it on and it's on now, I reckon we know what that means?"

"Mama's home," the girls chimed in again, the good time seeping out of them like air from a slow leaking tire.

"Give your Daddy a hug," he said as he put them down, holding each of them a little tighter and for an instant longer than he normally did.

"Keep those piggy banks out of sight. No use giving your mama anything else to throw," he continued as he planted one more kiss on their cheeks.

Chapter 19

Mary Helen had been home over three hours. She'd been there long enough for all the tender feelings from missing her husband to turn into a solid mass of anger. As early as it was in the day, she'd expected to find the girls with her Uncle Willie, but their home had been locked. No one's house was ever locked during the day. She went to Miss Mae Ella's house next. While her head and heart were still reeling from the news about her uncle's death the woman said, "Joe said he was taking his girls to the fair."

"Taking the girls to the fair?" Her uncle was dead and all he could think of was going to some damn fair?" Her uncle had been dead six whole days and Joe hadn't had time to let her know, but he could make time to take the girls to the fair.

This didn't make any sense. She knew her girls thought their Daddy was the fun one. He was the one who laughed and played with them while all she did was fuss and worry. She could be fun. At least she used to be. She decided to surprise them by finding them at the fair. That was it. She would got out there calmly and find Joe and the children at the fair. She wouldn't yell or anything. She would ask him just as quiet as could be, "Joe why didn't you let me know that my Uncle Willie had died?" Then when he gave her a sensible answer, she would ask him in the same quiet voice, "Joe, why you have these children at the fair when we got death in the family. And when he explained that he knew how the children loved their uncle. And that he was just trying to cheer them up. She would kiss him for being so thoughtful and they would all have a good time. She loved Willie too- maybe she needed to go to the fair as much as the children did.

She rode out to the fairgrounds with visions of Joe and her riding the Ferris-wheel and kissing every time it reached the top like they had that fall after they first got married.

Joe had said, "I liked riding this before, but riding it ain't never been this good. From now on I ain't riding it with no one but my girl."

When she got to the fair grounds, first she went to the donkey ride for children. They weren't there. Maybe he took them to the Merry-go-round she thought since it was about the only fair ride her children were big enough to get on. They weren't there. The only other place she could think of was the games. "If that man is over there losing all his pay trying to win those girls one of those cheap fair prizes, I'll... She stopped herself from finishing the thought. Remember Sister, you're not here to be the worry-wart messing up the children's good time by fussing at their Daddy. So, when she didn't find them there, she decided to take the bus back home and wait for them there. She was still as happy she could make herself be this soon after finding out about Willie until she looked up and saw her Joe on the Ferris-wheel with a woman wrapped around him.

She kept walking to the bus stop, but she couldn't remember getting on the bus or walking into her house. All she could remember clearly was taking the butcher knife out of the kitchen drawer and sharpening it over and over again with Joe's shaving strap and waiting for him to come home.

****

She started in on him as he walked through the door. You let my babies see you out with some slut? You got time to mess with some hussy, but you don't have a few minutes to let me know Willie was dead? Did you take my girls to some liquor house too?" she fired questions at him.

"I took them to the fair," he jumped in with an answer.

"The fair? You took just them-just them to the fair?"

"I just took my babies to the fair and I did send you a telegram about Willie."

"Then why didn't I get it and why did I see you there with another woman? Joe, you said you'd never go on a Ferris-wheel again with anyone but me."

She didn't know why, but somehow this seemed like an even worst betrayal than his sleeping around. All the nights that she had waited up for him, she'd go back in her mind to those two glorious nights when she still believed that he loved her- the night he sang to her at the club and that night on the Ferris-wheel when she believed he loved her in a way that made her feel like the most special woman in the world.

"I don't remember saying that." For Christ sake, why did women remember every word a man said when he was in a romantic mood?

"You don't? You don't remember? Joe, just give me the rest of the money for the rent and get out of my face. She put her free hand out and waited for him to put something in it.

When he didn't move she said, "Joe where's your money? We got bills to pay!"

"Always got bills to pay; fair don't come but once a year," was Joe's weary reply.

"I said how much you got of your pay?" I know you ain't spent all that money taking some woman and these children to the fair. How much you got Joe?" She was nose to belt buckle with him now and her nose caught the scent of honeysuckle, jasmine, rosewood, and some other ingredients only her Grandma Hester knew. Only three women in Greensboro wore that scent. She hadn't been here, and no one, not even Willie, got close enough to Aunt Daisy to get her scent on them. That left Glady.

Joe saw the look of pain mixed with more anger than he'd ever seen in anyone and he attempted to disarm her with humor. "How much I got? In money or in memories?"

"The one you can spend you fool!"

"Not one red cent," was his honest reply.

She didn't want to hear that. She didn't want to hear anything the lying, cheating bastard said for the rest of her natural life -for the rest of his life. She pulled out the knife that she had held down to her side in the folds of dress. She'd thought that she'd threaten him with it when she put it there but now her intent was to kill.

The fight began.

Since the children knew the routine, they rushed over to the sofa and pulled out what was left of their popcorn from the deep pockets of their pinafores. Usually, their Mama would throw everything that she could pick up and when she ran out of things to throw, she'd rush in on their Daddy like a raging bull, attacking him with her fists. He'd hold her- off by the top of her head with one of his thirty-five-inch-long arms until she became so angry and frustrated that she'd begin to cry. Then, he'd hold her. They never knew what happened next because he'd silently signal Gloria to put them to bed. And they went to bed thinking that fights always had happy endings.

But this night was different. Mary Helen was angry beyond tears.

"Woman, put that knife down! You're scaring the children," Joe said while flicking his eyes from Mary Helen's hand to their children's faces.

"Don't make the babies cry," he whispered that gentle way he'd always soothed away her anger before. This time it didn't work.

"Gloria, get out of here and take Josephine and Sandra with you!" he ordered as he struggled with Mary Helen.

The girls stood frozen in the doorway. They knew somehow that he wouldn't hurt their mother. They were afraid for their Daddy. There was no telling what that wild woman would do to him.

"I said get them out of here!" Joe nearly shouted this time. Even with the door closed the girls heard them. Their mother shouting words that they didn't even know she knew, their Daddy's deep whispers wrapping around her shouts like a too warm blanket. Finally, they heard a scream, then the metallic and wood thud of the knife hitting the floor,

"Joe, why you make me do this? Oh Joe. I didn't mean it. Why Joe?" Mary Helen wept. She hadn't cried when she read the wire about Claretha, she hadn't cried when she read Claretha's letter, she hadn't really cried since that first night she found out about Joe, but she cried now. "Why all the men I love leave me hurting? My brothers, Daddy, Robert Lee, but you most of all…"

"I ain't Robert Lee," Joe couldn't answer for the others, but he knew he would never do what his brother had done.

"Sometimes, times like these when you hurt me like this-when you make me so crazy mad- hurt me so deep I feel like I must be the biggest kind of fool holding on to a man that make me feel like this- times like these-I wish you'd just go on."

"You don't mean that. You can't mean that, he looked into her eyes hoping to see-he didn't know what − maybe just something of that sassy girl who'd met him at the door of Daisy's House that first night, but the eyes that looked up at him were old eyes and he hurt too knowing he'd done that to her.

****

Gloria eased the door open and her sister peeked around her. They had to know what had happened to their Daddy. There was a long slash from his elbow to his wrist.

Joe ignored the cut as he pulled a trembling Mary Helen into his arms. He spoke softly, calming her down. "It's all right, Baby, it's just a scratch. It's my fault, all my fault. I should have waited till you could go, too." Joe held her tight, trying to make up for all the times he'd hurt her.

Chapter 20

Joe told her about Weasel being there with Glady and how he would have ridden the Ferris-wheel with Weasel except Weasel was scared of every ride including the Merry-go-round. He swore up and down that was all there was to it.

Mary Helen wanted to believe him, but the way Glady said, "You know me, Sister," when she'd confronted her about it planted seeds of doubt in her mind which laid there dormant waiting for the spring of suspicion. She wanted to believe Joe. Going out with her cousin would be a low down dirty thing for him to do. But she couldn't convince herself that anywhere he could find a piece of pussy was too low for him to stoop.

He swore out that he had sent her a message about Willie dying and she believed him about that. When she thought about what Uncle Boy said about Grandma Hester being sick when she wanted something, she figured out that what Grandma had wanted this time was for her not to have to go to another funeral right after her sister's funeral. Sister wasn't mad at her grandma. She put the blame on herself for confiding how hurt and how tired she was. She had laid-around late every morning until those last days and let Grandma Hester make all the major decisions. Once Grandma Hester started making decisions she took over. Sister knew that about her.

At least Joe had said, "Yes" about moving into Miss Tunnie's house though. And it didn't bother her at all knowing that he'd done it to get on her good side again.

She'd made up her mind about one thing though. She needed something in her life to keep her from killing Joe. She decided that something was Jesus.

Mae Jo, James Robert's new wife had been nagging her about going to a tent meeting near the water tower up on Gorrell Street. She'd told Sister about it last night. They wouldn't even have to go that far, because the Holy Rollers, as people called them, had made sure they were as close to the sinners as they could get.

Sister had half heartedly said that she would go, but she was so tired and worn down from working and worrying that she just wanted to get her girl's clothes ready for the next day and go to bed.

She didn't know why, but getting their clothes all starched and prettied up comforted her. No matter how late it was when she got home, she'd starch and iron their pinafores, dresses, and crinolines. Then she'd polish Sandra's high-top white shoes and clean and polish Gloria's and Josephine's black patent leather shoes with day-old corn bread before she went to bed.

"Lord, if I can get in bed before eleven tonight I'll go to that tent service tomorrow night for sure." Sister lifted her eyes upward and firmly convinced herself that the Lord said, "Stay, home."

Evidently, the Lord didn't give the message to Mae Jo because she was there standing in the doorway two minutes later calling, "Sister, Sister, Let's go before all the seats be taken and we have to stand up. I'm coming back home if I got to stand up," Mae Jo said in the kind of fussy, whinny voice Mary Helen hated,

"Well, that's it. I'll have to go now. Mae Jo will never let me hear the end of it if I don't go, after she done walked a whole hundred yards out of her way to pick me up," Mary Helen thought to herself as she unplugged the iron and took off her apron. She'd wear the same dress she'd worn to work. It was clean. What did it matter that it fit her plump beyond pleasing body like a sack which had been gathered about the neck and arms. When she had her apron on, the tie at the back of it pulled the dress together just enough so that it hinted at a waist above a stomach which was rounded from seven months of pregnancy.

"Alright, Mae Jo," We ain't going to be too late. You know Colored folks never start nothing on time," she said as she eased her shoes back on.

Mae Jo was what Joe referred to as a "Big Old Gal". She was big boned with plenty of meat on those bones. So much meat that she kind of shifted from side to side when she walked like a wagon load of potato sacks that hadn't been tied down right

"See Sister, I told you. We almost
didn't have nowhere to sit?" Mae Jo grumbled
as she slid onto three of the last four remaining
folding chairs, then moved again leaving Sister
little more than a corner of the fourth one?

Mary Helen didn't say anything. She'd
listened to May Jo fuss the whole two blocks to
the big tent where the service was being held.
The lot on the corner of Gorrell Street and
Terrell Road had been used for revival after
revival since before Sister moved to
Greensboro. She hadn't paid them any attention
because she didn't set much store on traveling
preachers, there'd been one who'd come
through Salley every summer, a while back,
and four or five babies would be born the next
spring that looked a whole lot like him. Then
too, she'd been born and sprinkled with water-
African Methodist Episcopal Zion and that was
good enough for her.

She thought that if Mae Jo would get
quiet for half a minute, she might be able to get
some sleep after all.

"There he is Sister, Bishop Wyoming
Wells." Mae Jo shouted as she elbowed Mary
Helen awake.

Stepping up to the podium was the
biggest black man Mary Helen had ever seen.
He wasn't just tall, he was big. He was at least
four inches taller than her Joe who was six-
feet-one inch tall. He was wide big. His
shoulders were so wide she knew a yard stick
wouldn't be long enough to span them. It
wasn't his size or the fact that he was good
looking, dark, dark chocolate brown skin, even

white teeth and dimples an inch deep better
looking than her Daddy have been and she
never thought she'd think that about any man
that kept Mary Helen from going back to sleep.
It was his presence, the way that he stood up
there like he'd been born to be there.
Something about him made her know that his
smile wasn't just plastered on his face and that
everything he said came from a soul deeper
than a river.

Mary Helen Fullmore Evans considered
herself a sinner beyond redemption. She was
worse than the average sinner. She had almost
killed her own husband just a few nights ago.
She didn't suspect there was much anyone short
of Jesus in person could do for a woman like
her.

Then the preacher got up and began to
speak. It seemed to her that he was speaking
directly to her. Mary Helen leaned forward,
trying to get as close to the man as the six rows
of people in front of her would allow. Every
other soul in the tent seemed to fade away as
though it was just the two of them and his
message came straight from God specifically
for a woman so sinful that she had almost killed
her husband, for a woman who had sent one of
her daughter's teachers a note with more than a
few cuss words in it, a woman who had been in
more fights than she could count.

****

*"I'm not going to preach about what I'd
planned to preach about. As I walked up here,
God gave me a new message. God just gave me*

a new message- a message that someone in here
needs to know. God wants you to know that he
hears you. That he knows your heart, but he
wants you to know that there are some things
you must do.

Jesus said: "If ye abide in me and my
words abide in you, ye shall ask what ye will,
and it shall be done unto you." Anything you
want you can get from Jesus. Anything.

He wants you to know that he can make
that husband or wife who won't do right do
right by you. He can get that house that you
want for you. That car that you want. Anything.
That's a pledge that he made, but you have to
do something. His word must abide in you. He
must abide in you. Are you ready to let Jesus
abide in you?"

"Yes, I'm ready," Mary Helen heard a
voice that seemed to be hers join the multitude
of voices of others who believed that he was
talking to them.

Something touched way deep down in
her soul and started a fire. A fire that burned so
hot it lifted her out of her chair and sent her
running up and down the aisle crying and
praising His name.

"Sister, Sister. You're going to hurt
yourself and that baby running round here like
that. Sister, sit down," Mae Jo caught hold of
Mary Helen on her fifth lap around the tent.

"Leave her alone," Bishop Wells said,"
God has never let his spirit hurt one of his
children.

It took several other saints to get Mary
Helen and May Jo home that night because
once Mae Jo stopped worrying about Sister, she

rushed down to the front of the tent when Bishop called all the sinners to the altar. Both of them were crying, shouting, and praising His name all the way home.

Chapter 21

Mary Helen had religion.   Not that going-to-church-every-Sunday kind of religion, but that shouting, praying for hours, filled with the precious Holy Ghost kind of religion. The next Friday night when Joe came loafing in near midnight with his pockets empty and smelling like a gin factory, she used a weapon more potent than any knife.

She placed her hand on his chest since she couldn't reach his head and prayed, "Satan the Lord rebuke you. Get out of this man, devil he's a hard working man. He's a loving man. He loves his children. He doesn't want them going out here looking like they don't belong to nobody.   Lord, he knows I can't do it by myself. Jesus, tell old Satan to leave my husband alone."

Her words didn't faze Joe that night. He just thanked the Lord that he was too drunk to understand most of what she said during the two hours she prayed for him.

Mary Helen wasn't bothered by the seeming lack of effect her prayers had on Joe. She was new at this. Her failures with her husband just made her more determined to keep her mind set on Jesus until she got a prayer through for Joe.

Sister practiced praying every chance she got. She prayed for everyone, especially Old Lady Wilson. She'd thought when God saved her it'd been so she wouldn't rot in hell for killing Joe, but she knew now that He'd done it to keep her from wringing the old lady's stringy neck.

Old Lady Wilson was a trial and a tribulation. She'd started to forget where she put things and about every day the two of them had a heated discussion about why Mary Helen had started stealing things after all these years. Mrs. Wilson didn't even have the common decency to apologize when she later found things right where she'd put them.

"May Helen give me back my damn eye glasses? Girl, if you don't stop your thieving ways, I'm going to have to call the law in on you!" Old Lady Wilson screamed from the downstairs bedroom.

"Lord give me strength, if it is in thou perfect will," Mary Helen prayed before she answered the old Lady. "They probably under your pillow where you put them every night," she called back never pausing in her work.

"Where you put them you mean. Though I haven't quite figured out how you keep lifting my head without me knowing it. But when I do figure it out, I'm calling the law."

"Yes, M'am," Mary Helen kept working not missing a lick.

"Hurry up May Helen. We got an appointment." Old Lady Wilson called down the hall.

Mary Helen stopped what she was doing and walked back to the bedroom wiping the suds off her hands.

"M'am. We? What we got an appointment to do?" She'd never done much more than clean and fix lunch and breakfast for the Old Lady and she knew that she was too newly saved to take more than one car ride a week with Mrs. Wilson and they'd already been to get her groceries.

"Just be ready when I'm ready. You don't need to know more than that," Old Lady Wilson said as she pulled herself out of bed and steadied herself on the nightstand.

"Yes, M'am," Mary Helen said. But she didn't like it then and she didn't like it later when the old lady backed her Cadillac into two parking spaces in front a three story brick building on Elm Street.

"Come on May Helen, You've made us late already, taking my glasses like that," Mrs. Wilson said as she placed one leg outside the car and tried to coax the other into joining it.

"Yes M'am. I'm coming. Soon as I can," Mary Helen's voice was trembling; it always did when she was forced to ride in a car when Old Lady Wilson was driving.

They hadn't stopped for a single stop
sign or red light and had been the wrong way
on at least two streets.   Mrs.Wilson had
ignored the cussing, horns honking, and hands
waving, since she didn't know any of the
people who were doing it.   Mary Helen'd
motioned out her window for the first
policeman they passed to stop them, but he'd
driven on by.

The last policeman who'd been fool
enough to stop the old lady had spent the rest of
the month doing paper work.

She'd called the chief every time she
thought about the injustice of laws which were
applied to other people being applied to her.
She'd harangued him to the point he'd paid her
fine himself and ordered that anyone who
stopped that powder blue Cadillac would spend
the rest of his career on foot patrol.

"Where are you going, May Helen?" Mrs.
Wilson paused with her hand on the door Knob.

Mary Helen started not to answer.   Mrs.
Wilson had to know that she couldn't go in the
White folks' entrance.   "I'm going to find the
other door."

"May Helen, come on in here.   You're
with me. Nobody is going to tell me, I can't
take you anywhere I want to," she said using
her imperial Southern Lady tone.

Mary Helen followed her.   The people in
the waiting room looked up when Mary Helen

came in, but didn't say anything. Still, the sea of white faces made her nervous and she found herself edging closer to the old lady.

"Good morning Mrs. Wilson. I don't believe I have you down for an appointment today," the receptionist looked nervously from the old lady to the Colored girl beside her.

"I don't suspect that you do since I just decided to come this morning. Tell Dr. Wrighten that I'm out here," Mrs. Wilson kept standing as though she expected to go next even though there were several other clients in the waiting room ahead of her.

"Yes, M'am, The young woman rushed into the inner office looking relieved to have someone else handle the situation.

"Why, Mrs. Wilson, my nurse just told me that you were out here. So, sorry you had to wait. Come right on in," a thin man with an equally thin mustache pranced out into the waiting room and motioned Mrs. Wilson to come in.

"Come on May Helen,"

"Oh, your girl will be all right out there, Mrs. Wilson," the doctor said in his most ingratiating voice.

"Was I talking to you, young man?" Mrs. Wilson turned and gave him a look that had turned better men than him into pools of corn syrup.

"No, M'am. I - I. Well, if you want her with you I suppose it will be all right," he said, but he thought, "God I hate dealing with these old biddies."

"Like I didn't know that" Mrs. Wilson said as she huffed pass him. Mary Helen had no other choice but to follow.

"Sit down May Helen," the old lady said, motioning to a contraption that looked like what Mary Helen supposed bore a chilling resemblance to what an electric chair looked like.

"Now, Mrs. Wilson, you did find your glasses and the pearls too, and I swear before God I don't know what happened to that fork last week," Mary Helen pleaded, trying to reason with the old lady. She didn't feel that her reward for working for the old lady longer than anyone ever-had before should be death in that contraption.

"I know you are not sassing me. I said sit down, May Helen," Mrs. Wilson stared her back into the chair.

"Now, Mrs. Wilson, I appreciate your business, but I am not putting my hand in any nigger's mouth," the dentist said taking what he hoped was a firm stand. He didn't want to upset the old girl, but what would happen if the rest of his clients found out that he was using the same equipment on them that he'd used on a nigger?

Mary Helen didn't question his motives. In fact, she thought about kissing him right on the lips as she started to get up.

"Sit down. May Helen," Mrs. Wilson said, not taking her eyes off the young dentist.

"I say it's May Helen. I say I want you to pull those rotten front teeth and fit her for a partial plate. And if you say one more word to me about putting your hands in a nigger's mouth, I'll close this office down and you won't be putting your hand in anybody's mouth," she said as she kept those iron grey eyes on him daring him to defy her.

He didn't waiver long. He knew she owned the building, he knew that he'd been lucky to get such a choice spot in downtown Greensboro, but more than that he knew how vengeful her kind could be. She'd ruin him if it took her the rest of her life and with his luck he was sure that the bitch would out live him.

"May Helen, you tell me if he hurts you," Mrs. Wilson said as the dentist did as he was told.

Chapter 22

"May Helen, May Helen," I have been calling you for the last ten minutes!" May Helen! Why are you banging my pots and pans around like that? If something is dented, it's coming out of your pay. Are you ignoring me?" Miss Kay reached around and touched May Helen on the shoulder.

Mary Helen swung around with the pot still in her hand. "What? Lord, Lord, Miss Kay, you almost made me knock you upside the head with this here pan."

"And what would you have done next if you had?" Mrs. Kay asked recovering from the shock.

"I'd have finished you off and buried you in the back yard I reckon. I can't be going to jail for hitting no White woman. Your children and mine need me." She looked at Miss Kay with a half smile on her face. Although Mary Helen never lost sight of the fact that Miss Kay was White and she was the help, over the years she'd learned so much about Miss Kay that Miss Kay treated her like a confidant.

"You probably would. I won't even ask you what you'd tell Ben about my being gone."

"Why were you calling me anyway?"

"I don't even remember. I said why are you around here banging things?"

"I'm sorry." The half smile disappeared. "I need to hit something before I hit somebody.

I don't know when I've been this mad." She never told anyone about the time she' been mad enough to cut her husband. "They won't give me back my child."

"Who in the world would want to kidnap a Colored child?" Less you got some money I don't know about."

"My children are worth as much to me as any White child. Did I say somebody kidnapped her? I said they won't give her back to me."

"May Helen, you aren't making any sense. Who is this "they" you're talking about?

"My husband's mother and sister, Louise; they have my child and they won't give her back."

"Then why did you give her to them in the first place?"

"I never gave her to them. When Ma Mary had to have her breast cut off 'cause of that cancer, she was real sad and they said she just fell in love with my baby the moment she laid eyes on her 'cause she looked just like her first baby Louise looked when she was a baby. They said it would lift her spirits if I let her keep Mary Louise for a while. Then I had Sandra. Then my sister Claretha died and then when I tried to get Mary Louise back that next Thanksgiving, they asked me to let them keep her till Christmas. Then Joe got hurt at work and the roads were so bad with that ice we couldn't get anyone to take us down for Christmas. Then the next Good Monday and Mother's Day they claimed my baby cried after Louise's oldest daughter when she got ready to go see her husband's people that they let her take my little girl with her. Miss Kay, Joe don't understand why I want my baby so bad. He keeps saying, "We got three more girls and the baby you're carrying is probably another girl."

"Humph," Miss Kay said, "That's just like a man. I miscarried my first baby and Ben said, 'Don't cry Kay. We're going to have four or five more.' Like one child can take the place of another one. As long as I live, there will be a place in my heart where that child was supposed to be."

Mary Helen stood there nodding at Miss Kay. That's exactly the way she felt- as though a part of her was missing. Every time she combed her other girls' hair or starched and ironed their dresses she wondered if anyone was doing that for Mary Louise. She'd cried all the way home last night, but by this morning she was mad as all get out. She didn't know how, but she was going to get her little girl back.

"Where is your little girl May Helen?"

"York, South Carolina,"

"York, South Carolina? Now, where have I heard that before? Oh, Ben has an uncle on his mother's side of the family who's a big-time judge down there. Nunn, that's it Judge Nunn.

"I met him. He's the one who married Mae Jo and James Robert last August," But..."

Miss Kay cut her off with a hard look for interrupting, "A couple of years ago, I think he ran for Governor. I don't think he won though."

Mary Helen tried again, "Miss Kay, I don't mean no harm, but I don't see how Mr. Ben's family tree has anything to do with getting my child."

"Knowing someone who knows a judge might just do the trick. Maybe if I talk to Ben, he'll get his uncle to write up some official papers saying *by order of the court* they have to give your baby back."

"Do you really think so Miss Kay?" Mary Helen was almost afraid of getting her hopes up too high.

"Nothing beats a failure but a try. I'll ask him; and May Helen, don't call tonight checking up on me. I'll get to it."

"Yes M'am. They both knew why Miss Kay included this warning. Mary Helen could be pushy when she wanted something done. She did things the instant they came to mind, but Miss Kay would put things off until she could get to them. It could be the next day or the next month. It was all the same to her. Over the years, on several occasions Mary Helen had circumvented Miss Kay and carried a problem directly to Mr. Ben.

It took Miss Kay three nights to "get to it" and Mr. Ben's Uncle one week, three days, seven hours and 21 minutes to get the official looking papers to them. Mary Helen's only problem now was figuring out a way to get Joe to take off some time from work to go down there before the next holiday.

"God help me find a way to go get my child," Mary Helen prayed the same prayer fervently and continuously as she went through her regular work every day for the next week.

Miss Kay believed in God, but she didn't believe you had to keep begging him to do something. "May Helen, you have the papers.

He's made a way. Just go on down there this weekend and get her," After rushing her to get things done May Helen was standing around praying instead of getting about the business of getting her child back.

"It's not as easy as that. I'm not sure Joe won't wire them that we're coming. He's got this stupid idea about being 'fair' to them since they've had her almost three years."

"Men can be fools about abstract values like fairness. Could you get down there without Joe driving?"

"He don't drive no way. It's his cousin James Robert who takes us down home when we go."

"Joe's still working at that laundry, isn't he?"

"Yes M'am," May Helen almost rolled her eyes in disgust. She couldn't stand the way Miss Kay jumped from one subject to another no matter how important the first subject was.

"I saw that May Helen. You are just like Ben. If something isn't right before your faces you can't see it. Ben and I got an invitation to the Dicks girl's wedding next weekend. It wasn't from the Dicks but from the boys' family in Virginia. I've known them for years. Suppose I convince Muriel Dicks that she simply must have a house boy to show off to her son-in-law's family. They'll have the rehearsal party on Friday night and the reception will last late into the night since the wedding isn't until 4:00p.m. Joe will need to stay on the lot Friday night and work all day

Saturday. You could get Joe's cousin to take you to York to get Mary Louise."

"That won't work because I'm supposed to work for the Dicks that weekend," It was such a good plan she hated that it fell short. "Oh, wait a minute, I think one of the other girls might just be getting sick right about next week," Mary Helen came up with a plan of her own.

"You are such a good mother to know something like that this far ahead of time," the co-conspirators smiled as a bond formed between them that only a mother who has lost a child could understand.

****

"Sister, where's Joe? James Robert kept looking behind her as though one more look would make Joe appear."

"Do you see him, James?" Sister was careful not to lie. "We can't wait for him much longer. I got to get my little girl and get back home before dark."

"I don't know Sister. It don't seem right me taking Joe's wife out of town without him being in the car."

"It's all right James since I'm riding with y'all," Mae Jo had insisted on coming along even though her presence meant Sister would have to sit in the back seat with Gloria and Josephine.

"I got to get my little girl James. Every time we been down to York to get Mary Louise when they know we're coming or think we're coming 'cause it's a holiday, they take her somewhere where I can't get her. They know I can't stay down there looking for her but so long," Sister put her nail in the corner of her eye to make the tears flow. "James I'm so worried about my child. It's been almost a year since the last time they let me see her."

"Sister, I'm gonna stop one more place and see if Joe's there. If he ain't there we'll go on down to York."

James drove to a part of town with which Sister wasn't familiar. The houses seemed to be a bit better made and tended to than the houses off Gorrell Street where they lived. There were even shutters on some of the windows and awnings over a few of the front doors.

"Colored folks live over here James? Sister wanted to know why somebody hadn't told her about this.

"Yeah, Colored folks live in all these houses," Mae Jo said proudly. This was her side of town. She had never been on the side of town where she lived now until she met James at Shorty's Juke Joint.

"William's family is from over here too. They call it Warnersville. William's always bragging about how this is where some of the freed slaves came to live. They got a school, a church, stores, and about everything else they need to stay right here. May be Mae Jo and I will buy a place over here one day," James added.

Sister looked at him suspiciously. What was he nervous about? She's never known him to say that much at one time in all the years she'd known him. "It's like a city for Colored people?" Sister asked.

"I guess cause don't nothing but colored people live here."

"Why you think Joe might be here?"

"Ah, I'm just guessing," James Robert didn't want to tell her that William's sister Ruth was the first woman Joe stepped out with when he came to town and though Joe denied it, Ruth hinted that she still saw him once in a while. James was almost relieved when she came to the door and said she hadn't seen Joe in months. "Sister must be making me half crazy," James said under his breath. If Joe had been there, Lord there wasn't any telling what Sister would have done.

"Satisfied? Can we go now?" Sister knew her husband wouldn't be anywhere James would think to look. Mr. Dicks' daughter was getting married today and he'd offered Joe a job late yesterday evening as a kind of house boy for the weekend to impress his daughter's fiancé's parents. Joe wouldn't be home until well after midnight. By then Sister hoped to be back from York South Carolina with Mary Louise.

The six months that Joe's Mama was supposed to keep her baby had spread out to over three years. The last two times they had made trips to get her child Louise and Ma Mary had hid her away somewhere. Joe had so many kin folks down there that it was impossible to find her before they had to get back home to their other children and to work. But this time would be different. It wasn't a holiday so they wouldn't be expecting her.

"Yeah, I guess," Don't nobody seem to know where he is. Ain't you worried something happened to him," James Robert was still suspicious. Everyone thought he was a bit slow because he never liked going to school, but he was pretty sharp about most things.

"James, he's a grown man. I reckon he can take care of himself. Are you going to take me to get my child or not?

"Come on James. We're going to see Dank too, that woman sure can cook a sweet potato cobbler," Mae Joe encouraged James to get underway.

Eugenia or Dank as everyone called her was Joe's first cousin on his father's side. She grew up in the same house with Joe when her mother died in childbirth. Dank's food was legendary. They'd spent the night with Dank and her husband when Joe and Sister had accompanied James Robert and Mae Jo to South Carolina when they'd gotten married last August. They almost didn't get to Judge Nunn's house in time to get married because May Jo was finishing off the last chunk of one of Dank's cobblers.

That was the only time Sister and Joe had traveled as a couple without any of their children. Uncle Willie had just died and Daisy said she'd keep Gloria and Josephine and Miss Mae Ella kept Sandra. After the marriage, they went by Ma Mary's to get Mary Louise. That's when Joe's sister had asked to keep her until

Thanksgiving. That was also the last time Sister
had been allowed to see her little girl.

"Food may be your main reason for
going, but Mary Louise is mine. If we can get
by Dank's and she's got something cooked up,
we'll take time to eat. If not, I've got enough
food in this basket to last us until we get back
home."

"Sister you didn't say nothing about no
maybe we might stop at Dank's when you
asked me about James taking you," Mae Jo
remembered every conversation that involved
food.

"I know what I said, Mae Jo. Tell you
what, if she doesn't have anything ready to eat,
I'll make you two sweet potato pies," Sister
didn't feel bad about using anything she could
to bribe Mae Jo into getting James to take her to
York.

"Well, James what are you waiting for?
We got to get back here in time for Sister to
bake my pies."

****

Sister planned what she was going to say
all the way down there. She'd start off by
telling Ma Mary and Louise that she
appreciated them taking care of her child for so
long. She would give Louise and Ma Mary the
hats that she had purchased for each of them to
show her appreciation and then she would pick
up her little girl and carry her out of there. The
official papers were tucked away in her purse,
but she hoped it wouldn't come to that. Now

that she was sure she was going to get her child back, she was nearly over the anger that had been piling up over the last fifteen months. She had to admit that having four little girls so close together had been a little frightening for a 20-year-old. She'd spent hours each night starching and ironing their little dresses and polishing their Buster Brown shoes. No one would ever say bad things about the way she took care of her babies. Joe said she treated them like she was playing with dolls. Sister didn't know about that. She'd never owned a doll.

****

All those magnanimous feelings disappeared when they pulled up in front of the house.

"James, you told me you and Joe painted Ma Mary's house the last time y'all were down here. You said that was why y'all were so late getting home," Mae Jo looked from the house to James Robert suspiciously. It was clear that this house had not seen a drop of paint since the Civil War.

"We did. I ain't never seen anything like it. It seemed like the house was drinking the paint with a straw fast as we put it on it was gone. Tell her Sister."

Sister didn't hear them. She only had eyes for the five small children in front of the house. They were wearing the dirtiest, most raggedy undershirts and diapers in the history of the South and playing in a ditch almost in the road. Ma Mary was sitting in a rocking chair on the porch. She didn't even wake up when Sister jumped out of the car, scooped up Mary Louise, and jumped back in the car.

"Go on James. I got what we came for," Mary Helen urged James Robert.

"Aren't you going to wake Ma Mary and let her know you got the child?"

"I'll stop by Marie's Grill and call their pastor when we get home and tell him I got my baby. That's what Joe usually does when he wants to get a message to his family. Now go on." Sister couldn't believe the other children. They were standing there acting like they didn't have good sense- just looking at her getting ready to drive off with Mary Louise. If someone tried to take one of her girls out of their yard, they would have Josephine's teeth buried in their ankle and Gloria would be screaming and hollering loud enough to wake the dead.

"Can I go too? Why Little Mary gets to go on all the rides," One small boy about five years old asked.

"I wish I could take you, but I only have the right to take this one here." Sister didn't look back in case the child was crying. If she saw him crying, she knew she might make James turn around so she could take every one of them with her.

For the first time she felt guilty about leaving her child down here. Every time she'd seen her before, she had been clean and looked well cared for. Although it had been over a year since she'd been allowed to see her, Sister could not imagine what had happened to change the way her child was being treated.

"Sister, we got to stop by Dank's. I can't ride all the way to Greensboro with that smell in the car. I don't think I'll be able to eat anything the rest of the day," Mae Jo waved her handkerchief in front of her nose.

"She's right Sister. My eyes are watering from the smell," James rolled down his window. This was a major concession because he made a point of never rolling down his window no matter how hot it was while they were on a dirt road. James Robert prided himself on having a clean car.

"Alright," Sister couldn't object because she was feeling weak from the odor too. The weakness didn't keep her from holding the child tight against her bosom.

It took Cousin Dank, two-foot tubs of extra warm water and a whole bar of soap to get Mary Louise clean enough to satisfy Sister. The child's hair was so matted and filthy that they had to cut most of it off and wash what was left twice in a mixture of kerosene and Glover's Mange Treatment®. Sister had brought enough clothes in different sizes so that they had no trouble finding something for Mary Louise to wear. One of Josephine's play sets that consisted of a red and blue stripped shirt and a pair of shorts with an elastic waist was a perfect fit. Dank cut up an old pair of kitchen curtains for diapers since Sister didn't own any diapers large enough for a child Mary Louise's age. All her other girls had been potty trained before the age of two.

"Alright James, we're ready to go now. Where's Mae Jo?" Sister didn't want to waste another minute.

"She's already in the car. When she saw you putting clean clothes on the child, she knew she wouldn't smell bad anymore," James opened the door for Sister as he took the satchel of unused clothes. Dank had burned the undershirt and diaper Mary Louise had been wearing.

As soon as Sister got settled in the car she said, "We'll eat a late lunch as soon as we cross the line into North Carolina. And then she settled down to rock her baby to sleep. It must have been the excitement of the day and the last weeks of waiting and worrying that soon had her nodding off too.

****

"Lord, James. They gonna take us to jail 'cause you're speeding," Mae Jo's panicked cry woke Sister up.

"Mae Jo, I wasn't speeding. You ain't ever known me to speed," James was nearly as panicked as she was. No Colored man wanted to be stopped for anything by a South Carolina Highway Patrol or local Sheriff. He eased his car over to the side of the road and rolled the window down while he waited for the deputy to come to the driver's side.

The deputy didn't say anything just shined a flashlight in the car. "Where're y'all going?"

"I'm from Gastonia Sir. This here is my wife and Sister," James told the truth.

The deputy shined the flashlight on Sister and the child in her arms. "Y'all can take that little boy and those other two darkies and go on then. I'm looking for some people that stole a pretty little Nigger child out of her yard. I wouldn't be out here if the child's Mammy didn't work at the Country Club."

Sister started to say something about him calling her other little girls darkies but thought better of it.

James pulled back onto the highway but didn't get his speed past 45 miles an hour until he was ten miles north of Charlotte, North Carolina. He finally pulled over in a community where he saw some Colored folks sitting on the porches.

"Sister, what you got in that basket? I could eat a whole chicken by myself," James smiled for the first time since they got back on the highway.

"You're in luck then, because that's exactly what I have —a whole chicken, a dozen biscuits, and a whole apple pie."

"And they were real good too," Mae Jo confessed.

James Robert and Sister looked at her real hard. Neither one of them bothered to fuss about it. What good would it do? There wasn't anything left in the basket but some gnawed on bones and an empty pie plate.

"James, I'll fry you up some fish if you get us back home in time to go by the Fish Market.

"That sounds good," Sister, Mae Jo included herself in on the fish fry.

****

When Joe eased into bed a little after midnight, Sister waited until his breathing was almost even.

"Joe, I went and got Mary Louise today," she whispered. She was shocked when he whispered back.

"I saw her when I went in to check on my babies. Did Mama cry?"

"I didn't see her crying," Sister whispered.

"That's all I need to know," Joe said as he rolled over and went to sleep.

Chapter 23

Mary Helen was smiling again as she finished dressing in her Sunday-go-to-meeting clothes. She had four finely tailored suits that had been made by Helen Dean, who was the seamstress for a department store down town. The suits were black, navy blue, deep forest green and dark caramel. All were made from the same pattern with jewel necklines, jackets that were fitted where there should have been a waistline, flaring out and stopping at the hips, with straight skirts that stopped below the calf.

She changed the appearance of the suits with crocheted collars and cuffs, with bright costume jewelry, and with one of those fox thing-a-ma-jigs with the mouth that opened like a clip. She had given up her jewelry after she got saved. That was alright though, because she more than made up for their lost with her hats. All of them dwarfed her plump, round face. If the hat had feathers on it, they were large red, yellow, orange, or hot pink feathers. If the hat had fruit, there were at least five pounds, and if it had flowers, they were huge, cabbage-sized roses.

Mary Helen really wanted to look good this Sunday. It was her first Sunday back in church since the birth of her son, Phillip Ronald Evans. She had the son that she'd prayed for, Joe wasn't drinking that much anymore and she thanked the Lord for that. She knew now that anything that she asked, in His perfect will, the Lord was going to give it to her.

"Joe. Get that door," she called as she checked the girls for hanging slips and untied ribbons.

They were all pretty to her. Even the three who had coffee without cream colored skin and short, not quite black hair. She hadn't let the length of their hair keep her from putting a yard of ribbon and a bang ten inches wide in their hair.

Joe came to the door of their bedroom, "I think you want to come out to the front room."

She looked at him, trying to figure out who was dead or dying now. "It's not another letter or wire is it Joe? I don't think I could take another wire today, Joe,"

He'd planned on surprising her, but she was so near-hysterical he told her, "Baby, it's your brother, Oscar,"

"Oscar and Aaron?" she was so relieved, she could have fainted.

"Just Oscar," Joe said.

"Just Oscar?" She was beginning to get scared again; for as long as she could remember Oscar never went anywhere without Aaron. Never did anything without his big brother. When their mother died their father had allowed Uncle Boy to take Aaron into Columbia to find work. He had been hired on the spot at the first juke joint he went to. He could sing, he was sixteen, tall, straight, strong and dazzlingly good looking. Grandma said every generation had a Yeezhia. Aaron was theirs.

When word got back to Salley where Aaron was working, Oscar got himself in trouble doing the one thing he knew their father couldn't abide so he'd have an excuse to run off to Aaron. Of course the people didn't want Aaron's little brother hanging around. Aaron had told them that he wasn't staying anywhere without Oscar, so the Boss man had grudgingly taken-in the small, ugly fourteen year old Oscar who at five feet even, was as tall as he'd ever be.

The last time Mary Helen had heard anything about either of them, was when she'd found those letters in Claretha's things. Later someone brought word that they had joined the navy and that they'd both made it through that war in Korea because a cousin, had told a friend, to tell Grandma Hester and Sister that the boys were both all right.

"Oscar, Oscar." Mary Helen flew into his arms. He may not have been much to others, but he was a giant to her. It had been Oscar who fought beside her when the children at school tried to make sport of the "poor" Fullmores who lived in a shack, and it had been Oscar who went back with her to throw a rock through the teacher's window for whipping him and Sister for not knowing her given name. She had long since forgiven him for leaving her like that. Sister was fair minded enough to admit that if she had thought of a way to take Little Luke with her, she probably would have run away too.

"Oscar, where's Aaron. You finally let some woman come between you?" She paused looking expectantly over his shoulder. It was just like them to tease her this way. The fear didn't come back until she looked in Oscar's eyes.

"Where's Aaron?"

"Sister. I- I did all I could. I went back. I looked everywhere. I did all I could. You got to believe me Sister," Oscar said collapsing onto the sofa.

He was crying and this scared Mary Helen so badly, she didn't hear anything else he said. She'd only seen him cry like this once before--only when their Mama had died. Not when people talked about how black and ugly he was right with him standing there. Not when the bigger boys picked on him about his size. He and Aaron hadn't come to their Daddy's or Claretha's funeral so Sister didn't know whether or not he had shed any tears over either of them. She suspected that he had never forgiven their father for whipping him that last time or for allowing Uncle Boy to take Aaron away.

"It's all right Oscar. I know you wouldn't let anything happen to Aaron, same way he always took care of you," instead of comforting him her words made him cry harder.

"Sister, we was just coming home -paid for our tickets all the way to Salley to see you and to get the money you keeping for him. Aaron had it all planned. Then we was going up North to live with our cousins in Queens. No, I don't want nothing but to tell you what happened," he replied when Mary Helen offered him a glass of water. Oscar stared off like he was watching it happen...

The bus stopped in Alabama, didn't look like nowhere to be stopping. Wasn't even a gas station there, but some pecker-woods got on. Then before we'd gone two miles it stopped again and some more got on. They said it wasn't enough seats up front. Said all the niggers was going to have to stand. I got up Sister but Aaron wouldn't. He said he'd fought for freedom for some people with slanted eyes and he reckoned he deserved some freedom too. They started hitting him and when I tried to help; somebody hit me from behind with something. Next thing I knew, I was waking up and the bus was moving. I told the bus driver to stop, but he wouldn't until I went into my bag and got my gun. I run and run back there as fast as I could. Sister, nobody would tell me nothing. Wouldn't tell me nothing. Nothing.

"Don't cry Oscar. It's gonna to be alright," Sister said trying to comfort him though she was sobbing.

"They say the bus don't even stop nowhere near there, he continued as though she hadn't spoken. They say they ain't no White boys in that town what got red nappy looking hair. I couldn't find him Sister. I just couldn't find him. I shouldn't let nobody get behind me

like that.   Aaron done told me, 'Oscar watch my back and yours and I'll do the rest.'   It woulda took fifty more of those boys to take Aaron if I'd done my part."

Though Mary Helen thought that he was probably right about that last part, she didn't tell him. "I know you tried Oscar. There ain't nothing you can do about it now."

"Sister, give me the money you keeping for Aaron so I can go up North and start over." Oscar said as he finally took the glass of water.

"What money? I haven't heard anything since I read that last letter I found in a box Claretha had been keeping from me and she kept all the money Aaron sent me in those letters."

"Sister, Aaron had his allotment sent to you. He wrote and told you to spend what you needed, but to save some for a nest egg for him. Sister, don't tell me you ain't got no money." He looked around the living room his eyes greedily appraising everything in it.

Sister's eyes followed his around the room. It was an eclectic assortment of antique hand-me-downs from both Mrs. Wilsons and their neighbors. Every wooden surface was gleaming like new with polish and the fabric upholstery though worn in places looked better than anything they'd had growing up.

"Sister, you been getting a government check every month all these years. I don't believe you would do Aaron this way- spending all his money on yourself.

"Oscar, I swear I never got no government check from Aaron. I didn't know he knew I was living in Greensboro or that I was married."

"He didn't know. That's why we were going to Salley. Uncle Boy told me when I got there that you were up here. Sister how long you been up here?"

"Since, November of 1943. I came up here when Daddy gave Luke to Aunt Clare," Sister didn't add the part about her heart because Joe was close enough to hear.

"That explains it. We went in the navy January of 44. That's when Aaron had them start sending you the money at Daddy's house in Salley."

"That don't explain everything. Daddy died December 5, 1947 and Claretha December 5, 1952. Who's been getting Aaron's money since then?"

"I don't know Sister. It don't matter. Don't nothing matter." He put his head down and started to cry.

"Oscar, where's your money? I know you well enough to know you didn't send anything home to anyone," Sister couldn't understand any of this.

"You know me Sister. I gambled some and spent mine, but I wasn't worried. Aaron had enough coming to you for both of us to live off until we found work."

"I see," and she did see- more than those few words said. Like always Oscar had depended on Aaron to take care of him. Sister asked Oscar to stay with them awhile, but he said he was going on up to Queens because he knew the folks back home wouldn't want him around if Aaron wasn't with him.

She worried over Oscar and what had happened to all that money, and most of all she kept hoping that somehow Aaron had managed to get away, but it wasn't long before she had something else to worry about.

Chapter 24

"If that boy doesn't perk up today, take him to the doctor," Joe   said issuing a rare direct order.

"Yes,   Joe,"   Mary   Helen   wasn't in   the mood   to   fuss. She knew Joe was right. Besides, she'd used every tonic she knew of and some new ones from Aunt Daisy, but the boy was getting weaker by the day. She'd   noticed months   ago that   he   wasn't anywhere   near   as   sharp   as   her   girls had   been at   that   age.   But he was a boy and she knew that   men children didn't start getting   any sense until they were way on up there in the years. Still, she was worried. It just didn't seem right for an eighteen-month-old child, even a boy, not to be crawling.

"Gloria, when you get to school today tell your teacher to let you leave class about one o'clock so you can go get Josephine, then you meet me out front o-f the school," she didn't repeat her instructions. Gloria was as reliable as any grown up. Mary Helen told her what to do and considered it done.

At one-o-five Gloria and Josephine met their mother in front of Washington Street School. Mary Helen had already picked Mary Louise and Sandra up from the babysitter. She always took all of the children when one of

them was beyond her home remedies. It didn't
make sense for her to risk having to get off
work again if what the kid had turned out to be
contagious.

The doc tor checked each of the children
starting with Gloria and working his way down
to Phillip.

"Mary Helen, when you get the boy
dressed come over to my office, please," he
hadn't looked at her when he said this. That
wasn't like Dr. Redman.

"Yes, Sir. Do you know what' wrong
with my boy," she asked the last part to the
door because he was already gone.

"Gloria. Come in here and dress Phillip,"
Mary Helen leaned out the door and called
down the hall holding the naked baby in her
arms.

She handed the baby to Gloria and went
into the doctor's office. She came out crying so
loudly that the doctor put his arm around her
and guided her back in. When she came out the
second time, she was calm, but sad.

"What did the doctor say Mama?" Gloria
had already decided that she wanted to be a
nurse and the nine-year-old never missed a
chance to find out about any illness in the
family.

Mary Helen didn't answer. She didn't
know how to wrap her mind around the words.

Gloria didn't ask her again. She didn't recognize the look on her mother's face and for the first time in her life there was something that she didn't want to know.

None of the children said a word as they walked to the bus stop. They stood there like wooden soldiers, taking furtive glances at their mother.

They got on the wrong bus.

Gloria and Josephine knew that it was the wrong bus, but they didn't say a word. They were almost where the bus turned around before their mother noticed where they were.

Since she didn't have enough money to pay for transfers, the bus driver made them get off the bus when he turned around.

Josephine picked up a rock to throw at the bus, but Gloria held her arm until the bus was too far away.

The children were worried about this strange silent woman who wasn't behaving like their mother. This woman had silent tears rolling down her cheeks and their father wasn't even there.

Gloria and Josephine offered to take turns with her carrying Phillip. She simply shook her head and clutched him tighter to her bosom.

Their mother didn't take them back to school and this worried the older girls even more, because she usually insisted that they go back to school, even when there were only a few minutes left in the school day.

When they got home, Mary Helen didn't start dinner. She didn't iron. She didn't dust. She didn't sweep. She just sat holding Phillip. This wasn't like Mary Helen. She never sat still. Watching her sit there hour after hour frightened the girls more than the night, she'd cut their father.

She sat like that until Joe got home at about 6:30p.m. As soon as Joe saw her sitting down, he plopped down into the nearest chair instinctively knowing that he couldn't take what he was about to hear standing up.

Phillip was going to die. Mary Helen told Joe that the doctor said that Phillip had an incurable disease called leukemia and that he didn't have very long to live because he was already in the final stage of the disease,

The next six months, Phillip spent more time in the hospital than he did at home. Every Sunday afternoon, Mary Helen took all the girls with her to the hospital to see Phillip. Since they were too young to be allowed inside, she'd go in and hold him up to the window so they could see him.

They let Mary Helen take Phillip home so that the whole family could be with him to celebrate his second birthday. Mary Helen's heart wasn't in the celebration; the doctor had told her that there was nothing else they could do, other than keep him comfortable , so she might want to consider keeping him at home when she brought him home for his father's birthday in a couple of weeks.

That evening when they took him back to the hospital Mary Helen decided that she was finished with crying. Instead of going back home, she went to Benbow Road to see Bishop Wells.

"I need to see Bishop Wells," she told his daughter when she answered the door.

"He's in his study preparing his sermon for Sunday. We aren't supposed to disturb him," she was a polite child. Mary-Helen thought of her as a child even though there was only about ten month's difference in their ages.

"Tell him I've come to see him about healing my baby," Mary Helen tried to say it politely, but she sounded scared and a little crazy to the young woman.

"Daddy isn't a Doctor," she said as she tried to close the door.

"Let her in. Come on in Sister Evans," Bishop Wells said. Mary Helen hadn't realized that she was screaming until that very moment.

"I'm sorry Bishop, but..." she began.

"It's alright. DeOlia go get your mother," he said as he signaled f or Mary Helen to join him in his study.

"Bishop I need to know why. All these months I have been walking round here mad at

Joe. Mad at my children. Mad at everybody because I didn't want to be mad at God. Why? Why, he finally give me a son, then he gone take him away from me before he even had time to be a man? Why, Bishop?" Then she let go of all of her pain and anger and she wept before him as no man other than Joe had ever seen her weep.

"Why? You want to know why God allowed this to happen to your son?" Bishop Wells questioned her quietly.

She nodded.

"Well, I have an even more important "why" for you. I want to know why after all you've seen, why you don't believe God?" He asked her in that deep soothing voice of his.

"I believe God, I pay my tithes, I fast on fast days. I'm keeping all my vows to my husband, even the one about obeying-most of the time. Tell me what God wants. I'll do it. Anything. I'll never ask God for a house again if He will let me keep my son. Anything."

"If you believe God, you know that he never comes to the end of his resources. If you believe God, you believe He can heal your son no matter what those doctors say. Because a God that can't do any more than man can do isn't worth believing in at all. Do you believe He can do more than man can do?"

"Yes, Bishop."

"Then dry your eyes. Go get your son and meet us at the church," he instructed Mary Helen as he led her to the door.

Mary Helen checked Phillip out of the hospital and took him straight to the little church on Ash Street where Bishop Wells and several of the members were waiting -for them. They prayed for Phillip all night long and until sundown the next day.

"Saints, it's time to go. God has given me an answer," Bishop Wells said.

Although Bishop Wells hadn't told Mary Helen what the answer was, she was relieved and contented as she walked home. As soon as she walked through the door, Mary Helen handed Phillip to Gloria. Then she started cleaning the house. As soon as she finished that, she cooked and baked until there was nothing left to cook or bake.

Mary Helen took Phillip to the doctor to be examined the following week.

"Mary Helen, you don't have to spend all your days and nights nursing this child. When he has a really sick smell take him to the hospital," the doctor admonished her before he started the examination.

Moments later the doctor said, "Take him directly to the hospital. I'll meet you there as soon as I clear my office," the doctor said, puzzled by his findings.

The doctor ran some tests and then some more tests. And some more, but still, he could find nothing. The doctor gave some new experimental drug the credit for the cure, but Mary Helen knew who deserved the credit.

He'd given her what she asked for and she would keep her promise to him.

Chapter 25

Mary Helen didn't pray for a house anymore, but she did suggest to God that it sure would be nice if they had a place with a heater before winter came. They'd been forced to move into a four- room house on Hacket Street. Miss Tunie had finally died and the nephew who'd been taking care of her -found out that the only money he was going to get was from selling her house. They hadn't had enough money to pay down on it, so they had to move.

All the children were sleeping in a small bedroom that looked like a barracks. Miss Kay had given her two sets of bunk beds that were pushed against two walls and a day bed that Aunt Daisy gave her when she got married was up against a third wall. That left one wall for two dressers and no place for the children to play.

So, she prayed for a larger place, making it clear that it didn't have to be a house as long as the children had a place to play and some heat in winter.

She was so thankful that God had answered her prayer-and allowed her to keep her son, that she decided to spend most of the rest of her life on her knees and to keep her children on theirs.

At dinner time the children got a little weary of religion. Mary Heleñ didn't just say grace she blessed the food that was in the plant beds, and the food that was still in the seed bags. She blessed the people who didn't have food and prayed that they would have food. She prayed for the people who had food and weren't willing to share it: she prayed that God would soften the hearts of those people so that they would share His bountiful blessings with others. When she finished all of her blessings, each of the children were required to say a scripture. She didn't allow them to say the short ones. "Jesus wept," was not allowed and if one of them started with a Commandment, they had to say all ten. This whole service took anywhere from forty minutes to an hour.

Today, Mary Helen was sitting on the bus trying to decide how she could pray for relief from Old Lady Wilson without praying for one of them to die. The old woman had been fretting her so bad here lately that she didn't care which direction the relief came from. She couldn't recall how many times the old lady had fired her this week and it was only Wednesday.

"You look worried Miss Evans," she heard a loud brassy voice and knew without opening her eyes that the voice belonged to Margaret Jordan. A lot of the "girls" or day workers who rode the buses to places like Starmont Forest and Irving Park where the rich white folks lived, didn't like Margaret. She took pride in something most of them would have been ashamed to admit, her Daddy was a

White man who'd done the unheard of -
married a Colored woman.

Mary Helen liked her. Margaret made
her laugh. Margaret understood people the same
way that Grandma Hester and Aunt Daisy did
but she liked them anyway. The two women
had met in the maternity ward of L. Richardson
Hospital when Mary Helen had Josephine and
Margaret had her daughter Toni.

"I'm not worried, just tired," Mary Helen
said, following the unspoken code of day
workers - *When we ask about your worries,
we're just being polite. We don't want to hear
about your problems.*

"Mary Helen come on with me to put in
an application for those new housing projects.
That'll solve all your problems," Margaret
knew about the small house with no heat.

"I done talked to Joe about it and he said
people's names been on that list for years and
they still waiting for a house."

"Since when you started listening to
Joe? I don't see no reason to start worrying
about how long your name gone be on the list
till you put it on it." Margaret wasn't going to
let it rest.   Mary Helen was her only true -
friend. Her only friend period and this was her
way of thanking her. She knew some people
who worked for the Housing Authority, but
Mary Helen had to put her name on the list and
fill out some papers before they could help her.

"Come on Mary Helen. It won't take but a few minutes," Margaret said as she got up and walked to the door of the bus.

Mary Helen could see "the bright brick" buildings of the housing projects. Margaret's description made them sound like heaven on earth. Steam heat in every room, a living room, kitchen, and some had as many as four bedrooms for big families like hers,

"Oh, what will it hurt to put our name on the list," she thought as she followed Margaret off the bus.

She actually felt pretty good when she got home that evening. Like Margaret said, having their name on that list put her one step closer to getting a house with heat before winter than she'd been when she'd started out that morning.

"Mama, I cooked everything but the meat for dinner, bathed the children and got them ready for bed. Josephine's back there telling them some wild story she made up. I tried to get her to tell them a Bible story and you know what she said? She said, "I ain't telling no @%$# Bible story." Mama you gonna whip her for cussing?"

Gloria said all this without pausing for an answer from her mother. It was their usual routine. Mary Helen came in about six and cooked the meat while Gloria gave her a report of the day.

"I'll get her Saturday," Mary Helen said thinking that Gloria was too much like she'd been at that age -too old, too young. She hadn't meant for it to happen this way. Didn't she know what it meant to be robbed of a childhood? But it had been so easy to let the child slip into the role of mother's helper.

"Gloria, go get the children," she said as she set the table. She always set the table and placed the serving dishes on the table.

"Let us pray," she bowed her head when all the children were at the table.   Forty minutes later she was ready for the children to say their scriptures.

Mary Helen sensed that something was under foot when she saw Josephine take her fork and put it in her left hand under the table.

Gloria hadn't told her mother everything that'd happened that day.   Josephine had convinced them that they were tire d of eating cold food. She'd reminded them that grits were better when they weren't congealed.   They'd taken a vote before their Mama got home and decided they weren't going to say any more scriptures.

So now Phillip stood up and said what Josephine had coached him to say. "Mama, I don't have a scripture to say tonight."

Sandra and Mary Louise followed suit. Then it was Josephine's turn and she changed it a bit so that her mother wouldn't suspect a conspiracy.

"Mama, I didn't have time to prepare a scripture for tonight," she said boldly. Then she sat down and got her fork ready because she knew Gloria. Gloria would do anything to please their Mama. And Josephine wasn't sure she would follow through with their plan without force. So, she pressed her fork into the side of Gloria's leg, not deep, just enough so she would feel threatened. As soon as Josephine heard a scripture trying to slip out of her mouth, she pushed that fork a little deeper and gave Gloria the meanest look she could muster.

Gloria just whimpered, "Mama, I'm sorry. I don't have a scripture say for tonight."

Through all of this, Mary Helen hadn't said a word or changed the expression on her face one whit. When Gloria sat down, Mary Helen stood up.

"Well, children," she began. "Since most of you didn't see fit to prepare a scripture for this evening and one of you," she looked at Josephine, "Didn't have TIME to prepare a scripture, I will read one for each of you." All the children looked at Josephine; she hadn't warned them that something like this might happen. She stared at each of them daring them to say anything to her.

Josephine was more than a little ticked off that her mother was going to read her scriptures. She never let the children read theirs. They had to memorize those suckers and Josephine and Gloria had to help the younger ones learn theirs. Though she was more than a bit peeved, she didn't say anything. She was smart enough to know that a child could get her lips slapped to the back of her head if she said anything that her Mama might interpret as "talking back." Mary Helen read from the Bible:

> *Hear, O' heavens, and give*
> *ear, O' earth: for the LORD*
> *hath spoken, I have nourished*
> *and brought up children and*
> *they have rebelled against me.*
> *Ah sinful nation, a people*
> *laden with iniquity, a seed of*
> *evil doers, children that are*
> *corrupters: they have forsaken*
> *the LORD, they have provoked*
> *the Holy One of Israel unto*
> *anger, and they are gone*
> *backward...*

And she read and she read and she read. Josephine thought she read the whole Bible, but Gloria said she only read the -first two chapters of Isaiah.

Chapter 26

That Saturday night Mary Helen gave Josephine two extra licks during her weekly whipping for cussing and leading the *Bible Rebellion*. She had her mind set not to complain about the Lords plan for her in this life. She was just praying that she wouldn't have to walk around heaven all day with Old Lady Wilson and Josephine.

But it was Tuesday, and Josephine was usually still good on Tuesday since her Saturday night whipping hadn't worn off *yet,* so she wasn't expecting to see her waiting for her on the front porch. The child only did this when she'd done something really bad and wanted to confess *her* crime before Gloria told on her.

"Lord, give me strength," Mary Helen said casting her eyes upward.

"Mama, this was in the door when we got home. It's for you," Josephine said holding out the letter.

Mary Helen's hand shook as she reached for it. She walked through the - front room and sat on a kitchen chair before she opened it.

Come to Marie's Grill. I got to see you today.

She turned it over to see if there was more on the other side. There wasn't. No signature. Nothing.

"Who left it? Did you see anybody round the house?"

"No, Ma'am."

"You want me to go see who's at Marie's Grill?"

"You read my mail?"

"No, Ma'am. I mean - it just kind of fell out the door and I couldn't help but see it. Honest, Mama," Josephine gave her the most sincere look in her repertoire.

"Humph," Mary Helen said not quite believing her, but deciding to go along with her since it was easier that way and there was so much more of the week left for her to get into trouble.

"Gloria go on and fry some fatback meat for dinner and feed the children. I'll be back in a little while." She pulled herself up and started out.

Mary Helen couldn't figure out who it could be needing to see her today. She started to turn around and go back to her children, but something made her go to the tiny restaurant on Gorrell Street across from Bennett College. Something else made her stop, run her fingers through her hair and take off her apron before she went in.

"I'm over here," she heard a voice call to her from a dark corner.

"Glady, it's you," Mary Helen said sounding as relieved as she felt.

"Yeah, it's me Sister. You're not gone be so happy when I tell you why I had to see you. I'm pregnant and Joe the Daddy." Glady stood up and looked Mary Helen dead in the eye when she said this. It was clear that she was at least as pregnant as Mary Helen was.

"Joe? My Joe?" Mary Helen repeated the name tasting like bile in her mouth.

"Yours and everybody else's, but he gonna be mine now, me and Joe gone move back to South Carolina. Let him go Sister. Ain't no sense in you holding on to a man that don't want you." Glady sat there looking at Mary Helen with hard cold eyes.

"How you know Joe is the Daddy?' Mary Helen had to ask this. She didn't care what it inferred about Glady's character.

"I'm not that big a slut, Sister. Joe the only one I been with since I stopped going out with Weasel more than a year ago," Glady was still looking straight at her.

Surely, Mary Helen thought, no one, not even Glady would tell a lie that hurt this much. It must be true. No it couldn't be. She'd have smelled her on him. Wouldn't she? Not if he'd started bathing the smell off before he came home, Mary Helen argued with herself as she sat there wondering what Glady wanted her to do.

"Well, you gone let him go?" Glady asked like she'd already asked it more than once,

"Go where? Go where?" Mary Helen said to Glady and the entire room as she ran from the restaurant as fast as a woman six months pregnant could run.

* * * * * * * * * * * *

Sister was up walking the floor when Joe got home. Joe'd gotten a note too. He knew he was in trouble when he saw the light was still on. He'd gotten pretty drunk one night a few months ago. Weasel and James Robert had put him on a cot in the back room at Miss Teal's Place. When he woke up Glady was in the bed with him. Joe had been that drunk enough times to know that there was no way he could have done anything, no matter what Glady said.

"Hey, Baby. What you doing up this late?" Joe said as he went over to the stove to see what was left for his dinner.

"Joe, did you sleep with Glady? Joe look at me and tell me you ain't been in bed with Glady," Mary Helen had spent the last few hours convincing herself that she would believe whatever he told her.

"Listen, Honey."

"Lord. He's gonna lie. He's gonna lie to me. He never calls me that unless he's gonna lie," she thought as she looked at him and felt him searching his mind for the right words. It didn't matter what he said after that "Honey" part, she wouldn't believe it. She couldn't allow herself to believe it.

Joe called her "Honey" not because he'd planned on lying, but because he didn't know what to say to make her believe the truth. Then he made an even bigger mistake. He decided to lie.

"I ain't never been nowhere near Glady in a bed," He said hoping that this was the first lie he'd told right.

It wasn't even close.

"Just get away from me. Get away from me," cried holding her hand out like a shield when he tried to come closer to her.

Chapter 27

Mary Helen spent the next three months in a maze of hurt and hate. She knew hating wasn't a Christian way to feel. She didn't want to hurt. Jesus loved her and her children loved her. That should be enough love for one woman. It should not matter if Joe did not love her enough to be faithful, but it seemed to her that no one in her life loved her enough to stay with her- to be faithful to her. Her mother hadn't. Aaron and Oscar hadn't. Claretha hadn't. No one stayed. No one was there for her.

She spent every waking minute trying to pray her way through it, around it, and over it. Nothing worked.

She hadn't been to church in weeks. It wasn't that she doubted God. She doubted that she was worthy of having what other women took for granted. She spent all of her time hurting and hating. Hating Glady. Hating Joe. Hurting because she hated Joe so much that it made it hard for her to look at her own children without crying because each of them had a feature that reminded her of Joe. Gloria and Sandra had his lips. Josephine and Phillip had his eyes and Mary Louise looked like his mother and sister.

When she felt the hate spreading to her children, she'd cook them a cake or pie for dessert. They'd had dessert for 16 straight nights. Hating every attractive woman she passed became an obsession because she wondered if each and every one of them had slept with her husband. Hating. Hating. Hating. Hurting. Hurting. Hurting.

Joe came to her that morning in June, two weeks before their eighth anniversary. He was tired of trying to talk to her, but he knew he had to try one more time.

"Listen. Don't say anything. Just Listen. I don't know whose baby that is Glady had, but I swear it ain't no way it could be mine. I know I ain't got no right asking nothing of you, but I got to go to court today and if you aren't there the judge gonna believe Glady and make me take care of it until its grown. We need that money for our own children."

"You should have thought of that before you laid up there with Glady." Mary Helen didn't look up or stop plaiting Josephine's hair.

"You won't stand with me today?"

She didn't answer and Joe left without another word.

Mary Helen finished plaiting the rest of her daughters' hair and got ready to leave for work. This baby was more than two weeks late by her count and she was so big that each day felt like an extra month. After he'd watched her struggling to haul a load of clothes from the washroom in the basement, Mr. Ben had snatched the basket from her hands and ordered

her not to return to work until she'd had the
baby. Since he didn't say anything about paying
her for those days, Mary Helen had ignored the
order and made sure she got all the washing
done before he came home.

"Baby, if you'd stay still long enough to
let me get some sleep at night, I wouldn't be so
tired." Mary Helen always talked to her babies
while she carried them. Grandma Hester said
talking to a girl baby made her smarter and
made a boy baby listen to what women had to
say.

"Tired or not, I got to go to work. We
need the money too much for me to be lying up
in bed when I could be working," fussed at
herself as she tried to tie her shoes. She rested
her head on the back of the chair.

"You don't need the money all that bad
'cause you're willing to stand by and allow
Glady to take bread out of your children's
mouths.' The voice was inside her head, but it
sounded more like Grandma Hester's voice
than her own.

"Get out of my head, grandma. Gloria,
come here Baby and tie my shoes for me. I
can't bend down that far anymore."

"Mama. Mama a man is here to see
you," Gloria called from the front door.

"Who is it," Marx Helen didn't care
enough to look up from her work.

"Mr. William Bothwell, Mama. Do you want me to let him in?"

"Let him in," Mary Helen said still not caring whether he came in or stayed out.

"Sister, I need to speak to you in private," Weasel said in a voice so different from anything she'd ever heard come out of him, she looked up.

"See me in private for what Weasel? I've had enough of you and Glady's mess to last me two weeks after I'm dead."

"I think- No I know you need to hear this," he said standing there holding his hat in his hand.

"Children go to your bedroom and close both doors," Mary Helen instructed Gloria and Josephine.

"Go on and say what you have to say," she told Weasel after she checked to make sure both girls, but mostly Josephine, had done as they were told.

"That my boy. Glady had. Not Joe's."

"Weasel, don't I know you'd come here and say anything Joe told you to say. Everybody knows Glady ain't done nothing but let you carry her pocketbook all these years."

"It's been more to us than that. I been a fool for her, but ain't even a fool gone hang around twelve years without no pussy."

"Don't talk like that in my house," Mary Helen said forgetting that she'd said and thought a few unclean things herself during the last three months.

"How you know it ain't Joe's? Just cause you been there don't mean he ain't been there too," Mary Helen wanted to believe William but the doubt had been rooted so long ago that it was a weed in her soul.

"You can believe what you want to Sister, but I'm going to that courthouse and tell them that I helped Joe up to that room that night and he was so drunk he couldn't have got an eyebrow up much less anything else. Sides, Glady done told me more than two months before she climbed into bed with Joe that she was having a baby. Didn't say nothing about me not being the daddy until after that night. Why you think she went down to South Carolina to have him. She had him two days after we got down there," he finished and turned to leave.

"We- William, thank-you. You didn't have to do this and I thank you," she said.

"You wrong about that Sister, I did have to do this. Ain't no woman ever had my child. This probably the only son I'll ever have. Glady gone be alright once she see she ain't ever gonna get Joe. She gone be a good wife to me and a good mama to our son." He turned and headed toward the courthouse.

"You may as well take a snake home and try to breast feed it as to marry Glady and expect her to be a good wife," Mary Helen said, but he was too far away to hear.

Chapter 28

Glady sitting next to Joe on a bench outside the courtroom was the first thing Mary Helen saw when she got off the elevator. They made a striking couple. Joe was still as good looking as he had been that first night that he'd walked into her Aunt Daisy's Liquor House and Sister had pretended not to notice him.

Glady was leaning over almost in Joe's lap. Her dress was cut lower than any decent whore would wear in day light. The same way Sister noticed that Joe was still handsome she noticed that Glady wasn't ugly anymore. The sharp rough lines of her teens had given way to soft planes that defined features rather- than cut them up. Men had ways wanted her for her body- having a baby had actually improved her shape. Her breast seemed fuller-like she needed more tidies. Sister glanced down at her chest self consciously. She knew that the extra fullness of her breasts would evaporate like canned milk the moment she stopped breast feeding the baby. No, Glady wasn't ugly any more. Now she had the face to go with the body that men couldn't seem to resist.

Glady saw Sister before Joe did. She pressed her breast against his arm, "Joe, it won't be long before they call for us. Just say you'll leave here and go to New York with me. I'll drop the case."

"Get off me woman. I ain't going to New York or anywhere else with you with your lying self," Joe stood up leaving her alone on the bench.

"Joe, I love you. I want us to be together. I got family up in Queens. They'll put us up until we find work and a place of our own."

"What about Sister and my children. Are we all going to New York? They got room for eight people?" he didn't bother to comment on the I love you part. He'd heard Glady say it too many times. 'I love chitterlings'- 'I love Western movies'- 'I love me some jazz music'- she'd say she loved anything until the next something came along. "Gal, just get away from me."

When he turned his back on Glady, he saw Sister standing near the elevator.

****

Mary Helen looked around for William. She was about to get angry thinking that it'd been a trick of some kind, when she remembered that he couldn't read. "He's probably wondering around too shame to ask somebody where to go," she thought as she walked up and sat down beside Joe.

"Sister, what you doing here? This between me and Joe," Glady screeched.

"Glady, I've had my family taken away from me before piece by piece. I was too young to fight back then, but I'm serving notice right here and now; Joe ain't much but he's mine and I'm holding on to what's mine and my children's. You better take the best you can get and go on from here," Mary Helen said as she watched William walk up behind Glady.

Joe sat there watching Mary Helen. He wasn't sure whether to be proud that she was supporting him or insulted by what she said about him.

"You both gonna be sorry before I'm through with you. You're gonna be sorry." Glady refused William's arm as she walked into court.

The judge listened to Glady's story and she told it so well Mary Helen found herself almost having doubts again until Joe spoke.

"Sir, I haven't always been a good husband, but this woman standing next to me has always been a good wife, I ain't never worried about nobody going out my back door, that's why I wouldn't never sleep with her cousin. That isn't my child," Joe finished and stood there quietly,

"Are you his wife?" The judge asked Mary Helen.

"Yes sir," She wanted to say more but she didn't.

"Do you believe him?"

"Yes sir, I do."

"And who are you?" The judge said directing his question to William.

"I'm the baby's Daddy," he finally said. Then he said it again real loud and proud, "I'm the boy's Daddy."

"Are you supporting him?"

"No, sir. Glady won't let me. She say she don't want me to be the daddy. Say she wants Joe to be the daddy. I took her to South Carolina to have the baby three months ago. I got the birth certificate right here."

Sister expected a look of fear on Glady's face, but instead she looked triumphant as she grabbed the birth certificate from William's hand. "He can't even read Mr. Judge. I know what it says he doesn't. She began to read the birth certificate, "It says, "Baby boy Ervin born on March 26, 1955. That ain't right. It should be May. I told that old fool to..."

"Yeah, you told her to put May 26, 1955. You were thinking because I can't read, I would just go file it at the courthouse without knowing what you'd done. Girl, I ain't too proud to ask somebody to read something to me. I asked the man to read the date. When he said it was May 26. I said, "She just had him yesterday, Sir. He said, 'Half of you niggers couldn't read or write your name with a gun to your head.' Then he made it the right date," William smiled a big smile at Glady letting her know he wasn't the fool she thought he was.

The Judge's eyes got harder and harder, as William spoke the anger rang in his voice when he said, "March 26, 1956, that's not the date on this court document. Why the hell are we here? Gal, you got this boy here saying it's his baby and he want to take care of it. What are you wasting my time for? I have women in here every day begging a man that we had to about drag here to admit that a child was his. You got a man that came here on his own to claim your child. Now, I'm going to ask you one more time, and before you answer, I want you to know I'll slam your behind in jail if you lie to me again. Who is your baby's Daddy?"

"Who is your baby's Daddy?"

"Mr. Judge, I ain't lying. It's Joe's," Glady didn't bat an eye when she said this. Mary Helen looked at the judge, sure that he would believe Glady. After all, she'd believed her.

The judge looked Glady straight in the eye and said, "You're lying gal. I been a judge for over thirty years and I ain't ever had a man come in here and claim a child that wasn't his. I grant you no support and let it go on the record that this man - What's your name?

"William Bothwell, Sir."

"This man, Wiliam Bothwell is the father of this woman's child. Case dismissed."

Mary Helen and Joe walked out of court together. He wanted to hug her real close, but you didn't touch Mary Fullmore Evans in public. You had to know that if you were going to get along with her at all.

So, he said, "Let's get a taxi and go back home in style."

"You crazy, Joe I got to get to work." Mary Helen turned away from him and headed for the bus stop. She hadn't taken two steps before her water broke. Joe took her to the hospital in a taxi.

Chapter 29

They named the baby Daisy Marie. Hers was the first name they'd agreed on. Joe liked it because they'd met at her Aunt Daisy's place and he'd fallen in love with her all over again on the day the baby was born. Mary Helen liked the name because the child looked like her Aunt Daisy and Marie sounded good with Daisy.

It took her a little longer to get back to work after Daisy was born. She had gone to the doctor more times than she had with any of her other children. The doctor kept talking about *complications*. That word still struck fear in Sister's heart.

It was the same word her father used when he explained why they kept her mother so long in the hospital when she had Luke and it was the same word Aaron used when he tried to explain to her why her mother had died.

Sister was starting to have complications. How many babies could she have before she died like her mother did?

"Lord she prayed, please let me live to see all of my children grown. I don't want to leave my girls so they won't have time to be children."

She had to get Joe to agree to let her have that new operation where they tied a woman's tubes so she couldn't have any more children. She'd work on him some more when he got home this evening she decided.

Now, she had to get her mind back set to working. She wasn't looking forward to her first day back.   Every time she was out having a baby, Miss Kay would just leave things until she got back and Old Lady Wilson would be in bed starved half to death because she couldn't find her way to the kitchen. The old biddy wouldn't allow her sons to do what she was paying Mary Helen to do either. And she claimed any food Miss Kay prepared for her was poisoned.

Miss Kay had laughed her head off when Mary Helen told her that.

She said, "If I thought I could get away with it, she'd be dead as a door nail, but I would be the first suspect on their list if that old lady dropped dead from anything other than old age."

****

She put her key in the lock, but the door opened before she had time to turn it.

"I hope to God, you're May Helen!" A tall middle aged police officer said.

Mary Helen couldn't decide whether it was a statement or a question, but she answered anyway, "I am."

"Well, I'm getting the hell out of here," he said moving a lot faster than she'd have guessed someone his size could move.

"Young man, you come in here and finish filling out that report," Old Lady Wilson called from the bedroom.

"What report?" Mary Helen called back but didn't bother to go to the bedroom yet. She went to the kitchen and got the coffee going, made two rye bread toasts, and used the juicer to squeeze a half glass of juice from five of the sorriest looking oranges she'd ever seen, before she went in to check on Mrs. Wilson.

"Well, they found you. About time. Did you bring back all the things you took? Don't expect me to take you back this time. You've gone too far. Do you have something to say for yourself?"

"No, M'am." Mary Helen punctuated the rest of the old lady's speech with Yes M'ams and No M'ams while she helped Mrs. Wilson get dressed and ready to go sit out on the screened in porch where she had breakfast every morning -from spring to early winter for forty years.

Mary Helen heard a key turn in the lock in the back door and didn't bother to stop her work. She knew that it would be one of Mrs. Wilson's boys checking on her.

"May Helen, don't do this to us again. Mama's driven everybody crazy these last three weeks. Chief Foils had to assign two officers to take turns coming over here and filling out 'Missing May Helen Reports' and Creed hasn't been back since she slapped him for calling her a liar when he tried to tell her that you weren't missing," Mr. Ben finished as he accepted the cup of coffee she offered.

"I'm sorry about Mr. Creed getting slapped and all, but I got back as soon as I could. The police know I'm back. One was just leaving when I got here. You want some breakfast?"

He nodded yes and polished off four toasts and three sunny side-up eggs before he continued, "There's more, May Helen. Squeegie's slipped back to doing like he was when you first came to work, but only worst this time. He just jumps up and down all day making all kinds of scary noises. I don't know what to do. Kay won't let me get help for him 'cause she says she wouldn't be able to show her face at the Country Club again if folks found out she had a crazy son."

"Squeegie ain't crazy. He just as sane as most of the White folks I know."

"I agreed with you the last time, but it's different this time. It's gone on so long that the other two children are afraid to go near him. I don't have any right to ask, but would you come by today before you go home.

"Mr. Ben that would put me on the last bus and I…"

"Please, May Helen," He was the only one she worked for who said please when they asked her to do something extra.

"I'll come soon as I can," she sighed.

****

May Helen stood watching the boy jump up and down for a full twenty minutes.

"You tired yet?"

He didn't say anything just kept jumping.

"Do you want me to save you some of the molasses cookies that I made or will you be jumping until they're all gone?"

He didn't say anything just kept on jumping and adding a grunting sound every now and again.

"Cathy and Benjamin you can go on and get all of them cookies," Mary Helen yelled down the stairs.

He kept jumping but said under his breath, "Close the door May Helen and come close.

"I ain't getting but so close. They say you crazy. Ain't no telling what a crazy person gonna do."

"I'm not crazy just hyperactive. That's what Mother calls it. She says it makes me just like she was as a child. She said she bounced off the walls. I tried that but it hurts. She comes to talk to me every evening- just me not Cathy or Benjamin."

"So that's it. You up here jumping around and yelling like a plum fool to get your Mama to spend some time with you. You crazy as they say you is. I'm gonna fix fried chicken and a whole plate of biscuits before I go home and I ain't climbing back up these steps to bring any to a jumping fool!"

Less than twenty- minutes later he walked into the kitchen.

"Wash your hands before you sit down to eat," May Helen didn't look up from the pot she was washing at the sink or say a word of welcome to a child that she knew was so starved for attention no amount of chicken and biscuits would fill him up. But she'd try.

****

That evening when she got home she was three weeks worth of tired. All she wanted to do was go to sleep. The girls could cook the entire weekday dinner now so she got off the bus with her mind stayed on the bed.

And what should she see as she rounded the corner from Gorrell Street on to Hackett Street? Josephine-standing on the porch with another letter in her hand.

"What more Lord?" Mary Helen said, sitting down on the top step and reaching behind her for the letter.

"It's important Mama. You want me to open it for you? Josephine was just itching to know what was in that letter. It had a very important looking seal on it and she'd just - finished reading a story about a king who put his seal on all the letters he sent out using a ring and bee's wax. Wouldn't it be something if her very own Mama got a letter from a king? Her mother's voice cut through her day dream.

"Did I ask you to open it?"

"No, M'am."

"Then go on in the house." She was too tired to turn around to make sure that her order was followed.

She tore the letter open without looking at it in her hands. She held it open for several minutes before she could force herself to look at it.

Dear Mr. and Mrs. Joseph E. Evans:

We are pleased to inform you that your application for a unit in the Morningside Homes Housing Development has been approved, pending the completion of your application. The following is needed:

Verification of Mrs. Evans' income

If the application is not complete within forty-eight hours of this notification, the unit will be offered to another family.

Sincerely yours,
Mrs. M Brown

Mary Helen didn't know whether to be happy or start crying. She didn't remember what she'd done with that paper. She thought she'd taken it to Miss Kay, but so much was going on during that time she couldn't be sure. To make matters worse, there wouldn't be another bus going out to the Wilson's until 6:00 in the morning.

She was on that bus. But it didn't do her much good because it took her until 10:30a.m.to clean away enough stuff so she could find it.

"I found it Miss Kay, but Mr. Wilson hasn't signed it. Couldn't you write in how much I make and sign it?" Mary Helen wasn't above pleading in a case like this.

"Now, May Helen you know I leave all the business to Mr. Ben," she was arranging some fresh flowers in a vase. This seemed to be far more important to her than where Mary Helen lived since she didn't bother to look up when she said this.

"Well, would it be all right if I took it to him downtown?" Mary Helen said this while calling on the *Rock of Ages* for the strength to keep from slapping Miss Kay's red lips plumb off her face.

"It would be alright, if he was Downtown today. He had to go over to High Point on some business," she said still arranging her flowers just as unconcerned as you please.

"Where is he in High Point?" Mary Helen said struggling to keep what was left of her patience. Mary Helen had to ask even though she didn't have any idea how she could get to High Point. The 26 miles between the two cities may as well have been a thousand.

Miss Kay looked up then. "May Helen, I don't believe I like the tone of voice that you are taking with me. I don't know where he is in High Point and I don't want to hear anymore about it." She went back to her flowers dismissing Mary Helen.

Mary Helen wasn't angry at Miss Kay. For the first time in weeks, she was angry at Joe and Glady again. If Joe hadn't been drunk, Glady wouldn't have been able to trick him, and if he'd been a faithful husband, she wouldn't have believed Glady. And if she hadn't believed Glady, she wouldn't have forgotten about the paper. She wasn't being fair. She knew it, but she didn't care as she slammed pots and pans around in the kitchen.

The clanging could be heard a half a mile down the street.

Mary was standing at the sink washing pots that didn't even need washing because she knew better than to wash anything made of glass. She knew that in her present mood, she'd break every dish in the house.

"Who put a bee in your bonnet?" Mr. Ben said as he walked over and sampled the navy beans and ham in the big, blue speckled pot on the stove."

At first Mary Helen was too shocked to say anything. There she'd been the last few hours praying and fussing in about even amounts that Mr. Ben would come home before it was too late to get that paper in, but not believing that he would and here he was.

"Thank you Jesus," she said before she explained to Mr. Ben about the paper.

"But it's too late now," she ended sadly looking up at the clock's hands that were seconds from touching on five.

"No it isn't. Look up that telephone number and call them and tell them that I'm on my way with the paper," he yelled back as he rushed out to his car.

He called back to tell May Helen that she'd gotten the house and that her rent would be $33 a month. Four bedrooms and heat for $33 a month, it was more than she'd dared ask for since her promise.

Chapter 30

It'd taken Joe and James Robert two truckloads to move most of their belongings. Mary Helen left the children in Gloria's care in the house on Hacket Street and given her instructions to bring them with her on the last load.

Sister's initial impression of the projects was one of strength, of large, strong, solid brick structures housing strong, solid, hard working people like Joe and her. It was a place for a new beginning.

She was surprised by all the help her neighbors were giving her. She wasn't a trusting person and her first thought was to say "No" to their offers, but Margaret Jordan led the women in and got them started unwrapping dishes and putting food in the pantry before Sister could answer.

It wasn't long before she was glad that it'd been taken out of her hands. They helped her do what would have taken her all weekend and several evening after work before 10:00 that Friday evening. She was thankful but not totally trusting, she'd seen the way several of them eyed her things. She'd even heard one named Loosie speculating about how somebody who did day work had such nice things. Mary Helen could have explained how she came to have a Duncan Phyfe sofa, two authentic Queen Anne chairs, and a solid oak bed with a matching chest of drawers. She could have told them that the Wilson boys had decided to move their mother from that big old eleven room house to a small apartment off Market Street and none of their wives had wanted the heavy old furniture. She could have told them but she didn't.

The next day, instead of being worn out as she thought she would be she was rested and ready for her real initiation into project life - Wash Day. Saturday morning, Margaret had advised her to try and get up early, if she wanted to wash clothes on Saturday. It seemed that everyone wanted to wash on Saturday, and that everyone had a big family so lines were scarce. The women were already suspicious of her because she only had six children in a place where ten children was the average. If she wanted to wash her clothes she had to stake her claim to the number of clothes lines she needed and keep clothes on the lines all day *or* until she was finished.

Mary Helen was up and had her first load of clothes on the line by 5:00 Saturday morning. The children were up too, since she'd figured out that the easiest way to get four lines was to wash sheets first. Margaret was the only *one* who laughed when she got up and found that Mary Helen already had the lines that got the early morning sun.

By the time they moved into the projects most of her children were older and could do more for themselves. Mary Helen continued her habit of getting the children up, dressed, and fed by 6:00 every morning as she had done when they were little. She liked to make sure their hair was combed just right before they went out for school. She wasn't going to have anybody saying that she couldn't take care of her children. Nobody ever got her talked about but that Josephine.

"But that wasn't going to happen this day," Mary Helen thought as she determinly pulled Josephine's hair into tight plaits.

"Ouch, Mama that hurts." Josephine sat there painfully going through the ritual which made all black girls sure that they were part Japanese because all of them had slanted eyes. They thought it was a natural trait of young Colored females that they lost at puberty much like a tadpole lost its tail.

"Not half as much as it's gonna hurt if you sass back at me again," Mary Helen replied pulling the hair even tighter.

Josephine didn't say anything, but she sure wished her mother would understand that it wasn't her fault her hair wouldn't stay plaited. Josephine knew that a domestic worker's daughter's hair was the most public symbol of the quality of her work and of her undying devotion to cleanliness. She didn't set out to shame her mother. She'd tried stocking caps, extra grease, spit —still a few hairs would obstinately manage to escape and her Mama's enemy, Miss Loosie, would catch her with her hair messed up. Josephine put her head down and thought about yesterday, day before yesterday really.

****

"Come here, gal!" Miss Loosie screeched loud enough that most of the hearing people on that side of the earth were able to witness Josephine's humiliation.

"Look at yo head, gal yo mama know you is out here looking like this?"

"Hell no." Josephine thought, but she said, "No, Ma'am."

"Well, come here. Let me fix it so you won't be round here shaming' yo self and yo mama."

Then she'd whipped out the ever-present comb with the teeth set too close to get through Black folks hair, re-combed her hair, and plaited it so tight her eyebrows touched the top of her forehead.

To make matters worse Miss Loosie told her Mama what she'd done at the one time of day when she could embarrass Mary Helen the most — when she was waiting at the bus stop with her fellow workers.

As soon as all of them had assembled, Miss Loosie attacked.

"May Helen, you sho nuff must be doing more than you is able to do good. *I* caught that Josephine of yours going out to school yesterday morning with her hair standing all over her head. Next time you is too busy to take care of yo children, send them girls down to me and I'll fix em up right."

Though this was the ultimate insult — to imply that a domestic worker was ever too busy to take care of her own children-- Her Mama had handled it well, saying something like, "Thank you, Loosie. That gal must have been tomboying around after I left for the early bus."

Throughout the day, all of that graciousness festered and corroded. Josephine guessed that her mother had spent the entire day talking to herself in that way that Black mothers have perfected.

"Says I be doing more than I can do good. She don't know nothing 'bout what I can do. Should have told that slut that she can't do nothing good what ain't done in bed. Says I ain't got enough time to take care of my own children. Put mine up against hers any day. Should have told that hussy that least none of my children been left back three, four times like those dumb bunnies of hers.

"Send em down to her house so she can do what I can't, she says. Should have told that sorry excuse for a woman, your house is so nasty, I wouldn't send my children in there without gas masks," Josephine continued mimicking her mother in her mind.

By the time her mother got off work, she was ready to "jake" a knot into Josephine. She'd talked herself into such a mean state that steam was bellowing from the top of her head by the time she got off at the bus stop closest to their home that evening. The word had gone around the Projects that there was steam rising over the project buildings from the direction of the bus stop and every girl child who'd suffered a forced re-combing by anyone other than their mother's best friend, began putting the final touches on their excuses.

Josephine was ready with hers- she always was. This particular excuse had gone unused so many times that it had been polished to epic proportions. She frantically reviewed it, in hope that this time she'd get to use it.

She'd say, "Mama the Heady Headen boys, the Taylor girls and a bunch of Miss Loosie's own children tackled me and even though I put up a fight that Sugar Ray would have been proud of, they managed to pull a single hair loose."

She didn't get to use her story. When her mother got home, she was in one of those-I'll-ask-the-questions-but-if-you-even-open-your-mouth-to-answer-I'll-wear-your-little-narrow-behind-out-moods.

As soon as she opened the back door, without even unlocking it, she started, "Josephine, I want you to come here and tell me what you think you were doing going out of here with your hair standing all over your head? I'll tell you what you were thinking. You weren't thinking about nothing but yourself. What was on your little mind when you went out there like that? I'll tell you what was on your nappy little mind. You set out this morning to shame your mama. You were thinking about how you were going to give that hussy, Loosie, one more chance to put me down 'fore everybody. Well, I tell you what... I tell you what... (At this point she'd run out of things to say, but she wasn't about to let that stop her.) You want to get that comb and Royal Crown and come here so I can fix that hair? I know you do!'

"Not that comb!" she'd shouted when Josephine tried to bring back the wide-tooth comb that her sisters and she had chipped in together to buy.

"That's the comb I used this morning. Evidently, it didn't do a 1ickin-bit-of-good. Go getMY comb," her mother yelled.

HER comb was an extra, extra fine tooth comb that might have worked well on the straight hair of her white benefactor, but for Josephine it was an instrument of torture which captured every kink, and bit into every tight curl in its path. With this savage instrument, she smoothed and plaited Josephine's hair so tight that her eyes were so slanted they met at the back of her head,

"There, that ought to do it," Mary Helen said as she put two more dabs of grease in Josephine's hair.

Josephine moved away before her mother decided to tighten the plaits some more. Well, that wasn't nearly as bad as the last time Josephine thought as she made her way to the room she shared with Gloria.

The child would have been surprised to hear it, but her mother was in a very good mood. She was the happiest she'd been in a long time. So happy that she was scared something bad was going to happen. She'd doubled up on her prayers.

* * * * * * * * * *

"Kathy Wilson, how many times have I done told you about leaving your skates on the steps for somebody to fall on?" It was nearly noon and Mary Helen was in the middle of an already long day; so little things like retraining the Wilson Children to pick-up after themselves were wearing on her last good nerve.

"Enough times so I should know better?" Kathy said it like a question. Sometimes if you answered one of May Helen's questions with the right answer, usually with the same answer that she had told you a hundred times, she'd give you a big hug and say how smart you were.

Kathy was a pretty little thing. She was one of those rare children who take all of each parent's best features and ends up looking fairly good in spite of her parentage. She had her father's sea blue eyes and thick auburn hair and her mother's delicate bow shaped mouth and small ears. Mary Helen smiled thinking about the Wilson boys who had both inherited their father's ears. It was a good thing boy's were wearing their hair a little longer these days.

"That's right, Baby. Enough times so you should know better," She reached down and picked Kathy up squeezing her to a bosom that had filled out over the years. "Now pick em up and we'll go see what kind of lunch we can fix for a girl as smart as you." She turned to open the front door.

"Sister?" I knowed that was you," William Boswell rushed up the steps two at a time.

Mary Helen recognized the voice, but she didn't turn around. She didn't know what she would do if he was holding another telegram or letter. "What are you doing here in the middle of the day?"

"I come to tell you Joe got hurt at work and they took him to the hospital," William didn't mine talking to her back. He remembered what happened the last time he gave her some bad news and Joe wasn't here to catch her this time.

"Hurt how?" she asked as she finally turned to face him

"I don't rightly know. He's in the washing end of the laundry. They say it's something about his foot. I didn't see much blood though when they carried him out. So I guess it ain't been cut off or nothing,"

Mary Helen looked at him like he was a crazy man. Talking about folks getting a foot cut off in front of a child. "Kathy go on in the house. I'll be there in a minute. Go on now." She gently turned the three year old and pushed her toward the door. After she closed the door and steadied herself she turned to face William.

"Did that car bring you here?" Mary Helen looked over his shoulder at the black Oldsmobile parked on the street.

"Yeah, I rode in the back seat like a rich man. I was sitting back there smiling and waving to the people. I..."

"That don't mean nothing to me. All I want to know is whether or not you're suppose to take me to Joe or whether I got to wait until Mr. Wilson can get here.

"Oh, Mr. Dicks gave Albert directions to take you straight to L. Richardson Hospital and then take me back to work."

"Okay, let me go get my pocketbook and tell Miss Kay I'm gone," Mary Helen rushed into the house and was back out in less than a minute.

****

"Lord, Lord, what is this here now? Every time I pray my way through one mess, every time we turn one corner seems like something else jumps in the middle of the road. God, I know you ain't brought me this far to leave me," Sister prayed for strength. She prayed Joe wasn't dead. She prayed he wasn't hurt too badly. She prayed that if he was hurt so bad he couldn't get better that the Lord wouldn't leave him to suffer for months like her Daddy did. She prayed that God was God enough to make sense out of her prayers."

"Sister, Sister, we're here. Albert done told you four times to get on out so he can take me back to work and go get Mrs. Dicks at the

Country Club," William didn't mean to rush her but he didn't know if Mr. Dicks was going to pay him for all the time he'd been gone.

"I guess they took him to that new emergency part of the hospital," Sister said to no one in particular as she got out of the car. Any other time, she would have taken both men to task for failing to come around and open the car door for her. It was something James Robert and her husband did for May Jo and her that made them feel like ladies.

****

"Are you Mrs. Evans? I'm Dr. Blount," He continued when Sister nodded her head. "The wound wasn't as bad as we thought once we got it clean. I don't know how he stood the pain this long." The dark skin, round faced young doctor went on to explain that at some point Joe must have cut his foot and standing all day in the harsh soap had caused the wound to fester. This morning the wound had burst and Joe'd loss consciousness and hit his head when he fell. He said they thought they could save Joe's foot, but that he would have to stay off that foot for a couple of months.

When Sister called and told Mr. Dicks what the doctor told her, he said that he couldn't hold Joe's job for him that long and that since Joe's foot didn't get caught in a machine or something, he didn't have to pay Joe for all that time out of work. Nine years on the job and never missed a day and Mr. Dicks couldn't hold his job or give him a dime while he was home. Joe's boss at the Elm Street Building was much more understanding. He not only promised to hold Joe's job for him, he told Sister to come by every Friday and he'd give her half of Joe's $33 a week check.

Sister didn't know what she was going to do with six children and Christmas coming up while Joe was out of work. The first three weeks weren't so bad. Since Joe was at home, he kept the younger two children saving Sister the three dollars a week she paid May Jo to keep them and Sister had put away a little piece of change each week for Christmas presents for Joe and the children. But when that money was gone she let Margaret Jordan talk her into going to the Welfare Office for help.

Sister hated that place from the moment she walked through the door. It was in what had once been a mansion on Summit Avenue. The outside whispered of old South money, but the inside said the money was now controlled by tight fisted Crackers. The chairs were straight-back wooden chairs and none of the end tables around the room were part of matching sets. The huge fireplace on the back wall had been boarded closed in spite of the fact that with a little fire wood it was big enough to heat half the room. Instead, the women and children sat around the room wearing their coats on this cold November morning.

No, it wasn't a welcoming place. There is nothing about it that said, "Come in, we're here to help you." It was almost as though they wanted to make people feel as pitiful as possible. First, their hours were set-up so a person either had to take off from work or not be working at all. Second, there were dozens of children in the place, but it was eerily quiet. The rule said that when a woman applied for aide she had to bring her non-school age children with her. It seemed that every woman except Mary Helen had complied. There was no way she was going to bring Phillip and Daisy down here and then have to take them home before she could get to work. It didn't make sense and she'd tell them so. She had birth certificates for each of her children. That should be proof enough that they existed.

It was the third thing that made Mary Helen the most uncomfortable: nobody looked anyone in the eye. Most of the women either came in with their heads down like they had something to be ashamed of or they came in all loud and brassy like the world owed them something. Sister set up straighter. She didn't have anything of which to be ashamed. She worked too hard and Lord knew her Joe worked hard too. As for the loud and brassy part, two years with her Aunt Daisy had trained that out of her. Oh, she could get loud when she was rooting for Jackie Robinson or praising the Lord in church, but Mary Helen knew when and how to behave.

She recognized only one of the women sitting around in the big room. Although the woman recognized Sister too neither of them spoke. The woman's husband had walked off and left her about a year ago with 12 children.

At least he'd waited until the youngest child was nine years old.

"Evans," a voice called her name.

Sister followed the Southern twang of the voice to a cubicle that contained a small desk, a large file cabinet, and two chairs. A White woman with dyed hair and hone-rimmed glasses sat in one of the chairs behind the desk. The other chair was pushed against one wall on the other side of the room making it clear that the applicants were expected to stand submissively in front of the seated woman at the desk.

"I'll take the forms," the woman behind the desk reached for the forms as she said this and Mary Helen laid them in her hands.

The woman leafed through the papers without looking up at the woman who had handed them to her. After she finished looking through them a second time, she finally looked up at Mary Helen. She didn't seem pleased with what she saw. She looked back down at the neat handwriting on the forms. None of the ink was blotted or speared. Although she didn't want to believe that the woman in front of her was educated enough to fill out these forms on her own she had to admit that the woman standing before her looked capable enough.

The short Negro woman in front of her desk was wearing a camel colored suit with a matching hat and dark brown gloves. A light blue blouse under the suit appeared to be silk and the lace on the collar was interwoven with a slightly darker blue ribbon. The woman looked from the words on the paper to the woman standing before her dressed in clothes of a higher quality than she was wearing.

"It says here that you are 24 years old, but that you have 6 children," the woman eyed Mary Helen suspiciously.

"I am and I do." Mary Helen responded. She attempted to hand the woman her children's birth certificates.

"I don't need those. You people are always having more children than you can afford to take care of and then coming asking tax payers to take care of them for you," the woman stared up at the little woman expecting her to start crying.

Instead of crying, the woman stared back at her. "I am not asking anyone to take care of my children. Joe and me can do that. I need a little help until Joe can get back to work. That's all. It can be a loan and I'll pay you back some each week," Mary Helen wasn't going to cry and she wasn't going to beg.

"It doesn't look like you need any help dressed up like that." She didn't care if the girl was wearing her Sunday best because she was wearing her best too. The woman looked down at her serviceable wool skirt and cotton blouse that she simply added a jacket and her good black hat to on Sunday.

"I can dress like this because I work every day and my husband worked two jobs every day until he got hurt. I filled out all the answers to your questions. All I need to know is whether or not you can help us," That was as close to begging as Mary Helen was prepared to come.

****

Sister left that Welfare Office so mad she almost regretted being "saved sanctified and filled with the precious Holy Ghost" because if anyone ever needed a good cussing out it was that Welfare Lady.

She'd told Sister that the only way they could help her was if she put Joe out of the house. Sister explained again that Joe had always worked two jobs and that the reason his foot had gotten so bad was because he kept on working when he should have taken off work.

That woman didn't care. Rules were rules and the fact that Joe still had one of his two jobs cleaning up at the Elm Street Building meant with her $25 a week they made too much money to qualify for help.

"May Helen, what are you doing here," Mary Helen had almost walked into the long table with big Christmas stockings hanging along the front where Miss Kay Wilson was sitting in the hall outside the Welfare Office.

"Oh, Miss Kay, I didn't see you. I told you I'd be late today because I had some business to take care of. Where's Kathy? Miss Kay I know you didn't leave that baby at the house alone," Mary Helen was already fighting mad.

"Of course I didn't May Helen, I left her next door with the Hammer's girl. I told her to keep a look out for you," Miss Kay didn't notice May Helen's insubordinate tone but the woman next to her took notice and was insulted for her friend.

"Kathleen, I cannot believe that you allow the help to talk to you that way. Girl, you will apologize now," Trudy Galloway stood up and looked down her nose at this uppity Colored girl who had the nerve to be looking her dead in the eye.   Trudy fumed. Those Northerners and "new rich Whites" like the Wilson's and the Young's were spoiling their help to the point they were forgetting their place. Who ever heard of paying Day Help 75¢ an hour or paying a man to come in to wash windows and mop and buff the hard wood floors or spending good money on a cook and a girl to clean? Day help had been doing it all- the laundry, the cooking, the cleaning, and caring for the children for all her life and nothing was going to change if she could help it.

Mary Helen looked from Miss Kay's friend to Miss Kay. She knew both kinds of women pretty well by now. Miss Kay knew she needed Mary Helen, but she also needed her circle of friends too. Mrs. Galloway held the key to their circle. One word from her, and Miss

Kay would be an outsider; uninvited and unwelcome. It was a hard choice to make, but she made it. She said nothing.

Mary Helen looked from one woman to the other giving Miss Kay plenty of time to intervene on her behalf. And then she made her decision. She turned to speak directly to her employer, "Miss Kay if I have offended you in any kind of way I'm most sorry," Mary Helen turned to walk away. She liked Miss Kay well enough not to intentionally embarrass her in front of her friend, but she wasn't going to let this go unpunished.

"May Helen, give me the names of your children. I'll put them on the Empty Stocking Fund List," Miss Kay said brightly trying to get back into May Helen's good graces. Trudy didn't know the hell an upset May Helen could raise. Oh, everything that she was paid to do would still get done, but none of those special May Helen touches would get done. There would be no special honey frosted mint juleps or iced molasses cookies at her next bridge party and Ben wouldn't get any fried chicken for dinner or pound cake for dessert.

Mary Helen turned around, walked back to the table and gave Miss Kay the names of her children and then went to pick-up Kathy from the neighbors' house. After that she changed clothes, fed Kathy her lunch, and got a pot of pinto beans started for supper. She turned the beans up on high and waited until they came to a hard boil. This was the most important step in cooking pinto beans-where the cook skimmed that grey film off the top that gave people gas. Only this time, this cook didn't skim it. She cut up a small onion, added three tablespoons of sugar and some salt & pepper in with two ham hocks and turned the pot down to simmer. And then she settled down to make a few telephone calls.

By the end of the day, she had lined up two other day jobs cutting her time at Miss Kay's to only two days a week. When Miss Kay came home, Mary Helen made it clear that although she would only be coming two days a week, she still expected to be paid $25.00 a week. Miss Kay agreed.

Miss Kay suspected after Mr. Ben nearly blew her out of the bed five times that night that May Helen had done something different to the beans, but Mr. Ben insisted that they were the best beans he'd ever eaten.

Miss Kay was sure she had done something different when she told May Helen about how Mr. Ben had kept her up all night. May Helen baked him a pound cake for dessert that night to make up to him.

May Helen and Miss Kay remained confidants, but things were never quite the same between them.

****

With the additional work, they had enough to get them through until Joe went back to work the day before his 35th birthday. Mary

Helen was feeling really blessed. She'd tripled up on the number of services that she went to and joined the choir-she was determined to make a joyful noise since she couldn't sing, and joined the usher board. She was sure that God had listened to all of her prayers until February.

Chapter 31

At nine months pregnant Mary Helen looked more like a beach ball rolling along than anything else. It was all she could do to waddle up the three steps into her house that afternoon and sink into one of the blue, wing back chairs closest to the front door. Though the chairs were covered in plastic, no one, not even Mary Helen, was allowed to sit on them. So the girls knew how weary she was.

"That's good Baby, just let Mama sit here until she gets her next wind," she said as Gloria, slipped an ottoman under her legs. Her legs were so swollen it was impossible to determine where her ankles ended and her calves began. Cuts had been made on both sides of each shoe to made room for toes that looked like little pimples on the end of her feet.

The spring had been hot in Greensboro, the summer torrid, and it didn't look as though the fall was going to be much better. Heat furled around damp bodies like the warmth from a potbellied stove. As bad as the soaring temperatures had been for Gloria and Josephine, who had just spent their third summer in charge of the younger children, watching their mother get through carrying her seventh child in less than ten years was worst because they understood what most nine and ten year old children did not – this pregnancy was different.

Perhaps, because she'd been so young when she had them she felt almost as though the two oldest girls were her contemporaries. She confided in them about the complications that had started in her last pregnancy and doubled their training to take over "just in incase." Although she never verbalized what "just in case" referred to, the girls were smart enough to make the connection between their mother's complications and the complications she had told them about that had ended their grandmother's life when their Aunt Margaret was born.

They were terrified that their mother was going to die and each time she taught them a new skill that had up to then been something special that only she did for her family, their terror double.

Their terror more than tripled when she'd showed Josephine how to bake a cake from scratch and Gloria the secret to making her special Sunday dinner roast beef which came from a cut of beef so tough it could have been used to make leather come out of the oven so tender it would melt in your mouth. These were things only Mama could do.

When their mother was away at Workers Meeting or Convocation she left fried chicken and a pound cake, but since both were always eaten long before Sunday dinner, they usually wound up eating fried fish and sharing a box of Big Sixty Cookies for dessert.

Tender roast beef, fried chicken, and pound cake were their mother's special things.

They had not realized how special her chicken dinner was until she taught Gloria how to cut up and prepare one chicken so that each member of the family got their favorite piece- a thigh and a leg for Daddy, two wings for Josephine, the piece of the breast with the wish bone for Mary Louise, a side of the breast for Gloria, the other side of the breast for Sandra, a leg for Daisy and a thigh for Phillip. Only then did they realize that there was no favorite piece left for their mother. She ate the pieces that she had despised as a child: the neck, the gizzard and the liver.

It was a disgusting and scary thought that the "just in case" might involve Gloria and Josephine eating those parts of the chicken. This was reason enough for them to go along with their mother's plan.

This baby would be her last. There was an operation called *tying tubes* that would prevent her from getting pregnant again. The only problem was that their father refused to sign the papers.

He had never professed to be all that religious, but on this one point his religious fervor ran deep: Only God could decide how many children were enough.

So, their mother had come up with a plan. When she went into the hospital to have this baby, she would not be coming home until Daddy signed the papers for her to have her tubes tied. The girls' part in the plan was for them not to help their father in any way. No cooking, no cleaning, no combing and plaiting hair, no taking care of the younger children-nothing. The only amendment their mother had made to that decree was that they could give help if their father was about to make a fatal error. She let them know that if they helped and she determined after the fact that no one had been near death... She left that sentence hanging knowing that Josephine's very fertile imagination would conjure up a punishment far worse than anything she could think of or execute.

"Mama I started dinner and Josephine helped the children with their school work," Gloria stopped when she realized that their mother was asleep. "We'll let her rest until it's time to say grace and recite our scriptures."

Both girls stood for a moment looking down on a face that though still smooth looked much older than twenty-five. They prayed that "just in case" would not happen with this baby.

****

"It's time. I've got to take your mother to the hospital." Their father woke them up at 2:00a.m.the next day.

Gloria and Josephine knew the routine. They woke Mary Louise and Sandra up. Washed their faces and gave them their clothes and then each took one of the others to dress.

"The cab is here. I already went across the yard and woke up Miss Margaret. Stay there until I get back or until about time for y'all to go to school and to take Daisy and Phillip around to Mae Jo," Joe didn't wait to see if they would do as they were told. They were good girls and they had done it before.

****

On Friday morning September 6, 1957 another boy was born to Joseph Ervin and Mary Helen Evans. They named him Benjamin Andrew Evans. Joe liked the sound of the names and Mary Helen didn't tell him that those were the names of the Wilson boys. The boy was small, but Joe's mother had always said that he was much smaller than Robert Lee and either of his two older sisters when he was born so they guessed the boy took after him.

Joe thought the baby's timing was perfect. Since he was born at 4:16a.m., Joe got to work at his new job a Curtis Meat Packing Company on time and he wouldn't have to take time off to take his wife and child home, because he'd be able to take them home on Sunday.

He stopped by to see Sister and the baby on his way home after work. When he got home he expected the children to be fed and watching TV until he told them their bedtime story. But when he got home, there was nothing on the stove and the young ones were crying because they were hungry.

"Gloria, whose turn was it to fix dinner tonight?" Joe asked. He wasn't angry just puzzled.

"Yours," Josephine responded without explanation when Gloria couldn't seem to answer.

"Mine? What is she talking about Gloria?"

"Daddy, Mama told us not to do anything to help you while she was in the hospital," Gloria looked at her father with eyes pleading for him to understand that they were caught in the middle.

"I see. Boy, hush," He turned to Phillip, "I'll get something on the table in a little while. I hope your Mama doesn't think ya'll not cooking is going to make me sign those papers. I can cook as good as your mother." He turned and went into the kitchen.

The girls kind of felt sorry for him-underestimating their mother like that. Daddy had worked in the Mess Hall like many Colored soldiers during World War II. The only difference was that since his two older sisters were grown and married before he turned ten, and his mother had all she could do taking care of Big Mama, his grandmother, Joe learned to cook at an early age. His candied yams were way better than their mother's and his fried fish was poetry on a plate. Their mother knew he wouldn't mine cooking. It was the rest of her plan that would really try his last nerve.

Chapter 32

Joe was up early on Saturday morning and even though Gloria and Josephine did not help him by taking the linen off the beds and bringing it down to him; he had the first load ready to hang on the line by 7:00a.m. He was amazed to find every single line full.

"What am I suppose to do with all these wet sheets?" Joe asked Margaret Jordan.

"You have to wait until someone takes theirs down since you decided to sleep in this morning." As Mary Helen's best friend, she knew about the plan and had made sure that every line was taken by 6:30a.m.

"I have you know, I was up by 6:15a.m.," Joe suspected she was in on the plot.

"Like I said. You slept in. We've been up since 4:30a.m. When the sun gets up good the clothes will dry pretty fast," Margaret Jordan flounced off.

Joe went into the house to fix breakfast for the children. Although he kept an eye out for some free lines, each time he saw someone removing clothes from a line, one of her girls would be replacing the dried clothes with wet ones.

By noon, Joe was convinced that they were all in on it. "No one living in the Projects could possibly have that many sheets or clothes," Joe mumbled to himself. "If these women think they are going to get the best of me with these shenanigans they have another thought coming," Joe declared war on the women of the Projects.

He called two of the Herbin boys over. "Do you and your brother want to earn fifty cents?"

"Yes sir." Then one of the boys thought to ask. "What for?"

"As soon as you see someone taking clothes off the line, one of you start putting these sheets up there and the other one come to get me.

"It ain't worth fifty cents Mr. Evans. The word is out. Anyone helping you will have to wash his own clothes and ain't no telling when he'll see a cooked meal again."

"What word? What you talking about boy?"

"I don't know but the women are together on it.

"Well, did you ever hear of a bunch of women beating men at anything?"

"No, Sir."

"You help me and I'll see to it that you eat when I eat. I can cook as good as any woman around here. Us men got to stick together, Right?"

"Right," the boys said in unison. They shook hands on it and with the boys help Joe finally got some space on the lines a little after 1:00p.m., but by the time the sheets were dry, he had to leave the children's clothes on the line half wet.

****

This was the worst weekend Joe's had in a long time. Friday was still a problem because Joe liked to stop in at one of the liquor houses for a couple of drinks before he came home. Saturday was different. He and Sister had fallen into a very comfortable married couple routine on Saturday. Joe fried fish for dinner and Sister made coleslaw, mashed potatoes, and corn bread.

This Saturday there would be no coleslaw, but the mashed potatoes and pan fried cornbread more than made up for it as far as the children were concerned. Even though he continued the practice of making the children say a scripture, his grace was short enough that the food was still hot.

"I hope all the rest of our children are born on Friday morning. It makes everything easier all around," Joe congratulated himself on a job well done, in spite of the obstacles Sister and the other women had tried to put in his way. He'd fed his children, cooked dinner, washed the dishes and remade the beds. Although none of the bed clothes were dry enough for the children to sleep in, Joe was sure that if their faces and hands were washed, it would be alright for them to sleep in their clothes this one time.

"Well, Babies what story do you want to hear tonight?" he said when he had all the children settled down. Daisy climbed into his lap as she usually did and the others gathered on the floor at his feet.

"Goldie Locks and the Three Bears," the children shouted. This was their all-time favorite story because their Daddy never told it the same way twice and each time it was better than the last time.

****

I don't know why women make this seem so hard, Joe thought as he stretched out in bed that night. He'd pick his wife and the baby up early Sunday morning and everything would be back the way things should be.

But when he went to pick her up on Sunday morning, Mary Helen said, "I'm not going home until you sign these papers for me to get my tubes tied," she tried to hand Joe three sheets of paper.

"We already settled that. I said "no" and that's it. Now put on these clothes and let's go."

"I'm not going and the baby can't go home without me," Mary Helen stubbornly replied.

"I'm going out to the desk and to tell these people that I'm not going to pay one dime of the hospital bill after today. Then let's see how long they let you lay up in here. Call the house when they put you and the baby out," Joe said as he walked out of the maternity ward.

After he spoke to the ward clerk, he went straight home fully expecting to have to turn around and come straight back, but Mary Helen still hadn't called by 8:00p.m.

****

"Gloria and Josephine y'all get the children ready for bed and I'll come in and tell a story," Joe turned to the girls as he was washing the dishes.

"We can't Daddy. That's part of helping and unless you or one of the children is dying, we can't help," Josephine explained again.

"I see. Is it too much to ask you to bring me their night clothes?"

The girls looked at one another.

"I guess that would be all right," Gloria finally announced as she led Josephine up the stairs. A few minutes later they returned with two neatly folded piles of night clothes.

"Well?"

"Sir?"

"Well, what goes on which child?" All of the garments seemed to be about the same size and were so faded that he couldn't tell whether some were pink for girls or blue for boys. Some even appeared to be yellow.

Gloria looked at Josephine. Josephine hunched her shoulders and Gloria twisted her mouth in serious consideration.

"I don't think so Daddy. It sounds like too much help to me," Gloria finally said.

Josephine nodded in agreement.

"I see." Joe grabbed each of the smaller children up and put whatever he laid his hands on the child.

Gloria and Josephine decided that it was a good thing they were going to bed rather than outside somewhere people could see them. By the time he finished getting them ready for bed he was in no mood to tell or read them a story.

Each day, things got a little worst. Their hair became so matted and kinky the girls cried and carried on so when he tried to comb it out that after a couple of days he just pulled uneven clumps together with rubber-bands. Buck Wheat from those movies *Spanky and the Gang* looked better than they did. Josephine's friend Kenny offered to redo her hair but she felt it would be disloyal to her sisters to look that much better than they did.

By Tuesday of the second week, their father was getting up two hours earlier and their hair was so tangled and matted that he had broken every comb in the house. They were wearing their play clothes to school now because even though Joe had worked in a laundry, the gathered sleeves, skirts, and pinafores of little girls' dresses left him frustrated beyond hope.

"What is this?" Joe said when Gloria handed him a note.

"I don't know Daddy. The teachers put staples all around it and..." She started to say that even Josephine could not figure out some way for them to read it without him knowing that they had read it, but considering the fact that they were not currently in their father's good graces, she decided not to include that information.

Joe used his pocket knife to remove the staples, unfolded the note and began to read it.

Dear Mr. Evans,

Gloria has informed us that you are in charge of caring for them while your wife is in the hospital. You are probably

*unaware of our rules about little girls'
clothing. All girls must wear <u>skirts,
dresses, or jumpers</u> to school. If Gloria,
Josephine, Mary Louise, and Sandra
come to school in pants again they will
be sent home.*

Your truly,

*Mrs. Curry, Mrs. Nash, Mrs.
Eldridge,* **Mrs. Holly**

"I don't see where any of them are offering to come iron those damn dresses," Joe was cussing mad.

"Pants made more sense than dresses anyway," Joe thought remembering how much time he and some of his friends spent trying to look under those skirts when he was in school.

The girls went to school the rest of the week in their Easter dresses. The younger girls felt pretty, but Gloria and Josephine felt like fools. Even a tomboy like Josephine couldn't find a way to play right in a dress with enough ruffles and lace on it to make two dresses for Cinderella to wear to the ball.

After school that Friday, they decided to go talk to their Mother. If she wouldn't change her mind about coming home maybe she would at least amend the rules so that they could iron their school clothes.

When they got to L. Richardson Hospital, their mother was sweeping the hall outside the nursery. She'd made an agreement with the hospital administrator that she would do some light cleaning to pay for her and the baby's extended hospital stay.

"Is something wrong with your Daddy or one of the little children? What are you girls doing in your Easter dresses on a school day?" She fired questions at them as she ran down the hall toward them.

"No one's sick or dead Mama, but it's almost that bad. We're getting picked on at school and the teachers say that if we wear our play clothes to school again, they're going to send us home," Gloria intentionally talked about the two things that were most likely to get their mother riled up. No one messed with her children.

"Josephine, you're letting someone pick on your sister's and brother?"

"No, M'am," Josephine looked at Gloria appealingly. She had a reputation to uphold. Their mother knew that Josephine would beat up anyone who picked on one of the little ones. Every family in the Projects had an enforcer whose responsibility it was to look out for the younger siblings. In most cases it was an older brother, but since all the older children in the Evans family were girls the task had fallen to Josephine. Gloria was simply too small and didn't have the temperament to be a fighter.

Josephine was a natural and the fact that she was a girl gave her an advantage over most boys. It was a known fact that she had no respect for the "family jewels" and she kept her finger nails long and sharp. To add insult to injury, she would hit from behind with anything she picked up. No one male or female wanted to fight her. So, they usually left the Evans children alone.

Gloria sighed and handed their mother the note. They really hadn't expected the first part of their plan to work. "Here's the note our teachers sent to Daddy. All of them signed it so I guess its official," Gloria handed their mother the note that they had dug out of the trash.

"We'll see about that." Their mother said after she finished reading the note. The girls followed their mother down the hall to an office. "Dr. Hughes, could I please borrow a piece of paper and a pen."

"Certainly, Mrs. Evans. That husband of yours hasn't come to his senses yet?

"No, Sir, but it should be any time now. I appreciate your letting us stay here."

"My mother died in childbirth and the baby was still born. They divided the rest of us among ten relatives. It was a hard way to grow up so my sympathies are with you," he smiled kindly at her and the two little girls who had the most bedraggled church dresses and the most unusual hair styles he'd ever seen.

"Thank you." Their mother sat on a bench in the hall and turned sideways to use the bench to write on. "Now, take this to Margaret Jordan. She'll tell you what to do from there. Now, go on before it starts getting dark."

The girls never knew exactly what was in the note. All Miss Margaret told them after she read it was that they were to come over to her house each school day and change into clean freshly ironed school clothes and then return each afternoon and put back on whatever their father had given them to wear to school.

It worked for two whole days until that little tattle-tale Sandra said to their father, "Daddy, why can't Miss Margaret do our hair too."

"Do your hair too? What are you talking about Baby?"

"When she puts some of her girls' clothes on us for school," Sandra said innocently. Gloria and Josephine had decided that at six years old Sandra was too young to understand the intricacies of deception and had hoped that she wouldn't mention changing clothes to their father.

Their father just looked at Gloria and Josephine and said, "I see."

Gloria and Josephine were beginning to hate those two words. Each time he said, "I see," it seemed to them that the gap between the two older girls and their father widened. He barely spoke to them anymore other than to utter a simple "yes" or "no." When further elaboration was needed he kept the sentences as concise as possible.

Josephine missed him the most. She was a Daddy's girl in much the same way that Gloria had always been closer to their mother. Their father had this big old radio that could pick up baseball and basketball games all up and down the east coast. Gloria didn't care about the games, but Josephine spent most evenings lying on the floor at her father's feet listening to the games and having him explain what was going on to her. It was their time together. Lately he'd shoo her out of the room saying he was too tired, later she could hear his radio turned down low through the wall that separated the room she shared with Gloria from her parents' room.

Gloria tried to comfort Josephine saying that after Daddy signed those papers they wouldn't have to worry about losing either one of their parents. Their mother wouldn't die from complications from having too many babies and their father wouldn't be so mad all the time because he had to do their mother's work at home and his two jobs too.

But each, "I see" made Josephine less certain that she'd ever get her Daddy back.

They stopped going to Miss Margaret's for school clothes and wore their Easter dresses to school for the next three days in a row.

Chapter 33

"Enough is enough," Joe said the next Sunday morning. He couldn't spend another Saturday wash day fighting half the women in the Projects for line space and yesterday he hadn't been able to find those two boys who'd helped him the last two weeks. Besides, he looked at the pricks in his fingers from trying to sew the lace back on Josephine's church dress, "If I don't get that woman home I'm going to bleed to death or Josephine is going to trip and break her Tom-fool neck," he thought as he came up with a plan of his own.

He dressed up in his navy blue pin stripped suit. It was off the rack but it fit his 6'1' slim, muscular frame like tailor-made. By the time he shaved, trimmed his mustache and splashed on some Old Spice® after shave he was such a fine chocolate piece of manhood, Gloria and Josephine made up the bassinet for the new baby and started cleaning the house. They were certain that when he walked in there looking like that and flashed that Sam Cooke smile of his, their Mama would roll out of bed and run home.

Joe practically danced his way down the street stopping at a neighbor's to ask for flowers from her little garden. The girls looked at each other and smiled. He'd bring her home all right.

****

"James Robert, You are ready? William said he'd meet us at the front of the hospital," Joe stopped at his first cousin's place to pick up the final part of his plan to get Sister to come home.

"Joe, I don't know. Mae Jo says I'm wrong to help you against Sister."

"Mae Jo says? You're a grown man and you're listening to what Mae Jo says. I'm blood. Don't no woman come before blood. You coming or not?"

James Robert went back into the house to talk to his wife. Joe shook his head in disgust. James Robert wasn't hen-pecked. He was something worst; he was sensitive. A woman crying would about break his heart. He'd do anything to keep that wife of his from shedding a tear.

When James Robert finally came back out he said, "Yeah, Joe I'm coming, but since its Sunday Mae Jo says that if I go, we better not sing nothing but good old time gospel music. If you don't know no gospel music, I can't go," James Robert said this almost hopefully. Lord, he didn't want to get in no fuss with his wife about helping Joe against Sister. Mae Jo would cry all night long. Mae Jo and Sister were right close, like sisters almost and Mae Jo would talk to him about it for the next ten years if she felt he had wronged Sister in any way.

"I know just the song," Joe said grapping away James Robert's last hope of not going and keeping his manhood intact. "Do you know Wonderful by the Soul Stirrers?"

"You know I do Joe," James was affronted, just 'cause he mostly sang backup didn't mean he was less of a singer than Joe.

"Well, you just backup like you usually do and I'll do the rest."

James Robert, William, and Joe planted themselves right under the ward where Sister had been for too long.

They started out smooth as you please,

> Wonderful, God is so
> wonderful
> He's wonderful, God he's
> wonderful.
>
> The Lord is my shepherd,
> he's my guide
> Whenever I need, the Lord
> will provide
> And praise my lords name
> I know he's so wonderful
>
> And O, he's wonderful and
> I better believe
> The Lord is wonderful, oh
> yes he is
> And O, he's wonderful, I
> know the Lord
> He's so wonderful.

By the time they got half way through, all the windows on that side of the hospital were open.

"Which one is your husband Mary Helen? One of the new mother's who'd come in yesterday wanted to know?

Someone responded, "The tall one in the pin stripped suit."

"Girl, I'd jump out this here window to get to that one," one of the young nurses put in.

Sister didn't say anything. Her face was glued to the scene below the window. He did look good. He hadn't been to see her in over a week. She's heard from the nurse in the nursery that he'd been by every day to see his baby boy. Although she was glad that he wasn't blaming the baby, it hurt that his refusal was keeping her away from him and their children for so long. By the time they got to...

> And O, if you never tried
> God, try the Lord one
> day
> And see when my father
> come down and make a
> way
> And O, I can't help it but
> love God
> he's so wonderful,
> wonderful ...

> He's been my mother
> and my father too
> There's no limit to what
> my Lord can do
> and O, I love God, he's
> so wonderful.

Sister had made up her mind to go get their son and go home. She was still afraid of dying too soon and leaving her children to someone else to raise, but she didn't think she could bear to go on any longer. Just as she turned around, Joe, who had seen her in the window thought she was rejecting his plea and made the mistake salesmen often make; he over sold. He decided to change his tactics. He changed the words like Sam Cooke had done when he left the Soul Stirrers. He started singing...

Lovable
my girl
she's lovable
She's lovable
my my girl
she's so lovable
Candy's sweet and honey too
There's not another quite, quite as
sweet as you
I love my girl, she's so lovable
(she's so lovable)
I know she's
oh yes she is
I know she's lovable
yes she is
Love and fascination is her middle
name

To my heart to my heart a
sensational thrill she brings
I love my girl she's lovable
I know she's
Yes she is, I know
I know she's lovable
yes she is
I know she's lovable
yes she is
She's just an angel, a sweet little
angel to me
When I'm without her I know, I'm in
misery
I love my girl, she's so lovable.

"What did he say? What's he singing now?" Sister couldn't believe it. How could he shame her like this -changing the words from a gospel song to a honky-tonk song on a Sunday too. She raised the window and yelled at him, "Joe Ervin Evans, you heathen. I might not go home with you when you sign the papers. Now go on home and stop embarrassing me."

"I told you Joe. Mae Jo said sing only gospel on Sunday," James Robert said under his breath.

"Shut up James," Joe heard him any way.

When he returned home, he told his children, "That woman's crazy as hell."

****

On the seventeenth day of the Lay-in Movement, Joe signed the papers.

Mary Helen didn't see it as a win at Joe's expense, but as a victory for all of them. The only thing she regretted was not telling him about her enlarged heart. Maybe he would have signed it sooner, but maybe he would have made her stop working outside her house. She couldn't take a chance of that happening now.

Joe supplied the basics. He paid the rent, the water, and light bills and gave her money to put food on the table, but if she wanted anything beyond that, she had to pay for it. Her children would have Easter dresses, new school clothes, go on any school trips any of the other children went on, get at least one gift every Christmas, and get their pictures taken right along with the other children. Her $40 a week had to do a lot of little things for her children. She had to work. So, she convinced herself that it wasn't her victory, but a victory for her entire family.

Joe didn't see it that way. He felt that he had fought a good fight, an honest fight, but had lost to a woman who was willing to use any means, fair or foul. She had even used his children against him. When he looked at Gloria and Josephine his eyes called them "traitors".

But the worst thing was that everybody seemed to know. There were snide smirks of the faces of every woman in the neighborhood and all the men seemed to have come up with solutions that didn't involve Joe giving in and signing those papers-after the fact.

Joe knew in his heart that there was not a man among them who could have held out half as long as he had, but knowing in his heart didn't have much credence against the simple fact that he had given in to the demands of a woman barely half his size. To make matters worse, a couple of other women were demanding that their husbands sign the papers so that they could have their tubes tided. One of the women only had five children! What was the world coming to?

The guilt of his colossal failure was almost more than one man could bear. Joe had not only let the men in Morningside Projects down, he had probably done his part to wipe out the whole Colored race! If this thing caught on, women might decide to have only one or two children or God forbid, none at all.

Whenever someone would come up in his face about how Mary Helen had "made" him sign those papers, he would try to laugh it off with, "Only reason I signed was 'cause my girls hair was getting so nappy I was afraid that it would cut off the blood to their brains" or he would say, "I did it because my boy was getting so big he was beating up the other children in the nursery."

Instead of getting over it, as Mary Helen kept assuring the girls he would, he started coming home later and leaving for work earlier.

Gloria and Josephine became so desperate to see their Daddy they got up every morning as soon as they smelled the coffee, because they knew he always had coffee and a fried egg before he left. They'd press their noses against their bedroom window and wait for him to emerge from the house, then they would yell, "Good bye Daddy."

He never turned around, just gave them a backward wave and kept on walking.

Because they had taken their Mama's side for totally selfish reasons, Gloria and Josephine felt responsible for the problems between their parents. They knew that their mother would never have been able to pull it off if they had done all they could do to help their father. When their Mama finally got home from the hospital, she had been forced to cut their hair when she couldn't get all the tangles out and it hadn't really bothered them because they felt bald heads were a small price to pay for no more babies. But the loss of their Daddy was an almost unbearable price.

Chapter 34

The end of 1957 couldn't come fast enough for Gloria and Josephine. A new year might bring back their old Daddy. That's all both girls wanted for Christmas that year. Instead, they got snow on Christmas Day. The girls thought that this was a good sign, because a December snow in North Carolina was as rare as their father's smiles had become. It was so rare that their mother allowed them to play outside in the snow for as long as they wanted. They stayed outside for two hours. This was a mistake. It had been so long since any of them were sick that they'd forgotten about their mother's cures. By the middle of the week after Christmas, every child in the family except the baby, Benjamin had colds.

It was too late when they remembered that their mother had a cure for everything and that most of her cures were to be avoided at all costs. Every cure had at least one ingredient that stank to high heaven or that tasted like something had died in your mouth.

The cure for the common cold wasn't too bad as her cures went. First, she gave each of the children a ball of sugar and Vaseline that was about the size of a nickel.

"Swallow it," she commanded.

"We got to swallow this whole thing?" Josephine was the only one brave enough to ask.

"What did I say?" Mary Helen looked down the line of six children until the ball of medicine was placed in each mouth.

"Don't you choke," she dared when someone had trouble getting it down.

No one choked but Mary Louise and Gloria turned a little purple. Next, she rubbed each child's chest with a mixture of Vick's Vapor Rub and mustard oil. And then she put two undershirts, a long sleeved flannel night shirt, and two pairs of wool socks on each child.

After she assured herself that they were all still breathing, she seated them in a circle in the kitchen. She put a quilt over the opening between the kitchen and the living room. When this was done, she filled two big pots with water and put them on the stove to boil. She turned the oven on high and opened the oven door. All the while the water was boiling she kept throwing herbs into the pot.

Sister hadn't put them in the kitchen because the rest of the house was cold. One of the good things about living in the Projects was that all of the rooms were always warm in the winter. The wood burning stoves that gave off little fingers of heat which barely reached five feet beyond the surface of the stove were replaced in the Projects by steam heat radiators that popped and whistled with warmth. Better yet, there was one of these heaters in each room. So, it was usually warm enough so that if a sister or brother hogged the covers, the youngun left with their butt out did not have to worry about getting cold. This had never been the case when we had lived on Cruz Street where only the front room with the large potbellied stove was warm all the time and the kitchen was warm when their mother was cooking a big meal or baking.

Since it had already been quite warm in the kitchen before Mama closed it off and opened the oven, it wasn't very long before we were perspiring - No, we were sweating like horses. After a while the steam from the herbs in the pots had our eyes watering like spigots. The undershirts and nightshirts were as wet and clingy as fat, spoiled two year olds who refused to walk.

Nearly an hour had passed before the first of the children fainted from the heat and from the effects of the herbs. Before that youngun hit the floor, Mary Helen grabbed her by the collar and started stripping off the nightclothes, undershirts, and socks. She dipped the child in a washtub that had been filled with tepid water and redressed her in a single undershirt and panties. The procedure was repeated each tine one of the children dropped until all of them were ready to be carried, pulled, pushed or dragged upstairs to our beds. Once they were in bed, their mama gave each of them a dose of cod liver oil and garlic extract. This not only cured the colds but it also made them cold proof for about ten years.

Mary Helen's cures were not only effective in healing all manner of diseases they were also invaluable as preventive medicine. Although wellness health programs did not begin until the mid-eighties according to some uninformed medical historians, such a program was in full force in the Evans household during the fifties. Lord knows, her children did everything that they could do never to get sick, and if failing in this they tried to keep their mama from finding out that they were sick unless they were sure that they were at death's door. A young entrepreneur could really make some serious money when a child in the family got sick. Most of the time the "Sickie" would be willing to give up their entire fifty-cent allowance to keep their mama from finding out that they were sick.

No one ever complained of a mere stomach ache because Mary Helen would cure it with a cure that was too foul to mention and send them to school anyway. In order to stay home from school, a child had to have a temperature of at least 102°. Staying home from school was not to be taken lightly. Mary Helen was determined that no child of hers would ever be left back because of missing too many days of school. She did everything in her power to make staying home from school as terrifying a thought as getting your Halloween treats snatched at the end of a hard night of trick-or-treating.

A child who was too sick to go to school was not allowed to go anywhere after school hours - not to the Annual County Fair, not to the Christmas Parade, not even to the Saturday Rock Fight if they happened to be sick on a Friday; Nowhere. A child who was too sick to go to school was too sick to hold a telephone; too sick to keep down anything more filling than a bowl of Mary Helen's special Sick-Children's Soup (It looked and smelled a whole lot like warm dish water, but since no one was allowed in the kitchen when she made it rumors ran rampant. One sister claimed to "know" that cat guts were a key ingredient.

Perhaps the worst thing about staying home from school was that and a child who was too sick to go to school was too sick to raise their head to look at the television. Now, that their father no longer told them stories every night, television was the children's only form of entertainment. They watched the *Howdie-Dooie Show*, *The Lone Ranger*, and *Hop-A-Long Cassidy*, *The Roy Rogers Show*, *Lassie*, and of course Josephine's favorite *Mighty Mouse*.

Josephine convinced the rest the children that the cartoon character was really the first Colored hero on television and that Mighty Mouse was his nickname. It made sense because there were some pretty strange nicknames in the Projects- Tootle Lips Towns, Stick Man Floyd, and Big Feet Deecie to name a few. The fact that Mighty Mouse actually looked like a mouse only made Josephine's explanation more believable because Stick Man Floyd wasn't much wider than a stick and Big Feet Deecie had to wear men's shoes because they didn't make women's shoes big enough for her. Mighty Mouse was their hero until they had an episode about his tail being the source of his powers. Not even Josephine's fertile imagination could explain away a tail on a Colored man.

The thought of being too sick to watch television made the children extra careful about getting sick or doing anything that was even remotely dangerous-except playing one of the two National Sports of the Projects – stickball and rock fighting. The children never messed with bees or reported any kind of insect bites because they knew that their Mama's cure for insect bites and bee stings called for a glob of that stuff from Miss Tunie's spit can. It didn't matter to their Mama where the injury was, even if it was on a child's mouth, she would still put that junk on it.

Somehow, Gloria and Josephine escaped most of the illnesses that the younger children got, but their luck ran out the spring of 1958.

Mary Helen decided to give Gloria a birthday party. She couldn't give either of the older girls back all the time that they had spent helping her around the house and taking care of their younger siblings, but she could help them enjoy what was left of their childhood a little bit. Both girls had been moping about since the "Lay-in of 1957 and she felt guilty for enlisting their help. She was determined to make April 11, 1958 special. Margret Jordan's oldest daughter, Yvonne had made birthday invitations for all of Gloria's friends and Josephine had managed to deliver them without her sister finding out. The manager of the Projects had agreed to allow the party to be held in the meeting hall of the Office Building. The decorations were being made in blue and yellow- Gloria's favorite colors. Everything that could be planned had been planned right down Gloria's grand entrance. But then something no one could have planned for happened.

****

"Does my face look fat to you?" Gloria asked Josephine who was waiting impatiently to brush her teeth

"Fat for you or just plain fat?" Josephine didn't want to scare Gloria but her face was much rounder than usual.

"Don't play. I want to know if it's any kind of fat. My throat hurts so much that I can't swallow anything."

"Girl, if you think you're getting sick you better stay out of Mama's sight. You know what she does to sick people," Josephine advised.

"Don't I know it? But you've got to help me. I'll come home from school, do all of my house work, and go to our room. If you'll trade weeks cooking with me, then I won't be in the kitchen washing dishes when Mama gets home."

Josephine agreed because they had to keep Gloria well for her "surprise" birthday party. Although it wasn't much of a surprise because Gloria knew that she was going to have a birthday party (Some dumb hussy had asked what they were supposed to wear), she didn't know all the details about how special it was going to be. Josephine wanted this party almost as much for herself as she wanted it for her sister.

Just when they thought that they were going to make it to the birthday party without being detected, Gloria's legs blew up like cantaloupes. They got so big that she needed help to stand up. Josephine became afraid that she was going to die and get her in trouble with their Mama, so she told on Gloria.

The trouble with getting close enough to tattle was that it gave their mother a chance get a good look at Josephine. The girls had spent so much time keeping Gloria's sickness from their mother that they hadn't noticed that Josephine's face and throat were swollen too. One look at Gloria and Josephine and their Mama diagnosed that both of them had the mumps and that the mumps had dropped on Gloria. Mama set about curing her after she finished fussing about how she would have killed both of them if they had died without telling her that they were sick.

It must be true that what "goes around comes back around" because the cure for mumps gave the other younger children plenty of fuel for getting back at Gloria and Josephine for teasing them when they had been cured.

"This will make the swelling go down Mary Helen said as she rubbed them down in sardine oil and tied sardines in rags underneath their chins.

"Here eat these she commanded as she held pickled pig's feet to their mouths until each girls chewed a couple of bites, but neither of them could swallow what they had bitten off. Next, she gave them a double dose - a dose from a tablespoon rather than a dose from a teaspoon- of a thick, herb, castor oil, and sulfur solution. This stuff nearly knocked them out, but before either one could reach blissful unconsciousness, she grabbed Gloria's thighs and rubbed them in a salve that made the sardines smell like roses. And then she did the same thing to Josephine's thighs just in case the mumps dropped on her too. Every hour or so throughout the night she tapped up and down the front, back, and sides of each girl's legs with the sides of her hands continuously for five to ten minutes. The rest of the night she sat in a straight back chair between their twin beds changing the cold wash clothes to keep the fever down.

"You want me to sit with them awhile?" Joe asked after watching her nod off.

"What time is it? Don't you have to go to work in a little while?"

"It's three-o-clock in the morning. I got another two hours before I have to get going. I fed and changed Ben, so he won't be waking up again tonight.

"I appreciate it. Joe I..." She knew what she wanted to say. She'd been thinking about how to put it into words for what seemed like forever, but she was so tired at this moment that she couldn't remember her name.

"Go ahead. I got them," Joe pulled her up and pushed her out of the room.

****

"Lord it stinks in here. I got to leave myself enough time to wash-up again and change clothes," Joe muttered to himself as he leaned down and kissed each girl on the forehead.

He sat in the chair between the twin beds watching the girls toss and turn fitfully. Thirty minutes into his watch, he exchanged the warm wet cloth on each of their foreheads for a cool one from the bowl of half melted ice. He repeated the routine every thirty minutes.

When they woke up the next morning he was gone. Gloria missed her birthday party, but all of her friends said they had a real good time.

Chapter 35

Things went on like that for so long-over two and a half years- with their Mama saying, "Give him time" and their Daddy saying nothing at all until the girls reached a numbed state of resignation. When they had given up hope completely, everything changed.

One Sunday Bishop Wells preached about some people who were staging a sit-in at the Woolworth's downtown.

"Saints, he said, there is no place among them for people like us. There is no place for Saints who have been saved, sanctified, and filled with the precious Holy Ghost. It doesn't matter. I said, it doesn't matter, Saints, where we sit or eat down here. Jesus. I said Jesus has gone to prepare us a better place."

Bishop preached that Sunday. And the chorus of Amends gave testimony of the willingness of the Saints to wait on the Lord.

That evening when Mary Helen told Joe about the sermon, he showed more fire than they had seen from him in months.

"Woman, sometimes it ain't about being a Saint - not even about being a man. It's about doing what you have to do. My pastor said (Joe was Baptist, not Holiness like Mary Helen and the children) that we should stand with those boys and I think I will."

"Why are you getting into it? It ain't got nothing to do with us. They say those Colored people gonna end up in jail. Joe, I ain't coming to get you out of no jail for something like that!" Mary Helen said.

Joe just shook his head as though it was a waste of time trying to talk some sense into her and went back to reading the paper.

Before, Mary Helen never would have allowed this kind of summary dismissal to stand, but now she simply left him with his paper.

Three days later, when she walked in right after Gloria and Josephine had put the children to bed, she was beaming.

"Things are going to be better girls." Mary Helen said.

Then she told them about the events that had magically ensured that their old Daddy would come home to them that evening.

"I been feeling extra tired here lately," she began. "I know I been acting like I wasn't worried, but your Daddy staying mad this long really been whipping me down. Most days, I've just been getting on the bus closing my eyes. I never talked much anyway so everybody has been leaving me alone. They know I don't want to talk about what happened anymore and I never wanted any congratulations for doing what I had to do. No, I never talk and I don't listen neither - No need to —It's the same old talk every day about how much Miss So and So wants -for the five dollars a day she pays. Here lately, I just been sitting there wishing my head would stop aching, wishing they would all stop talking, but mostly wishing things would be the same between your Daddy and me.

Gloria offered her a glass of water. She shook her head no.

"When the bus pulled up in front of Woolworth's, nobody could hardly get off 'cause so many people were crowded around the place.

"I say to Sister Turner, them A&T students still sitting-in there?" and she says to me 'Yeah, and some Bennett College and Greensboro Women's College students done joined them sitting at the counter."

"They'll be waiting a long time to get something to eat, I says. Then May Ruth tells me all this stuff about how it ain't about food. About how it's about something called Civil Rights. Said how they are even talking about boycotting old man Mayfair's Cafeteria for having a Dutch door in back for Colored folks instead of letting em sit inside and eat. Didn't make any more sense to me then than when your Daddy was talking about it. Why would anyone go to that kind of trouble to eat food cooked by somebody they don't even know?"

They hunched their shoulders to let her see that it didn't make a-lickin'-bit-of-sense to them either.

"Ain't no telling where their hands have been," she went on, "Besides, I remembered what Bishop Wells said about those children sitting in where they weren't wanted. Remember?"

They nodded "yes" they remembered and "yes" get on with the story.

"They should wait on the Lord," I said to May Ruth. I was fixing to close my eyes when a voice in my head said, "You didn't wait."

I got mad and I told that voice in my head, "I wasn't thinking just about myself. I did it because I was thinking about how if I had waited and kept on having children, I would have died like my Mama died - bleeding her life away 'cause the Colored hospital didn't have no more Type 0 Colored blood. I explained to that voice that I couldn't stand the thought of my children being spread out to relatives all over, never getting to know each other like family is suppose to. But that voice wouldn't let me be. The voice kept saying, "You didn't wait on the Lord to decide how many children you should have."

I told that voice, "I was right!" Then I stuck my head out the window and let the world know.

"I was right! There's a time to lay down and there's a time to sit down! You boys are right! Sit down! Lay down if you have to!"

"As the bus pulled off, I saw your Daddy next to Woolworth's under the sign at Edmond's Drug Store and when I looked into his eyes I knew he understood."

"You girls go to bed now. I want to spend some time with your Daddy. I want to explain to him something I should have told him a long time ago about why I was so afraid."

Gloria and Josephine lay stiffly in bed. They were not fully convinced that things were going to get better, until they heard the

almost forgotten thump-thump of their daddy's
rich bass alternating amiably with the tap-tat of
their mama's alto. The cadence of their   voices
droned the girls into the best sleep they'd had in
over three years.

The next morning when Gloria and
Josephine yelled, "Good bye   Daddy," Joe
turned around, gave them a two finger-salute
and   flashed that perfect smile.

Chapter 36

"Mama, there's a big ole Cadillac out here." Josephine was standing in the screen door offering an open invitation to all the flies in the neighborhood.

"Close the door with you on one side or the other." Mary Helen continued icing the cake. She didn't have time to be fooling with Josephine today. Tomorrow was Convocation Sunday, which meant the sisters of the church were responsible for serving a big meal after the service to all of the out of town delegates. Her pastor was the state Bishop. Mary Helen had been up since four-o-clock that morning washing clothes, baking, and cooking. And she wasn't half way through her list of things to do.

"A White man got out of the Cadillac. It looks like he's coming to our house Mama." Josephine kept up an unwanted running narrative.

"Yes, Sir, She's home. May I tell her who is calling?" Mary Helen listened to the child greeting whoever it was using manners she'd taught her, but up to this point hadn't been sure had taken.

"Tell her it's Mr. Ben Wilson," The voice on the other side of the door said.

Mary Helen was at the door before he finished telling Josephine who he was.

"Mr. Ben? Did something happen to one of the children? Is something wrong?" She'd never expected to see him at her house.

"Calm down May Helen. Nothing is wrong unless you count my mother as something wrong with the universe. May Helen, Mother wants you to come be with the family today. It has something to do with her will. She says anyone who doesn't come today will be cut out of her will, if she hadn't already cut them out."

"What's that got to do with me?" Mary Helen said eyeing her pot of divinity icing. It had to be spread while it was still hot or it couldn't be spread at all.

"I don't know, May Helen. She told me to come and get you. Said she wouldn't start until I did. So, here I am."

"Lord. Lord. Mr. Wilson, I don't mean any harm, but I have to fool with your Mama half a day a week. I don't much want to be round her on my days off."

"I know May Helen. But if you don't come so she can do whatever the hell it is she wants to do, nobody is going to have any time off this weekend. Please, May Helen I'll pay you for your time."

"All right, Mr. Ben. Josephine, go wash your hands and finish spreading this icing for me. And hurry up. It's 'bout too hard to spread already," she called back as she left.

Half of the Projects were standing around outside trying to figure out what was going on and the other half were peeping out their windows or hanging out their doors. Mary

Helen held her head proudly as she stood near the rear-door of the Cadillac. Mr. Ben opened the door for her and chauffeured her out of there like she was somebody. She suppressed the urge to wave like she'd seen those politicians and beauty queens do in the Christmas Parade because she knew that no matter how much style she left there in she would have to come back and live among these people. Nothing made life harder living in the Projects than giving people the idea that you thought you were better than they were.

Mary didn't want that. They had lived in the Projects long enough that she felt that she and her family were a part of this *Village.* Although Loosie still made her crazy sometimes meddling- for the most part the people here had won her respect. That was one of the things that made living here so special. They gave one another a level of respect Colored people only got from their own. Her neighbors called her Miss Evans and she called them by their last names too. It didn't matter that it was Miss instead of Mrs. It was the use of the last name that set her and the rest them apart from their work. Respect and people who looked out for your children just like their own- a body couldn't ask for better neighbors than that.

Mary Helen sat back and started planning out how she could make up all the work she was getting behind on- frying two chickens, making a potato salad, ironing Sunday dresses, washing and straightening the girls' hair, polishing patent leather shoes... The list seemed to get longer as she closed her eyes.

****

"It's about time you got back here. Always was slow. I don't know how a child as slow as you came from my loins," Old Lady Wilson started fussing at Mr. Ben as soon as they walked through her bedroom door.

There was more light filtering through the shades into the room than the old lady usually allowed Mary Helen to let in. Most of the time, Old Lady Wilson kept the apartment as dark as a tomb. She'd gotten rid of all the dressers with mirrors years ago. She told Mary Helen that she wanted to remember herself the way she'd been during her prime. Mary Helen didn't know when her prime had been, but she was sure that it was long before she'd started working for the Wilsons.

Mary Helen had thought that Mrs. Wilson looked at least seventy-five back then and she was sure she looked every day of a hundred now. Although the old lady had on a fancy bed jacket-she owned a different pastel colored bed jacket for each day of the week-her face was made-up like she was going somewhere. In some places the heavy powder on her face covered some new wrinkles, but in most places the powder sank to the bottom of the craters and turned darker emphasizing the lines of demarcation that mapped times victorious march. Her wrinkled, pencil thin lips were the same shade of cardinal red that she'd worn when she'd met her husband seventy years ago when he'd said that her lips looked like rose petals.

"Y'all get out so I can talk to May Helen." Mrs. Wilson ordered. No one stopped to question her before leaving.

"They all think I'm about to die, but I've got news for them. I'm not dying until I'm good and ready."

Mary Helen started to tell the old lady that she was talking blasphemy, but decided that if anyone was mean enough to make God wait for them to die Mrs. Wilson was the one to do it.

"May Helen, what do you want?"

"M'am?"

"I said what do you want?"

"I want my children healthy and happy. I want to serve God best I can." Mary Helen stopped not sure what Mrs. Wilson wanted to hear.

"I mean what do you want that I can give you?" Mrs. Wilson said in a voice that implied that she had clearly given Mary Helen credit for having more sense than she had.

"I can't think of anything right off M'am." Mary Helen lied, but she hoped that it was a lie that God would forgive. The one thing she wanted was what she'd promised never to ask God for again. She wasn't sure whether telling Old Lady Wilson was the same as asking God, but she knew enough about how the Lord worked through people to suspect that he might count that as a back-handed way of asking Him.

"Well, call the others back in. I'll give you what I want you to have," the Old Lady said while reaching under the pillow on the left side of the bed and pulling out her glasses.

"I got all of you here to hear me read my will. I don't want any fighting after I die. Besides, I have decided not to die any time soon. My last joy in life will be watching you spend my money." She began as soon as everyone had filed back into the room.

I Eunice Cottier Wilson being of sound mind." She paused to stress the sound mind part. **"Do here by bequeath...**

And she continued to give her sons even shares of everything she owned with one stipulation that the one who would take her into his home for her last years would receive an additional two hundred thousand dollars.

"That's not nearly enough." Miss Kay said before Mr. Ben could stop her.

...To May Helen I bequeath the down payment and closing costs on any home she chooses subject to my approval.

"Now, pull those blinds down and get the hell out of my house." She dismissed them as she rolled over and pretended to go to sleep.

Mr. Ben took Mary Helen back home. She kept thinking: *Ye shall ask what ye will and it shall be done unto you.*

And sometimes you don't even have to ask.

Epilogue

Many of the places and events mentioned in the novel are actual historic locations and events in Greensboro, North Carolina. For example, my mother Mary H. Evans actually carried out a 17 day lay-in at L. Richardson Hospital to force my father to consent to the early birth control strategy of tying a woman's tubes and one of my brothers was miraculously cured from leukemia through prayer. Here is a little of the history that inspired portions of this book.

Morningside Housing Projects

After World War II, many of the returning soldiers moved with their families to urban areas to attend College on the G.I. Bill or to find work. In order to fulfill President Truman's promise of decent housing for soldiers who had served their country so well, government subsidized housing or public housing was built in cities throughout the country. The first two public housing developments in Greensboro, North Carolina were completed in 1951 as segregated communities. Smith Homes served the White community, while Morningside Homes served African Americans.

Morningside Homes, built in the eastern section of Greensboro, included 400 units. The units contained 1-4 bedrooms. For many of its occupants, these townhouse or single level units represented a step up in housing because each room was heated with a radiator and the kitchen was large enough for a dining table and were equipped with modern electric appliances. With the government subsidy, rent which included all utilities was about $33.00 a month for a 4-bedroom unit. This community was demolished in 2002 to make way for Willow Oaks, a mixed-income community.

Warnersville Community

Yardley Warner, a Quaker missionary from Philadelphia, bought 34 acres of land outside of the city limits of Greensboro in 1867 to establish a planned community for African American freedmen. For almost 100 years, the community was a model for African American prosperity and neighborhood pride. Today, the J. C. Price School is all that is left of this part of African American history in Greensboro. Almost the entire neighborhood was destroyed in the 1960s through urban renewal, when a modern subdivision and wide thoroughfares replaced the homes, gardens, and community church. The school built in 1922, was named for Dr. Joseph Charles Price (1854-1893), the son of a slave who served as a minister, lecturer, and founder and president of Livingstone College in Salisbury, North Carolina. The building is one of the oldest schools in the city.

L. Richardson Hospital

Charles H. Moore, a veteran Greensboro city school teacher for whom a present day city school is named, is credited with having begun the movement for a Negro hospital to serve the needs of the African American citizens of the city. Dr. S. P. Sebastian, a practicing physician who with physicians J. W. V. Cordice and C. C. Stewart had operated the private Trinity Hospital for Negroes and layman Watson Law were two other Negro leaders of the pioneer group.

In January of 1923, a group of individuals organized the Greensboro Negro Hospital Association. On May 4, 1927, L. Richardson Memorial Hospital opened. The hospital received donations from families in Greensboro. Mrs. Lunsford Richardson's family donated $50,000 to assist with building the hospital. Mrs. Emanuel Sternberger contributed $10,000 to purchase equipment for the operating room and X-Ray Department. Additionally, donations received from the Rosenwald and Duke Funds were used to finance a nurses' residence built in 1929.

The A&T Four/Sit-in Movement

On Monday, February 1, 1960, David Richmond, Franklin McCain, Jibreel Khazan (formerly Ezell Blair) and Joseph McNeil all freshman at NCA&T at the time entered a segregated Greensboro, North Carolina F.W. Woolworth's lunch counter and demanded to be served. This protest re-ignited the Civil Rights movement with sit-in campaigns throughout the South. It was a new tactic added to the peaceful nonviolent measures employed by Martin Luther King

Jr. Such nonviolent measures helped African American activists win supporters across the country and throughout the world.

The Negro Public School System of Greensboro

Although the public schools of Greensboro, North Carolina were segregated like other public schools in the South, because of the leadership of educated freedmen, African American business men and some Whites the Negro Public Schools of Greensboro were always a cut above other schools for Blacks in the South. As early as 1873, when Bennett Normal School was founded as a co-educational school to educate newly emancipated slaves the African American community was served by established schools. From 1923-1926 when Bennett College became a college for women, a co-educational high school program was held on the campus. From 1926 until December of 1929 the high school was housed on the Washington Street School campus. In 1929 James Benson Dudley Senior High School opened as one of the first public high schools for African Americans in the state.

One cannot talk about public education for African Americans in the City of Greensboro without beginning with one man- Charles Moore (1855-1952). Moore came back to his home state of North Carolina after graduating from Amherst in

1878, determined to work against educational and financial inequality. In addition to his work with the North Carolina Agricultural and Technical State University, he was the first principal of the first "negro graded school" in the state. Percy Street School the permanent black graded school was erected in Greensboro in 1880 five years after the first permanent graded public school for Whites opened. Moore also helped to organize the Negro North Carolina Teachers' Association, became the regional director of the Julius Rosenwald Fund, in which role he helped to build schools for black students in rural areas, helped establish the L. Richardson Memorial Hospital and worked with Booker T. Washington as vice-president of the national Negro Business League.

Moore's 1916 inspection and report on rural schools in North Carolina was groundbreaking, and showed that thousands of public dollars earmarked for black education had gone instead to build schools, hire teachers and increase resources for white students. [1] Wherever Moore traveled he encouraged people in African American communities to "take charge" of educating their children by demanding that tax money be spent on their children and by becoming better educated themselves.

[1] From the Biographical Files of Charles Henry Moore, December 14, 2011 by Sara Smith.

The Agricultural and Mechanical College for the Colored Race

In 1895 the North Carolina legislature appointed Dudley to the Board of Trustees for the college. Later that year he was made secretary of the board, a position he served in until 1896 when the President, John O. Crosby, resigned. At the next meeting of the board, Dudley was voted unanimously to become the second President of the college. While President, Dudley focused on modifying the curriculum. He believed that it was best to aim the curriculum towards jobs that were currently available. He wanted the men and women who attended his college to be able to get jobs and "raise the standard of living among their people". His additions to the curriculum included the teaching of carpentry, wood turning, bricklaying, blacksmithing, animal husbandry, horticulture and floriculture, mattress and broom making, shoe making, poultry raising, tailoring, electrical engineering, and domestic science. As well as adding these specific classes, Dudley also added an entire teaching department to the school, that taught pupils to be a teacher while placing special emphasis on "courtesy, manners, and an appreciation to culture in general." Dudley himself was praised for his politeness. He also added a summer school program.

About the Author

Jo Evans Lynn, a native of Greensboro, N.C., taught nearly every grade level and every form of English/language arts during her 37 years in education. Her diverse experiences as a language arts teacher reinforced her belief that even fiction should be based on real life experiences. In all of her books, the reader shares her experiences during the 1950s & 1960s as an African-American child growing up on the "Colored" side of town in the segregated South. In Holding On, she shares her parents us. She says "I was always a "Daddy's Girl" so I didn't realize how special my mother was until I began writing this book. Although it is a fictional account of their romance and life together, like all my books, it is based on fact-they met in my Aunt Daisy's Liquor House, and my father was a handsome womanizer who took years to "settle in."